STEPBROTHER

Penelope Ward

First Edition, September 2014

Copyright © 2014 by

Penelope Ward

CHAPTER 1

Cold air fogged the bay window in our living room as I nervously waited in front of it and struggled to see outside. Any minute now, Randy's Volvo station wagon would be pulling into the driveway. He'd gone to Logan Airport to pick up his son, Elec, who would be living with us for the next year while his mother took a yearlong work-related assignment overseas.

Randy and my mother, Sarah, had only been married a couple of years. My stepfather and I got along well enough, but I wouldn't say we were close. Here's what little I knew about Randy's former life: his ex-wife, Pilar, was an Ecuadorian artist based in the San Francisco Bay area, and his son was a tattooed punk who, according to Randy, was allowed to do whatever he wanted.

I hadn't ever met my stepbrother before and had only seen a picture of him that was taken a few years ago, shortly before Randy married my mother. From the picture, I could see he inherited dark hair, probably from his South American mother, along with tanned skin, but had Randy's light eyes and fine features. He was clean-cut then, but Randy said Elec had entered into a rebellious stage as of late. That included getting tattoos when he was only fifteen and getting into trouble for underage drinking and smoking pot. Randy blamed Pilar for being flighty and too focused on her art career, thereby allowing Elec to get away with murder.

Randy claimed he had encouraged Pilar to take a temporary position teaching classes run by a London art gallery so that Elec, now 17, could come live with us.

Although Randy took two short trips out west a year, he wasn't there on a daily basis to discipline Elec. He struggled with that and said he looked forward to the opportunity to set his son straight over the next year.

Butterflies swarmed in my stomach as I stared out at the dirty snow that lined my street. The frigid Boston weather would be a rude awakening for my California-bred stepbrother.

I had a stepbrother.

That was a weird thought. I hoped we would get along. As an only child, I had always wanted a sibling. I laughed at how stupid I was, fantasizing that this was going to be some kind of fairytale relationship overnight, like friggin' Donny and Marie Osmond or Jake and Maggie Gyllenhaal. This morning, I heard an old Coldplay song I never even knew existed called *Brothers and Sisters.* It's not about siblings per say, but I convinced myself it was a good omen. This was going to be okay. I had nothing to be scared about.

My mother seemed just as nervous as I was as she repeatedly ran up and down the stairs to get Elec's room ready. She had turned the office into a bedroom. Mom and I had gone to Walmart together to buy sheets and other necessities. It was weird picking stuff out for someone you didn't know. We decided on dark navy bedding.

I started muttering to myself, thinking about what I would say to him, what we would talk about, what I could introduce him to here. It was sort of exciting and nerve-wracking at the same time.

A car door slammed, prompting me to jump up from the couch and straighten my wrinkled shirt.

Calm yourself, Greta.

The key made a turning sound. Randy walked in alone and left the door cracked open, allowing the freezing air to seep into the room. After a few minutes, I could hear feet crunching on the sheet of ice that covered the walkway but no Elec yet. He must have stopped outside before entering. Randy stuck his head back out the door. "Get your ass in here, Elec."

A lump formed in my throat when he appeared at the doorway. I swallowed hard and took him in for a few seconds, my heart pounding harder and harder as the realization hit that he looked nothing like the picture shown to me.

Elec was taller than Randy, and the short hair I remembered from the photo was now a tousled inky black mess nearly covering his eyes. He smelled of cigarettes, or maybe it was pipe smoke because it was sweeter. A chain hung from his jeans. He wouldn't look at me, so I used the opportunity to continue examining him as he dumped his bag on the floor.

Thud.

Was that my heart or the bag?

He looked over at Randy, and his voice was gravelly. "Where's my room?"

"Upstairs, but you're not going anywhere until you say hello to your sister."

Every muscle in my body tightened as I cringed at the term. There was no way I wanted to be his sister. For one, when he turned to me, he looked like he wanted to kill me. And two, once I got my first look at his chiseled face, it became abundantly clear that while my mind was wary of him, my body had been instantly put under a spell, one I would have given anything to come out from under.

His eyes bore into mine with daggers in them, and he didn't say anything. I took a few steps forward, swallowed my pride and reached out my hand. "I'm Greta. Nice to meet you."

He said nothing. Several seconds passed before he reluctantly took my hand. His grip was uncomfortably hard, almost painful before he quickly released it.

I coughed and said, "You look different…than I pictured."

He squinted at me. "And you look pretty…plain."

My throat felt like it was going to close up. For a quick second, I thought he was paying me a compliment before he followed the word "pretty" with "plain." The sad part was, if you'd asked me how standing across from him made me feel, "plain" might have been the term I would have used.

His eyes were looking me up and down with an ice-cold stare. Despite the fact that I detested his personality, I was still in awe of his physical likeness, and that sickened me. His nose was perfectly straight, and his jaw was defined. His lips were perfect—too perfect—for the filth I was sure came out of them. Physically, he was my dream and in every other way, my nightmare. Still, I refused to let him see that his words had an effect on me.

"Would you like me to show you to your room?" I asked.

He ignored me, lifted his bags and headed toward the stairs.

Great. This was going well.

My mother came down the stairs and immediately pulled Elec into a hug.

"It's so nice to finally meet you, honey."

His body stiffened before he ripped himself away from her. "Wish I could say the same."

Randy stormed toward the stairs pointing his finger. "Cut the shit, Elec. You say hello to Sarah in a decent way."

"Hello to Sarah in a decent way," Elec repeated in a monotone voice as he walked up the stairs.

My mother put her hand on Randy's shoulder. "It's okay. He'll warm up. Let him be alone. This cross-country move can't be easy. He doesn't know me yet. He's just a little apprehensive."

"A little disrespectful prick is what he is."

Whoa.

I had to say, I was surprised to hear Randy speaking that way about his son regardless of how badly Elec was acting. My stepfather had never used words like that with me, although I had never really done anything to deserve it. But Elec *was* being a disrespectful prick.

That night, Elec stayed behind closed doors. Randy went in there once, and I heard them arguing, but Mom and I decided to let them hash it out and stayed out of whatever was going on between them.

On my way up to bed, I couldn't help stopping to stare at Elec's closed bedroom door. I wondered if his alienating us was indicative of how the entire year would go or if he would even last the entire year here.

Planning to brush my teeth, I opened the bathroom door and jumped at the sight of Elec wiping his wet body down from the shower. Steam and the smell of men's body wash filled the air. For some God forsaken reason, instead of running out, I froze. More disturbing, instead of covering himself with the towel, he let it fall nonchalantly to the floor.

My mouth dropped.

My eyes were now glued to his cock for a few seconds before my gaze traveled up to the two shamrocks inked on his ripped torso and then to the full sleeve tattoo on his left arm. His chest was dripping with water. His left nipple was pierced. By the time my eyes landed on his face, they were met with an evil smirk. I tried to speak, but the words just wouldn't come out.

Finally, I whipped my head away and said, "Uh…Oh my God…I…I'm so…I better leave."

As I turned around to head out the door, his voice stopped me in my tracks. "You act like you've never seen a guy naked before."

"Actually…I haven't."

"How disappointing for you. It's gonna be really *hard* for the next guy to measure up."

"Cocky much?"

"You tell me. Don't I deserve to be?"

"God...you're acting like—"

"A giant dick?"

It was like a bad car accident impossible to turn away from. I was looking down at him again. What was wrong with me? He was stark naked in front of me, and I couldn't move.

Holy hell...his tip was pierced. What a way to be introduced to my first live one.

He broke my stare. "There's really nowhere to go from here, so unless you're planning on doing something, you should probably leave and let me finish getting dressed."

I shook my head in disbelief and slammed the door shut behind me.

My legs were shaking as I fled to my room.

What just happened?

CHAPTER 2

"How is stepbrother dearest today?" Victoria asked.

The bed squeaked as I plopped on my stomach and sighed into the phone. "Up to his usual assholery."

I hadn't told my best friend Victoria about Elec's show and tell in the bathroom Friday night. It embarrassed me to no end, and I decided to keep it to myself. A Google search of pierced penises ended up keeping me up the rest of that first night. Let me tell you, anyone who innocently searches "Prince Albert" is in for a big surprise.

It was now Sunday, and tomorrow Elec would be starting at my high school where we would both be seniors. Soon enough, everyone would get to meet my jerky stepbrother.

Victoria sounded shocked. "He's still not speaking to you?"

"No. He came downstairs to pour some cereal this morning and brought it back to his room."

"Why do you think he has such a stick up his ass?"

You should see his other stick.

"Something's going on between him and Randy. I'm trying not to take it personally, but it's hard."

It's hard alright. God, I can't get it out of my head!

Pierced mushroom head.

Shit.

"You think I would like him?" Victoria asked.

"What do you mean? I told you...he's the devil," I snapped.

"I know...but do you think I would *like* him?"

Honestly, I knew he was exactly Victoria's type. She loved dark and brooding guys even when they weren't as good-looking as Elec. This was another reason I had to keep the details of the bathroom encounter to myself. All she needed to hear was that his cock was pierced, and I'd never get her out of my house. But she'd find out what he looked like soon enough, so I figured I'd be honest.

"He's really hot, okay? Really...fucking...hot. In fact, his looks are just about the only thing he has going for him."

"Okay, I'm coming over."

"No, you're not." I laughed, but deep down, the idea of Victoria throwing herself at Elec made me really uncomfortable even if I didn't think he'd return the attention.

"What are your plans for tonight, then?"

"Well, before I actually met him and realized he was an asshat, I was supposed to be making Sunday dinner for all of us. You know…my one specialty."

"Chicken Tetrazzini."

I laughed because it was the only thing I knew how to make well. "How did you guess?"

"Maybe you can serve up a can of whoopass on the side for stepbrother dearest."

"I'm not engaging him. I'm gonna kill him with kindness. I don't care how much of a…dick…(oh goodness) he wants to be to me. The worst thing I can do is let him think he's affecting me."

***

Mom helped me set the table while we waited for the Tetrazzini to bake. My stomach was growling, but it was more nerves rather than the smell of cream sauce and garlic emanating from the oven. I really wasn't looking forward to sitting across the table from Elec, that is, if he even agreed to join us.

"Greta, why don't you go upstairs and see if you can get him to come down."

"Why me?"

My mother screwed open a bottle of wine. She was the only one who would be drinking, and she likely needed it. She poured a little, took a sip then said, "Look, I can understand why he doesn't like me. He sees me as the enemy and probably blames me in some way for his parents not being together, but there is no reason for him to be treating you poorly. Just keep trying to get through to him, see if you can get him to open up a little."

I shrugged. She had no idea how all out in the *open* things were in the bathroom the other night: balls to the wall open.

As I walked up the stairs, the theme song to *Jaws* rang out in my head. The thought of knocking on his door terrified me, and I didn't know what I would be faced with if he even opened the door.

I knocked.

To my surprise, he opened right away. A clove cigarette was hanging out of his mouth. The sweet smell of the smoke traveled quickly up my nostrils. He took a long drag then slowly and intentionally blew the smoke right in my face. His voice was low. "What?"

I tried to seem unaffected until an uncontrollable hacking cough broke out.

Very cool, Greta.

"Dinner is almost ready."

He was wearing a tight, white ribbed tank top, and my eyes drifted down to a tattoo that said "Lucky" on one of his muscular biceps, which was now leaning against the door. His hair was wet, and his jeans hung low, showcasing the top of the white boxer briefs underneath. His steely gray eyes stared into mine. He was breathtaking…for a bastard.

I had zoned out when he said, "Why are you looking at me like that?"

"Like what?"

"Like you're trying to remember what I looked like the other night…like you'd rather have *me* for dinner." He snickered. "And why are you winking at me?"

Shit. My eye twitched whenever I was nervous and made it look like I was winking.

"It's just a twitch. Get over yourself."

His expression turned angry. "Really? Should I? My looks are all I have going for me, right? So, I should capitalize on that."

What was he talking about? I stood there speechless.

He continued, "What's the matter…too hot in here for you? Then, he said in a mocking tone, "So…fucking…hot." He flashed a wicked smile.

Shit.

Those were the exact words I had used to describe him on the phone to Victoria earlier.

He had been eavesdropping on my conversation!

My eye twitched.

He continued, "You're winking at me again. Am I making you nervous? Look at your face! Red's a good color on you."

I immediately left to go back downstairs.

He yelled after me. "We'll match, seeing as though I'm the DEVIL!"

**

Elec picked at his meal without saying a word as I fixated on his lip ring. Randy was glancing over at him with a look of disdain. My mother refilled her wine glass more than once. Yup, our very own version of the Brady Bunch.

I pretended to be enjoying the Tetrazzini while ruminating over the fact that he'd overheard me talking about him that way and therefore, now knew I was attracted to him.

Mom was the first to speak. "Elec, what do you think of Boston so far?"

"Seeing as though I've ventured nowhere but this house, it sucks ass."

Randy slammed his fork down. "Can you show some respect to your stepmother for five seconds?"

"That depends. Can she stop boozing it up for the same amount of time? I knew you married a cheater, *Daddy*, but a lush, too?"

"You worthless piece of shit," Randy spewed.

Whoa.

Once again, Randy had floored me with his choice of words toward his son. Elec was surely being an asshole, but it still shocked me to hear that kind of language coming out of my stepfather's mouth.

Elec's chair skidded back as he threw his napkin on the table and got up. "I'm done." He looked over at me. "The Titty Zinni or whatever the fuck it's called was wonderful, *sis*." The word "sis" had rolled off his tongue with sarcasm.

After he left the table, the silence was deafening. My mother put her hand on Randy's, and I was left pondering what could have happened between Elec and his father to cause such a rift.

I impulsively got up and walked upstairs. My heart was pounding as I knocked on Elec's door. He didn't answer, so I slowly turned the knob and found him sitting at the edge of his bed smoking a clove cigarette. He had headphones on and hadn't seen me enter. I stood just past the doorway and observed him. He was bouncing his

11

legs nervously, looking frustrated and defeated. Eventually, he put the cigarette out only to immediately reach into his drawer and grab another one.

"Elec," I shouted.

He jumped and removed his headphones. "The fuck? You scared the shit out of me."

"Sorry."

He lit the cigarette and gestured toward the door. "Leave."

"No."

He rolled his eyes and shook his head slowly, returning the headphones to his ears and taking a long drag.

I sat down next to him. "Those are gonna kill you."

Smoke billowed from his mouth as he said, "Perfect."

"You don't mean that."

"Please leave me alone."

"Okay, fine."

I left the room and went back downstairs. Seeing him looking so down when he didn't know I was watching him made me more determined than ever to break through to him somehow. I needed to know if this was just a façade or if he were truly a genuine asshole. The meaner he was to me, the more I wanted to make him like me. It was a challenge.

I returned to the kitchen and asked Randy for Elec's cell phone number before programming it into my phone. I then typed out a text.

You don't want to talk, so I'll text.

Elec: How did you get my number?

Greta: Your father.

Elec: Fuck him.

I decided to change the subject off of Randy.

Greta: Did you enjoy the meal?

Elec: Scramble the letters of meal. You get LAME. Your meal=lame.

Greta: Why are you so mean?

Elec: Why are you so lame?

What a jackass. This was going nowhere. I threw the phone on the counter and marched up the stairs. Now, he'd put me in the mood to do something that would piss him off.

He was still sitting on the bed smoking when I opened the door after neglecting to knock. I headed straight for the drawer, grabbed his box of cigarettes and ran out.

I was laughing all the way back to my room. That is, until my door burst open. I quickly stuffed the cigarettes into my shirt. Elec looked ready to murder me, although admittedly, the glare in his glowing eyes was pretty sexy.

"Give them to me," he said through gritted teeth.

"I'm not giving them back to you."

"Yes the fuck you are, or I'm reaching into your shirt and getting them. You choose."

"Seriously, why do you smoke? It's so bad for you."

"You can't just steal my shit. But then again, like mother, like daughter."

"What are you talking about?"

"Go ask your mother," he muttered under his breath. He held out his muscular, tattooed arm. "Give me my cigarettes."

"Not until you explain why you just said that. She didn't steal Randy. Your parents were divorced before my mom even met your dad."

"That's what Randy wants you to believe. She was probably fucking around on your father too, right? Poor gullible bastard."

"Don't call my father a bastard."

"Well, where was he when Sarah was fucking my father behind my mother's back?"

My blood was starting boil. He was going to be sorry for asking. "Six feet under. My father died when I was ten."

He was silent then rubbed his temples in frustration. His tone eased for the first time since I'd met him. "Fuck. I didn't know that, okay?"

"There's a lot you're probably assuming. If you'd just talk to me…"

Elec almost looked like he was going to apologize. *Almost.* Then, he shook his head and turned right back into evil Mr. Hyde. "I'll be fucking damned if I have to talk to you. Give me my cigarettes, or I'm ripping them out of your shirt."

My body buzzed when he said it. *What was wrong with me?* A part of me wanted to see what that would be like, his rough hands pulling at the material on my shirt, ripping it off. I shook my head to rid the thought and backed away as he slowly approached. He was just inches from me now. The heat radiated from his body as he moved up against me, squishing the cigarette box into my chest. My nipples instantly turned to steel. I had never felt so out of control of my own body and was silently begging it to stop reacting so intensely toward him. Let's face it. My body was an imbecile with poor judgment. How could it want something so badly that hated it right back?

His breath smelled like clove. "That was the last package of that brand. They're imported from Indonesia. I don't even know where to buy them here yet. If you think I'm difficult to deal with now, you're not gonna want to see what I'm like with no cigarettes tonight."

"They're so bad for you."

"Ask me if I give a shit," he said uncomfortably close to my mouth.

"Elec…"

He backed up a few inches. "Look…smoking is the only thing that has brought me any peace since walking into this hell hole. Now, I'm asking nicely. Please."

His eyes softened, and with each second that passed, my resolve weakened. "Okay." His gaze followed my hand as I reached into my bra for the cigarettes. I handed them to him and instantly felt the cold air replace the heat of his body as he walked away.

If I thought giving him back the cigarettes would initiate a truce, I was wrong.

He turned around one last time to face me, and his eyes were no longer soft. They were piercing. "You're gonna pay for that."

CHAPTER 3

The start of school went exactly the way I expected. Elec ignored me anytime we were in the same class or in the cafeteria. Girls flocked around him everywhere he went, and he instantly became popular while barely having to say a word. Probably the least surprising development was Victoria's covetous reaction to him.

"What do you think my chances are?"

"Of what?"

"Of bagging Elec."

"Don't get me involved in that venture, please."

"Why not? I realize you don't get along with him, but you're my only in."

"He hates my guts. How am I going to be able to help you with this?"

"You could invite me over, set it up so we're all in the same room and then leave us alone."

"I don't know. You don't understand how he is."

"I mean, I know you don't get along with him, but does it really bother you if I try to make a move? It might actually help your relationship with him if I ended up dating him."

"I don't think Elec is the dating type."

"No…he's the *fucking* type, and that's okay with me, too. I'll take that."

My heart was beating faster, and I hated myself for it. Every time Victoria would bring this up, it made me insanely jealous. It was like a secret struggle I was constantly battling. I could never admit this to anyone. Which part bothered me most was unclear. Was it the thought of my friend screwing Elec, getting to touch him and living out my darkest fantasy? That bothered me, sure, but I think what upset me the most was the thought of Elec connecting on a deeper level with someone else while he continued to apparently despise me.

I hated that I cared.

I lifted my backpack out of my locker. "You're crazy. Can we please change the subject?"

"Okay. I heard Bentley wants to ask you out."

I slammed the locker hard upon that news. "From whom?"

"He talked to my brother about it. He wants to ask you to the movies."

Bentley was one of the popular preppie guys. I couldn't figure out why he would be interested in me since he usually dated girls from his own crowd. I didn't really belong to their group or any group for that matter. There were the people like Bentley from the rich side of town in one clique. Then, there were the artsy and theatrical ones. Then, you had the international exchange students. Then, there were those who were just popular because they were good-looking, intriguing or acted out (Elec). Victoria and I were sort of in a class of our own. We got along with everyone, got good grades and stayed out of trouble. Unlike my best friend, though, I was a virgin.

I'd only had one boyfriend, Gerald, who ended up breaking up with me because I wouldn't let him get past touching my boobs. Word got out that I was a virgin and certain people around school would joke about it behind my back. While I still saw Gerald in the halls from time to time, I tried to avoid him.

Victoria snapped her gum. "So, anyway, if he asks you out, we should totally invite Elec. He could go with me, and you could go with Bentley. We could go see that new scary movie."

"No, thanks. Living with Elec is all the scary I need."

***

My words would come back to haunt me the next morning. I was getting dressed for school, and when I opened my underwear drawer, it was empty.

I threw on some yoga pants commando-style and marched into Elec's room as he was putting on a shirt.

"What the hell did you do with my underwear?"

"It doesn't feel good when someone takes your shit, does it?"

"I took one box of cigarettes for less than five minutes and gave it right back, by the way. You took every single piece of underwear I own! There's a little bit of a difference there."

I couldn't believe I assumed he wasn't going to get back at me for that one. Lately, he had been ignoring me especially well, and I just assumed all was forgotten.

I started searching his drawers. My hand quickly retracted after touching a strip of condoms.

"You can look in here all day until the sun goes down. They're not in here. Don't waste your time."

"You'd better not have thrown them out!"

"Those were some hot pieces. I couldn't do that."

"That's because they cost a fortune."

Good underwear was probably the only thing I splurged on. Each and every pair came from a pricey online lingerie boutique.

As I knelt down to look under his bed, he laughed. "You have a wedgie, by the way."

I leapt up and clenched my teeth. "That's what happens when you don't have any fucking underwear!"

I wanted to pick it so badly, but that would have made this worse. I stood up to face him.

Elec gave me a once-over. "You'll get them back when I'm ready to give them to you. Now, if you'll excuse me…" He brushed past me and ran down the stairs.

I didn't even bother to stop him because he wasn't going to budge. I went to Target on the way to school and bought cheapie panties until I could figure out how to get mine back.

I came home from school that day in a really anxious mood. Between the missing underwear and my actually getting asked out by Bentley, I was seriously in need of ice cream—not just any ice cream, but the homemade kind I'd make occasionally on the machine I got for Christmas last year.

I dumped every piece of leftover Halloween candy into it and ended up with a delectable Snicker, Heath bar, Almond Joy concoction with a vanilla base.

Once it was ready, I sat down at the counter with my gigantic bowl and closed my eyes, savoring each bite.

The front door slammed and shortly after, Elec strolled into the kitchen. The scent of clove cigarettes and cologne wafted in the air. I hated his smell.

I fucking loved his smell, wanted to drown in it.

As usual, he ignored me, just headed to the refrigerator, took out the milk and drank it straight from the carton. He eyed my ice cream and walked over to me, taking the spoon out of my hand. He placed it in his mouth, devouring a huge dollop. The metal from his lip ring clinked against the spoon that he licked until it was dry. My insides were quivering from just watching it. Then, he handed the spoon back to me. His tongue lightly brushed across his teeth like a snake. Even his goddamn teeth were sexy.

I opened the drawer, grabbed another spoon and gave him his own. We both started eating out of my bowl while saying nothing to each other. Such a simple thing, but my heart was beating a mile a minute. This was the longest amount of time he'd ever willingly graced me with his presence.

Finally, in the middle of a bite, he looked at me. "What happened to your father?"

I swallowed my ice cream and tried to fight the emotions creeping up. His question caught me totally off guard. I rested my spoon in the bowl. "He died of lung cancer at 35. He'd been smoking since he was 12."

He closed his eyes briefly and nodded to himself in understanding. He obviously now realized why I'd hated his smoking so much.

After several seconds of silence, he was looking down at the bowl when he said, "I'm sorry."

"Thanks."

We continued sharing the ice cream until there was nothing left. Elec took the bowl from me, washed it in the sink, wiped it and put it away. He then left to go back upstairs without saying anything else.

I stayed downstairs in the kitchen alone for a while replaying that strange encounter. His interest in my father really surprised me. I also thought again about when he first licked my spoon and how I'd felt when I licked it after.

My phone chimed. It was a text from Elec.

Thanks for the ass cream. It was really good.

When I returned to my room that afternoon, a single pair of my underwear was neatly folded on my dresser. If this were his version of extending an olive branch, I'd take it.

***

The "sweet" Elec was short-lived. A few days after our ice cream social, he showed up at the café where I worked right in the middle of the after school rush. Kilt Café was down the street from our high school and served things like sandwiches, salads and coffee.

If Elec's showing up wasn't bad enough, he'd brought with him probably the most beautiful girl in our entire school. Leila was platinum blonde and tall with huge breasts. She was the total opposite of me looks-wise. I had more of a dancer or gymnast's body. My long strawberry-blonde hair was poker straight and simple as opposed to her big, bouncy Texas-style do. You'd think she'd be a bitch because of her looks, but she was actually really nice.

Leila waved. "Hey, Greta."

"Hey," I said as I placed their menus down. Elec gave me fleeting eye contact but was trying not to acknowledge me. I don't think he knew that I worked there, because I never told him.

A pang of jealousy hit me when I noticed Elec locking Leila's legs in with his under the table.

I wasn't sure if Leila realized he was my stepbrother. I never spoke about him to people at school and figured he never mentioned me, either.

"I'll give you two a few minutes," I said before walking back toward the kitchen. I watched as Leila reached across the table and planted a kiss on his lips. I felt sick. She pulled on his lip ring with her teeth. It looked like she might have purred. *Ugh.* I'd never wanted to disappear into thin air so badly.

I reluctantly walked back over to them. "Have you decided what you want?"

Elec glanced over to the chalkboard that listed the daily specials and smirked. "What's your soup of the day?"

That bastard.

"Chicken."

"That's not correct. You're misrepresenting it."

"It's the same thing."

He repeated, "What's…the soup…of the day?"

I stared at him long and hard then clenched my jaw. "Cock a Leekie Soup."

The owner was from Scotland, and apparently, that was a specialty there.

He flashed a mischievous grin. "Thanks. I'll have the cock soup. Leila?"

"I'll have the garden salad," she said, looking back and forth between Elec and me confused.

I took my sweet time before bringing them their food. It didn't matter to me if the soup was cold.

After a few minutes, Elec lifted his index finger for me to come to the table.

"Yes?" I huffed.

"This cock is leaky. It's also bland and cold. Can you please replace it and ask the cook to actually put some flavor in it?"

He looked like he was stifling a laugh. Leila was speechless.

I took the soup back to the kitchen and dumped it violently into the sink along with the ceramic cup. Instead of talking to the chef, I had a light bulb moment and decided to take this into my own hands. I grabbed the ladle and put more soup into a new cup. I opened a bottle of hot picante sauce and poured it more than generously into the soup.

It was piping hot in more ways than one now. I walked back out and placed it carefully in front of Elec.

"Anything else?"

"No."

I walked back over toward the kitchen and waited in the corner to watch him. The anticipation was killing me. His tongue would practically fall off when he got one taste of my specialty.

Elec took the first spoonful. He had no reaction.

How could that be?

He took another spoonful then his eyes sought me out. His mouth curved into a sly smile before he took the entire cup and started drinking the soup like a beverage. He wiped his mouth with the back of his hand, whispered to Leila and excused himself.

Leila's back was turned to me when Elec walked over and dragged me by the arm into the dark corridor leading to the bathrooms.

He backed me up against the wall. "You think you're so smart?" My heart was slamming into my chest. Speechless, I shook my head as he said, "Well, the joke's on you."

Before I could respond, Elec grabbed my face with both hands and smashed his lips into mine. The metal from his lip ring scraped my mouth as he nudged it open with his tongue hungrily and started kissing me deep. I moaned into his mouth, both shocked and excited by the ambush of his hot tongue assaulting me. My body was shaking. He smelled amazing. I felt like I was going to collapse from the sensory overload.

Within seconds, the heat from the picante sauce on his tongue began to penetrate my own, which was now burning. Even though it felt like my tongue was about to fall off, I didn't ever want to pull away.

I'd never been kissed like this.

Then, just like that, he ripped his mouth away from mine.

"Don't you know by now not to fuck with me?"

He walked away, and I stayed panting in the corridor with my hand over my chest.

Holy shit.

My mouth was on fire along with every other orifice. I was throbbing between my legs. When I finally gained enough composure to walk back out, I realized they needed their check at some point.

I decided to get it over with and took the leather bill binder to their table, placing it in front of Elec without making eye contact.

I overheard him telling Leila to meet him out front and that he'd take care of everything. He reached into his pocket and slipped something in the folder and soon after, he took off.

He probably didn't even leave me a tip. I opened it and gasped when along with a twenty-dollar bill was my favorite black lace thong and written in pen on the check:

Keep the change, or rather, change into these. I'm guessing your current ones are a little wet.

CHAPTER 4

Elec and I never spoke of the kiss even though it ran through my mind constantly. I was pretty sure it didn't mean anything to him, that he was just trying to make a point. Still, the sensations I experienced were the same as if the kiss had been based on real passion. Knowing what his lips felt like on mine and how he'd tasted wasn't a memory that could so easily be erased. I craved that feeling again. It made the battle between my mind and body much more difficult than before.

It was a curse having a crush on someone you had to live with, particularly when he brought girls from school back to the house.

One afternoon, while our parents weren't home, he'd brought Leila over, and they were in his room messing around. Another afternoon, it was Amy. Then the next week, it was a different Amy.

I'd be in my room covering my ears so that I didn't have to hear the sound of his bed squeaking or the stupid girl giggling. The particular day that Amy number two exited his room to go home, I texted him immediately after.

Really? Two Amys? Will Amy #3 be coming tomorrow? What are you thinking?!

Elec: I'm thinking you're wishing your name were Amy…"sister."

Greta: Step! Stepsister.

Elec: Scramble the word step, you get PEST. step=pest.

Greta: You're a moron.

Elec: You're a pest.

I got up from my bed in a huff and walked right into his room without knocking. He was playing a video game and didn't even look at me. "I really need to get a lock on that thing."

My heart was racing. "Why are you such a fucking jerk?"

"Nice to see you, too, sis." He patted the bed next to where he was sitting at the edge with his eyes still fixed on the game. "If you won't leave, by all means, have a seat."

"I have no desire to sit on your dirty bed."

"Is that because you'd rather sit on my dirty face?"

My heart nearly stopped.

His mouth spread into a devious smile as he continued to play the game. He had rendered me speechless. In fact, I had rendered myself speechless, because as soon as the words "sit on my dirty face" came out of his mouth, I had the urge to cross my legs to curb my arousal. My vagina was a hopeless fool. The cruder he was, the stronger its attraction to him.

Instead of dignifying his question with a response, I looked around the room, headed straight for his drawers and began rummaging through his things. "Where's my underwear?"

"I told you, they're not in here."

"I don't believe you."

I continued searching around until I stumbled upon something that caught my eye. It was a binder with a large stack of papers inside. Printed on the front were the words *Lucky and the Lad by Elec O'Rourke.*

"What's this?"

For the first time, Elec stopped his video game and practically flew off the bed. "Don't touch that."

I flipped through it as fast as possible before he ripped it out of my hands. There was dialog and some lines were crossed out and corrected in red pen. My eyes widened. "You wrote a book?"

He swallowed and for the first time since I'd met him, Elec looked truly uncomfortable. "That's none of your business."

"Maybe you do have more going for you than your looks," I joked.

My eyes wandered to the tattoo of the word "Lucky" on his right bicep, and the wheels began turning in my head. The tattoo was connected to the story he apparently wrote.

Elec gave me one last death stare before walking over to his closet and placing the binder on the top shelf. He sat back down on the bed and resumed his videogame.

Desperate to connect with him in some way, I sat next to him and watched as he destroyed his virtual enemy in combat.

"Can two people play?"

He stopped for a moment and froze, then sighed in exasperation, before handing me a controller. He changed the setting to two players, and we began battling it out.

It took me a while to figure out how to play the game. After multiple wins on his part, my character finally killed his off, and he turned to me with a look of amusement and dare I say…admiration. He cracked a reluctant but genuine smile, and I felt like my heart was going to disintegrate. That one little gesture, and I was a lost cause. What would I have done if he were actually really nice to me: lose my mind altogether and start humping his leg? Upon that thought, I decided it was time for me to go back to my room.

I spent the rest of the night trying to figure him out and concluded there was definitely more to *stepbrother dearest* than met the eye.

***

Several weeks passed before I'd accepted Bentley's offer to take me out on a date. I'd finally conceded that a.) there were no better alternatives at the moment and b.) a distraction from my unhealthy obsession with my stepbrother would be most helpful.

My attraction to Elec was at an all-time high. Almost every night after dinner, I'd go to his room and play that videogame with him. It was a harmless way for us to take out our frustration toward each other without anyone actually getting hurt. The surprising thing was, he seemed to be the one initiating it now. The one night I decided to stay in my room and read, he'd sent me a text.

Are you coming to play or what?

Greta: I wasn't going to.

Elec: Bring some ass cream too and put extra Snickers in it.

That message would have seemed really odd to someone on the outside looking in. The text had made me giddy, though.

That night, we shared another bowl of ice cream and played the game until I couldn't keep my eyes open. I even managed to kill Elec off two out of the 17 times we played. Even though he didn't really open up to me, the gaming sessions seemed to be his own special way of saying he didn't find my company deplorable anymore and that maybe, he even enjoyed it

But in typical Elec fashion, just when it felt like we were finally connecting, he had to go and ruin it.

***

It was a couple of days before my Friday night date with Bentley. Victoria and I were hanging out in the kitchen when Elec walked in and did his usual drinking out of the milk carton routine.

Victoria's eyes fixated on Elec's shirt riding up as he lifted the milk. The two shamrock tattoos on either side of his rock-hard abs were exposed.

She was practically drooling. "Hey, Elec."

Elec grunted in response through the carton before putting it back into the fridge. He then began rummaging through the snack cupboard.

Victoria dipped a pretzel in some nutella and spoke with her mouth full. "So, have you decided which movie you're going to see with Bentley Friday night?"

"No, we haven't discussed it."

From across the kitchen, I couldn't help but notice that Elec stopped sifting through the cabinet for a moment and froze. It seemed like he was trying to listen to what we were saying. He glanced over at me for a fleeting moment with a troublesome expression.

"Well, I think you should see that new Drew Barrymore romantic comedy. Make him suffer through a chick flick. What do you think, Elec?"

"What do I think about what?"

"What movie should Greta see on her date with Bentley?"

He ignored her question and looked at me. "That dude's a fucknut."

He started to walk away, but Victoria called after him. "Hey, Elec…"

He turned around.

"Would you want to join? I mean…we could go with them. It might be fun. Like a double date."

He chuckled and just stared at her for the longest time with a look that screamed, *not a chance.*

I shook my head. "I don't think that's a good idea."

He turned to me with a malicious grin. "Why not?"

Why not?

"Because it's my date. I don't want anyone else tagging along."

"It would really upset you if I went?"

"Yes, actually."

He looked over at Victoria. "In that case, I'd love to go."

The look of satisfaction on her face sickened me. She thought this was her big chance to make a move on him. Meanwhile, he'd basically admitted he was just doing this to torture me.

"See you Friday night," he said before disappearing.

Victoria opened her mouth in a silent scream then tapped her feet excitedly on the floor, and it made me want to vomit. I now had to gear up for what would surely be one of the most awkward dates of my life. But nothing could have prepared me for what actually transpired that night.

CHAPTER 5

Elec was supposed to be meeting us at the cinema. He had taken a part-time job at a bike shop and would be going home to shower first after work.

Victoria, Bentley and I got his ticket before they sold out.

"Victoria, are you sure your date's showing up?" Bentley laughed.

"He'll be here." She looked over at me with uncertainty. Truthfully, I had no clue whether Elec was actually planning to show up and prayed he didn't. When Victoria texted him that we planned to go inside the theater early to secure seats, he'd never responded.

As we waited in the concession line, Bentley put his arm around my shoulder, causing me to stiffen. It seemed a little forward since we were just getting to know each other. He did smell nice and looked really good in jeans and a black dress shirt. His short light brown hair was spiked with gel. I remember I used to think Bentley was really cute. Nowadays, every single guy seemed to pale in comparison to Elec on the physical attraction meter. I wanted to crush that meter with a sledgehammer.

Victoria was under strict instructions not to tell Bentley that Elec was my stepbrother. Since Elec never spoke to me at school, most people still had no clue that we lived together. I preferred it that way.

Relief set in when the theater darkened, and the previews began to play. I put my phone on vibrate. Maybe he wasn't going to show after all. My body started to relax while Victoria checked her phone every two seconds and looked around for him.

The opening credits to the movie started. I sank deeper into my chair and kicked my feet up on the empty seat in front of me. Bentley gestured for me to have some of his popcorn. I'd been munching on it for a while and was actually enjoying the movie until I nearly choked on a whiff of clove cigarettes mixed with cologne.

Then, there he was.

My knees trembled as he slid past them in the darkness making his way to the empty seat on the other side of Victoria.

I wanted to smack the look of joy off of her face. When Elec leaned in and kissed her on the cheek, my appetite for the popcorn transformed quickly into nausea. I handed Bentley the bag and pretended to be interested in the movie. In all honesty, I was staring straight at the screen, but Drew Barrymore might as well have been speaking Mandarin Chinese.

All I was really doing was ruminating and breathing in Elec's scent. His presence had made me angrier than I anticipated it would.

At one point, Bentley grabbed my hand and wrapped it inside his. I froze.

Victoria, who had downed a giant Diet Coke before Elec arrived, whispered in my ear that she was going to the bathroom.

My heart began to pound faster once she left because there was no longer anything blocking my view of him. I could feel from the corner of my eyes that he was looking at me. Despite laughter erupting around me from the audience, the weight of his stare seemed to drown it all out. I wouldn't look at him or even move.

Just keep staring at the screen, Greta.

My phone vibrated on my leg.

Are you practicing to be a store window mannequin?

I couldn't exactly respond to the text because Bentley would have seen me. I did, however, look over at Elec and regretted it. His normally unruly hair was gelled and styled. He was also more dressed up than normal in dark jeans and a leather jacket.

His mouth spread into a rare genuine smile that made me feel as if something were squeezing at my heart. Then, he chuckled, causing me to laugh at myself, too. He was right. I had been sitting there stiff as a board tonight. I was acting ridiculous.

Victoria interrupted my moment with Elec when she slid past my legs and sat down, once again obstructing my view. She leaned into him, and that was my cue to stare back at the screen.

I wanted to be the one with him.

It didn't make sense, but it was proof that desire and logic were two very separate things.

What if Victoria tried to kiss him tonight? What if he responded? I couldn't deal with this jealousy already, and nothing had even happened yet. His dating girls from school had become something I'd forced myself to accept. I mean, he was my stepbrother, supposedly disliked me and would be moving back to California after graduation. The reality was, nothing could ever happen between us. Despite that, his messing around with my best friend would not be okay for me. She'd tell me every last detail and wouldn't hold back.

Somewhere in the midst of my thoughts, the movie finally finished. Drew Barrymore was smiling, so it must have been a happy ending.

Bentley's hand rested on my lower back as we exited the theater. In the bright florescent lights of the crowded lobby, Elec looked even more stunning. Victoria grabbed onto his arm possessively. I wanted to hate her for it, but she had no clue about my feelings for him.

This situation was overwhelming me. I needed to be alone for a few minutes. "Guys, I'm just gonna go freshen up. You should decide where we're going to eat."

Upon entering the safety of the bathroom, I let out a deep breath. After I peed and washed my hands, I was reluctant to head back outside, so I stayed staring at myself in the mirror.

Anger and frustration coursed through me the more I thought about this fucked up date. I picked up my phone and texted Elec.

Why are you really here? Do you even like Victoria?

I immediately regretted that impulsive move. My phone vibrated.

Elec: What if I do?

Wishing I'd never said anything, I had no answer and just stared at my phone. He texted again.

Elec: I don't.

I hadn't realized I was holding in so much breath until a massive sigh of relief escaped me.

Greta: Then, why are you here?

Elec: To get a rise out of you.

Greta: Why?

Elec: Because I get off on it.

Greta: Why?

Elec: I can't answer that question any more than you can tell me why you look at me the way you do even though I've treated you like shit.

Oh. God. Until now, I hadn't realized how obvious my feelings were, how stupid and desperate I must have looked to him all this time.

Elec: Have some self-respect.

What. The. Fuck. Now, he'd seriously pissed me off. Wow.

Greta: Don't worry. I won't be looking at you anymore.

I just couldn't believe he'd said that to me. My eyes started to water, but I was determined not to let him see me upset. It took a few minutes to compose myself before walking back out to the lobby. As hard as it was, I refused to look at him. *Refused.*

"What the heck took you so long?" Bentley asked.

"I ran into a little glitch. But it's over."

Victoria put her hand on my shoulder. "Everything okay?"

"Yup. Let's go."

Victoria and Elec walked in front of us. She was still hanging onto his arm while both of his hands were in his pockets.

The four of us packed into Bentley's Prius and drove to an all-night diner. Avoiding my stepbrother became a much bigger challenge in the confines of a small booth where he was sitting right across from me. Still, I kept to my word. I'd focus on his sleeve tattoo or play with the salt shakers but never looked up. I pretended to enjoy being immersed in conversation with Bentley, who was sitting to my left.

We ordered our food, and so far, I'd been successful in not making eye contact with Elec.

"So, Greta, there's this party next Friday at Alex Franco's house. I wanted you to come with me," Bentley said.

"Sure. Sounds like fun."

"Good." He leaned in and lightly kissed the side of my face.

Elec was mindlessly playing with some sugar packets. If I were Victoria, I'd find it peculiar that my "date" wasn't even talking to me. But what did I know?

She tried to make conversation. "Elec, what are your plans after graduation?"

"To get the hell out of Boston."

And that was all she got.

A few minutes later, he seemed to be texting under the table. Then, my phone vibrated.

Bet I can get you to look at me.

I ignored him and didn't text back.

A few seconds later, our food arrived, and we all dug in. I was happily ensconced in my pancakes when I heard Elec say to Victoria, "You have some milkshake right there."

"Where?"

"Here," he said before pulling her into him and tongue kissing her right in front of me. I watched in horror as he did to her mouth, the same things he'd done to mine during the encounter at the cafe. My face burned up in anger as he slowly and sensually moved his mouth over hers.

"Damn, you two, get a room," Bentley said.

When Elec finally backed away, Victoria covered her mouth and said, "Wow…and here I was, thinking you weren't interested." She laughed.

My stare burned into Elec's, and he silently mouthed, "Told you."

"Excuse me," I said to Bentley as I exited the booth and promptly asked the waitress where I could find the bathroom. Before I could grab my bearings, Victoria came in after me.

"What was that?" she asked.

I leaned against the sink. "What was what?"

"That whole thing…Elec kissing me like that, and then you running off. Did it upset you that he kissed me?"

I dodged the inquiry. "He can do whatever he wants. He just bugs me."

"You didn't answer my question."

Sure, why don't I just admit that I'm obsessed with my stepbrother, so much so, that it turned me on a little watching him kiss you, because everything he does seems to make my body react.

"You know things between him and me are rocky, Vic. I also don't want to see you get hurt."

"Don't worry. I'm a big girl. I'm just having a little fun. I know he's leaving."

This was exactly what I was afraid of.

"Don't mind me, okay? Elec just gets under my skin. It's no big deal. I just needed a breather."

"Okay, if you say so." She crossed her arms. "Are you feeling good about Bentley, though?"

"We'll see. He's…nice. I think I'll definitely give him a chance."

"Good."

When Victoria hugged me, I could smell Elec on her, and it made me crazy. It was my reaction to that whiff of smoky musk that served to remind me that he was driving me insane and that it needed to end. I vowed in that moment to do whatever it took to shake this thing I had for him.

"You ready to go back out?" she asked.

"Yeah." I nodded and took a deep breath. "Yeah, I'm ready."

The events that took place next seemed to occur in rapid succession. As we walked back toward the booth, I heard silverware flying and then a loud crashing sound. A crowd of people gasped before I caught sight of Bentley on the ground and Elec kicking the shit out of him. Bentley's face was bloody, and Elec's mouth was also bleeding.

"Elec, what are you doing?!" I screamed.

He continued kicking Bentley with all his might.

The restaurant manager ran toward us along with a waiter who assisted him in pulling Elec away from Bentley who was keeling over on the ground in pain.

I bent down. "Bentley, what happened?"

"That lunatic punched me for no reason and so, I hit him back. Then, he just started beating the shit out of me. I tripped, and he started kicking me when I was down."

"Are you okay?"

"I'll be fine."

"You don't look fine."

I helped him up, and he leaned against me. The two men were still holding Elec down as police sirens approached in the distance.

What was happening?

Victoria walked over to Elec. "What the hell is going on?"

He spit some blood onto the floor. "Do *not* let her leave with him."

I looked over at Bentley. "What started this? I don't understand."

"Nothing. That freak just attacked me."

"You fucking liar," Elec spewed as he lunged forward to charge at Bentley again, but the men holding his arms restrained him.

Two officers walked in and began questioning each of the guys in separate corners. Victoria and I just stood at the sidelines, dazed and confused as to what could have possibly happened in the short time we were in the bathroom to have caused this. I'd wished I could have heard what they were saying to the officers, but they were too far away.

After they were released, Elec walked straight past Victoria and over to me. "Let's go. You're not getting in his car."

"Who the fuck do you think you are, trying to take my date home?" Bentley shouted.

"I *am* her home, fucknut."

CHAPTER 6

The cab ride with Elec and Victoria that night had been extremely uncomfortable. Bentley had freaked out and taken off in his car after he found out Elec was actually my stepbrother. The cause of what happened in that diner remained a mystery to me. The entire way back, Elec said nothing to either one of us. He sat in the front while we sat in the backseat.

When we got home and he went upstairs to his room, he slammed the door so hard, it made me jump. I'd thought about trying to talk to him, but my better instincts told me to just let him be alone.

By the time I woke up the following Saturday morning, Elec had already left to work the entire day at the bike shop.

My mother sat at the granite island in our kitchen on the stool next to me. "Do you wanna tell me what happened last night? Randy got a call from his cop friend saying that Elec was involved in a fight over at the diner and that you were with him?"

I put down my coffee and rubbed my temples. "We were having dinner…Elec, Victoria, myself and this guy, Bentley, from school. Elec and he got into a fight. We don't know what started it because it happened when Vic and I went to the bathroom. So, I really don't know much more than you."

"Well, your stepfather is fuming, and I don't know what to do about it."

"He needs to just let it go. Guys get into it sometimes, and it may not have been Elec's fault. You need to explain that to him."

"There's no talking to Randy when it comes to Elec. I don't understand it."

"Neither do I."

***

I'd decided I was going to talk to Elec that night and had been waiting for him to come home all day. The bike shop closed at six, so I'd expected him back by seven, but he never came home.

Unable to sleep, a sinking feeling came over me. Finally, around midnight, I heard footsteps and the doorknob to Elec's room slowly turn.

At least, he was home.

About a minute later, came the sound of his door busting open.

"What the fuck, Elec? You reek of alcohol," I heard Randy yell.

I jumped up and plastered my ear to the wall.

"Hey Da-da," Elec seemed to be slurring his words.

"Boy, you just continue to make me so damn proud. First, you start a fight and humiliate me in front of this entire community and now, you have the gall to set foot in my house tonight drunk? Well, you're gonna wish you never came home."

"Really? What are you gonna do? Hit me? That's the one thing you haven't done. I'm so ready for it."

"You would love that, wouldn't you? No. I'm not gonna hit you."

"Right…you're not going to hit me. You're just gonna *hate* me…like you always have. Sometimes, I wish you'd just hit me once and for all then leave me the fuck alone."

"You're a loser, Elec."

"Tell me something you haven't before."

"Okay, then, I've got news for you. I'm not going to help you pay for college after all. You're on your own. I've made the decision tonight. I'm taking the money I would have allotted you and giving it all to Greta."

What? No!

Randy continued, "I'm not wasting my hard-earned money on a fuck-up who wants to be a pansy writer. If you decide you want to have a real career some day, come talk to me. Until then, I'm not spending a dime on you."

"You were never planning on paying for my college anyway, and you know it."

"Why would I want to…for someone who's done nothing but disappoint me from the day he was born?"

"That was the start, wasn't it…the day I was born? I never even stood a fucking chance, did I? Because Mami never aborted me like you asked her to."

"That's a fucking lie. Did she tell you that?"

"Even if she hadn't told me, I could have guessed it. Is that why you've been slowly killing me with your words my entire life to make up for it?"

My heart was breaking.

"Have I? Then why aren't you dead yet, Elec?"

I gasped in horror. I couldn't stand back and listen to this anymore. I ran into the next room and was even more horrified to find Elec sitting at the edge of his bed with his head in his hands. The smell of alcohol on him was pungent. His back was rising and falling with the heavy breaths that escaped him.

"Randy...stop! Please *stop!*" My stepfather stood there with his arms crossed, looking at me blankly. In that moment, the man standing in front of me might as well have been a total stranger. "He's your son. Your *son!* I don't care what you convince yourself he did to deserve it, there is nothing that could *ever* justify talking to your child like that."

"Greta, you don't understand our history..." Randy said.

"I don't need to know anything to understand that the words that came out of your mouth tonight cut deeper than any weapon ever could. And I'm not gonna stand here and let you abuse him like that."

Neither of them said anything. The room was silent. Elec's breathing seemed to have calmed down and with that, so did mine.

I turned back to Randy. "You need to leave."

"Greta—"

"Leave!" I screamed at the top of my lungs.

Randy shook his head and walked out of the room, leaving me alone with Elec who was still in the same position.

I ran to my room and returned with a bottle of water, putting it up to his mouth. "Drink this."

He gulped it down in one sitting then crushed the plastic and threw it. I kneeled down to pull off his shoes.

He was slurring his words and muttering something I couldn't understand.

I stood up and pulled his blankets down. "Lie down."

He took his jacket off, throwing it clumsily onto the ground and crawled over to his pillow. He lay on his stomach and closed his eyes.

I sat at the side of the bed and was still shaken by what I'd walked in on. I felt so badly for Elec and was so ashamed of Randy. I knew I needed to talk to my mother tomorrow. How could she have not overheard and intervened tonight?

Elec's breathing had evened out. He had fallen asleep. I ran my hand once through his silky black hair, relishing the ability to touch him freely without his knowing it. My index finger brushed lightly over the cut on his lip that he sustained from the fight with Bentley. It was right around his lip ring, and I shuddered when I realized that his lip must have torn.

The reason for the constant anger he exhibited was now clearer to me than ever, yet I still felt like I knew nothing about Elec's life.

He looked so innocent in his sleep. Without the smirking or the glare of his eyes, it was easier to see past his harsh exterior in order to catch a glimpse of the boy hiding beneath—the same boy I now realized had been damaged by the man married to my mother.

A teardrop fell down my cheek as I adjusted his blanket before exiting the room.

Back in my own bed, I thought about how ironic it was that this guy who'd done nothing but try to chase me away and intimidate me was the one person in the world I felt like I wanted to protect.

***

By the time I got up the next morning, Randy and my mother had already taken off for an overnight trip out to the Western part of the state.

Mom had left me a note on the kitchen counter:

Randy surprised me in the wee hours of the morning with an early birthday trip to the Berkshires. He'd already packed the car by the time I woke up! I didn't want to wake you. It will only be one night. We'll be back late Monday. There are plenty of leftovers for you and Elec in the fridge. Call my cell if you need anything. Love you.

How convenient. I was sure my stepfather had arranged this to avoid having to deal with what happened last night. I immediately grabbed my phone and texted her:

Enjoy your trip, but when you get back we seriously need to talk about what's going on with Randy and Elec.

Elec didn't come downstairs until two that afternoon. He looked like death warmed over as he dragged his feet over to the coffeepot, his hair disheveled and his eyes bloodshot.

"Good morning, sunshine," I said.

His voice was groggy as he whispered, "Hey." He poured some coffee into a mug and nuked it.

"So, apparently, our parents took off on an overnight trip. They'll be back Monday night."

"That's too bad," he said.

"That they went away?"

He took a sip of coffee and said, "No, that they're coming back."

"I'm sorry abou—"

"I can't do this." He shut his eyes and held out his palm. "I can't talk to you. Every time you speak, it sounds like a chainsaw."

"Sorry. I get it. You're hungover."

"Well, there's that, too."

I rolled my eyes, and he winked, causing my heart to flutter.

I sat with my legs crossed on the sofa adjacent to the kitchen. "What are your plans today?"

"Well, first I have to find my fucking head."

I laughed. "And then?"

"I dunno," he said, shrugging his shoulders.

"Would you want to get some takeout later?" I asked, trying hard to seem casual.

He looked apprehensive and rubbed the scruff on his chin. "Um…"

"What?"

He checked his phone. "No, actually, ugh…I have a date."

"With who?"

"With, um…"

"You don't know?" I laughed.

He scratched his forehead. "Give me a minute…"

I shook my head. "That's sad."

"Oh! With Kylie…yeah…Kylie."

If Kylie only knew how interchangeable she was. I was just secretly relieved he didn't say Victoria, because I knew she still had it in her mind to contact him despite the scene he caused on our "double date." She'd texted him at least once yesterday, and her desperation really annoyed me.

Early that evening, I'd curled up on the couch with my book when Elec walked downstairs. I instinctively sat up and straightened my clothing. His cologne wafting through the room was enough of an aphrodisiac before I even turned to look at him. He was dressed in black pants and a fitted maroon shirt rolled up at the sleeves. His hair was styled into a controlled mess, and aside from the cut that remained on his bottom lip, he looked better than I'd ever seen him. Actually, even the damn cut was sexy. The energy in the room seemed to change anytime he walked into it. All of my senses were hyperaware of him.

I remembered his text from the other night: *Have some self-respect.* Ugh. I forced myself to return to my book since apparently, I couldn't seem to hide my attraction whenever I looked at him. Just thinking about that text again had put me in a bad mood. I had kind of forgotten about my vow to never look at him again after everything that happened with Bentley and Randy.

He grabbed his keys. "I'm headed out."

"Okay," I said, making sure to keep my eyes fixed on the book.

The door slammed shut, and I breathed out a sigh of relief. It had been a long time since I had the house to myself and although the pathetic side of me wished Elec had stayed in, there was something to be said for privacy.

I ended up ordering some Chinese takeout to be delivered. Shortly after I opened the carton of shrimp lo mein, the text alert on my phone sounded.

I had this flashback from last night.

Greta: Oh?

Elec: You were on your knees at the foot of my bed. Did you take advantage of me?

40

Greta: You'd better be kidding. No! I was taking off your shoes, drunkass.

Elec: Kinky. A foot fetish?

Greta: You're not serious...

Elec: ;-)

Greta: Aren't you supposed to be on a date?

Elec: I am.

Greta: Then, why don't you pay attention to her?

Elec: Because I'd rather bug you.

A phone call interrupted my thoughts before I could text him back. It was Bentley. *Crap.* I wasn't sure whether to pick it up.
"Hello?"
"Hey, Greta."
"Hi. What's up?"
"Elec isn't there, is he?"
"No. Why?"
"You left your jacket in my car the other night. Can I come by and give it to you?"
"Um...sure. I guess that would be okay."
"Great. I should be there in about twenty minutes."
I hung up and noticed that Elec had sent several more texts while I had been on the phone with Bentley.

Elec: Actually, my date is a dude.

Elec: A dud! I meant to type my date turned out to be a dud.

Elec: LMAO

Elec: #notadude #eleclovespussy

41

Elec: Where the fuck r u?

Laughing hysterically, I typed.

Greta: Sorry, that was Bentley. He called. I left my jacket in his car the other night and he's dropping it off.

A couple of seconds later, my phone rang.

"The fuck he is! You're not letting that guy into the house."

"He's just dropping off a jacket."

"Call him back and tell him he can leave it on the doorstep."

"I'm not gonna do that. There's no reason to. Whatever happened is between you and him."

The call dropped. *No, he hung up!*

He had some nerve trying to tell me what to do like that without a good explanation.

Ten minutes later, my feet flew off the couch when the front door opened.

Elec was out of breath. "Did he show up?"

What the heck?

"Not yet. Why are you here?"

"You didn't sound like you were paying attention to me. So, I had no choice but to come home."

"If you won't explain to me why you want me to stay away from Bentley, how do you expect to me listen to you?"

He ran his hands through his hair in frustration.

The doorbell rang, and Elec beat me to the door and opened it.

Bentley's face turned white. "What are you doing home? She said you weren't here."

Elec swiped my jacket out of Bentley's hands and slammed the door in his face. Then, he locked it.

"I'm going after him. Get out of my way," I said.

He crossed his arms in front of the door. "You'll have to get past me. And can't you hear his car taking off right now? He's a fucking sissy."

I let out a breath and gave up, deciding to move past it. I didn't really want to see Bentley but remained annoyed by Elec's

42

controlling behavior. He didn't have a right to interfere in my life when he only closed himself off to me in return.

The tension in the air was thick as I walked back over to my plate of food on the coffee table. We didn't speak for several minutes before I broke the ice. "There's some takeout Chinese on the counter if you want some."

Elec still looked irate and didn't respond. He walked over to the counter, grabbed the container of lo mein and started inhaling it.

"Hungry? Didn't you eat on your date?"

He slurped a noodle into his mouth. "Nope."

"Was she upset that you basically abandoned her?"

"No," he said with his mouth full.

Leaning my elbows against the counter, I asked, "If you didn't eat, what did you do? Or do I really want to know?"

"Um...Riley wanted to go bowling."

"I thought you said her name was Kylie."

He grinned guiltily as he bit into a spring roll. "Whoops."

Unsure of what to make of that, I rolled my eyes at him and reached for the last spring roll before he inhaled that, too. I took a bite. "I'm getting a movie on Netflix if you want to join."

He stopped eating for a moment and then just glared at me. "What the fuck is wrong with you?"

"Excuse me?"

"It doesn't matter how shitty I treat you...you still try to hang out with me."

It felt like steam was about to blow out of my ears. "No one asked you to come home tonight! I was actually enjoying having the house to myself."

"Really? Were you gonna lie on the couch with your vibrator or something?"

My heart dropped. *My vibrator.*

Shit!

It was in my underwear drawer, too. I had forgotten I'd moved it in there after I cleaned out my bedside table. I hadn't used it in a while and had totally forgotten about it.

He'd taken that too!

He continued, "Look at your face. You just realized it was missing? How have you been getting off? Either your fingers are sore or you must be in serious need of tension relief."

My face must have turned a hundred shades of red. "You bastard."

My eye twitched.

"You're winking at me again. Sorry, I can't help you out. Maybe you need to watch…a different kind of movie tonight? That might get you off. I have some if you want to borrow one to—you know—wet your whistle."

His words from the other night once again replayed in my head. *Have some self-respect.*

I'd decided I was done with him tonight. I'd take the high road and go back to my room without saying another word but not before I grabbed the container of noodles and dumped it all over his lap. "Wet that, dickhead."

His raspy laugh cut through me as I made my way up the stairs.

That night, I was still fuming as I squirmed around in my sheets. Who did he think he was with his passive aggressive behavior? He'd tried to play it off like I was the one seeking his attention, when he'd been texting me during his date before coming home early to intrude on my encounter with Bentley.

My obsessive thoughts continued until about two in the morning when I was interrupted by what sounded like yelling coming from Elec's room.

CHAPTER 7

Elec was tossing and turning as he cried out, "Mami, please. No! Wake up! Wake up!" His breathing was erratic, and all of his bedding had fallen on the floor.

"Pleeeeease," he screamed.

My heart was pounding as I shook him. "Elec! Elec. It's just a dream."

Still in a state of semi-sleep, he gripped and squeezed my arm so hard that it hurt. When his eyes flew open, he still seemed to be in a haze. Beads of sweat glistened on his forehead. He sat up and looked at me in shock as if he didn't know where he was.

"It's Greta. You were having a nightmare. I heard you yelling and thought something was wrong. It's okay. You're okay."

His breathing was still intense and slowly regulated. When his grip loosened on my arm, clarity returned to his eyes.

He let go of me. "This is the second time I've caught you in my room when I've been in a state of semi-consciousness. How do I know you're not just hanging out here doing things to me while I'm sleeping?"

Are you kidding me?

I'd had enough of his shit.

Maybe it was the fact that I was wired from no sleep or maybe it was because I'd just hit my limit with all of his jabs, but instead of responding, I pushed him with all my might. It may have been a juvenile thing, but I'd been dying to do it, and this moment seemed to be the straw that broke the camel's back.

He laughed heartily which pissed me off even more. "Well, it's about damn time."

"Excuse me?"

"I've been waiting for you to lose it on me."

"You think it's funny that you've caused me to resort to that?"

"No, I think *you're* funny…like really funny. Nothing has ever given me more amusement than busting your chops."

"Well, great. Glad I could do that for you."

Fuck. Tears were forming in my eyes.

45

This could not be happening.

It was almost that time of the month, and there was nothing I could do to control these emotions. I tried to cover my face but knew he had seen the first teardrop fall.

Elec's smile faded. "What the fuck?"

I needed to just leave. There was no way to explain my asinine reaction to him if I didn't even understand it myself.

I turned around and left, slamming my bedroom door behind me. I climbed into bed, pulled my blanket over my head and shut my eyes even though sleep surely would be impossible.

My door slowly creaked open, and the lamp was turned on.

"Peace offering?" I heard Elec say.

When I turned around, to my mortification, he was standing there with a dick in his hands. Not any dick. *My dick.* My vibrator. My purple life-sized rubber penis.

Elec waved it. "Nothing says I'm sorry like a dick and a smile."

I turned back around and hid under the blanket.

"Come on. Were you seriously crying in there?"

The room was silent as I stayed under the covers. I assumed he'd just leave if I ignored him. I knew I was wrong when I heard a click and a buzzing sound then felt the weight of him on my bed.

"If you won't smile, then I'll just have to tickle you with your little boyfriend here." He touched it to my hip, and I flinched, pushing the blanket off of myself. I tried to grab the vibrator, but he wouldn't let it go. He continued to tickle me with it in quick movements: behind my leg, the back of my foot.

I was fighting the urge to laugh. "Stop!"

"Not a chance."

All control was lost when he placed it under my armpit, which caused me to giggle hysterically. His own laughter vibrated against my ear.

How did I end up rolling around in bed in the middle of night with Elec holding a rubber cock against me?

I was laughing so hard that I thought I might die from it.

Death by dildo.

He finally clicked the off button, and it took me several minutes to catch my breath and calm down.

"Why stop now?"

46

"The point was to get you to laugh. Mission accomplished." He handed it to me. "Here."

"Thanks."

He lifted his brow. "Party in your pants tomorrow night? Should I bring chip n'dip?"

"Very funny," I said, placing it in my side table drawer and making a mental note to find a better hiding spot for it tomorrow.

He stayed lying next to me with his head leaning against the headboard. Even though we weren't touching, I could feel the warmth of his body as we lay side by side in silence.

As my eyes wandered to his tanned chest and prominent six-pack, desire started to build inside of me. His briefs were peeking out of the top of his gray sweatpants. His long feet were bare, and it dawned on me for the first time how damn sexy that was. I forced my eyes off him and stared up at the ceiling.

His voice was low. "I really didn't want to come here, Greta."

It was the first time he'd ever said my name.

It sounded so good coming out of his mouth. I turned to him as he continued staring away from me when he spoke.

"I was this close to skipping that flight and going somewhere else."

"What made you change your mind?"

"I couldn't do that to my mother. I didn't want her to have to worry about me while she's away."

"I see why you didn't want to be here now. I didn't understand it at first, but after listening to the way Randy spoke to you, I can understand why you have so much anger toward him. I guess, what I can't understand is why you took it out on Bentley the other night."

"Why do you assume that the fight was my fault?"

"Because you won't explain it to me, and you were the one kicking him when he was down."

He let out a single angry laugh. "I also *look* like the bad guy, right? So, every person in that diner just assumed I flew off the handle for no fucking reason other than to beat up that pretty boy for fun. I may have a record...for underage drinking and smoking weed once. But never in my lifetime have I ever attacked someone or even thrown a punch before that night."

Wow.

"Why won't you tell me what happened?"

"Because despite what you think and despite the fact that I love messing with you…I don't *really* want to see you hurt."

"I don't get it."

He finally turned his body toward me and looked at me for the first time. "That first day when you walked in on me in the bathroom, I wanted to shock you. You said you never saw a guy naked before. I assumed you were kidding. Now, I actually feel guilty about pulling that shit on you."

I repositioned myself, feeling a little nervous about where this was going. "Okay…what does that have to do with what we were talking about?"

"Fucknut didn't know I was your stepbrother, so when you left the table, he started bragging about how he was gonna take you to that party next week, get you drunk somehow and fuck you. Your ex-boyfriend made a bet with him that he couldn't get you in bed because you're a virgin. If you ended up giving it up to Bentley, your ex was gonna give him 500-dollars."

I covered my mouth. "Oh my God."

Elec nodded slowly with a sympathetic look. "So, yeah…I fucked him up."

"You let everyone think you were to blame. You took all that shit from Randy over it! You were just protecting me?"

"I didn't know how to break that news to you about what they were planning. But clearly, tonight, my warning to stay away from him wasn't getting through to you, so I needed to tell you."

"Thank you."

"I like to give you a hard time. It started out as a way to get back at my father…torture Sarah's daughter. But eventually, getting under your skin sort of just became this fun little game. Tonight, when you cried, I knew I'd taken it too far and that for you, it wasn't a game. As hard as it may be to believe, I never meant to hurt you, and I sure as fuck wouldn't stand by and let someone else hurt you, either."

He looked up at the ceiling again, and his lips bent into a frown as he pondered what he'd just said.

I lifted my index finger and brushed it softly across the spot on his lip that got torn in the fight. He closed his eyes, and my heart started to pound furiously as his breathing quickened with every stroke of my finger over his warm lip. "I'm sorry you got hurt."

"It was worth it," he said without delay.

I stopped touching him, and he looked at me. The sarcastic glare he used to give me was replaced with a look of sincerity.

Since I had his attention, I used the opportunity to change the subject. "You want to be a writer?"

He returned his gaze to the ceiling. "I *am* a writer. I've been writing since I was a little boy."

"What's *Lucky and the Lad* about? Why were you ashamed to show it to me?"

Looking uncomfortable, he repositioned his body. "I just wasn't ready to talk about it." He smiled and hesitantly said, "Lucky was my dog, actually."

I couldn't contain my smile. "You wrote a story about him?"

"Sort of. It's like a supernatural version of my life with him. Lucky was not only my best friend, but he was the only thing that could calm me down when I was younger. I suffered from pretty bad ADHD back then and had to be on medication for a while. When my mother brought Lucky home, my behavior improved dramatically. So, while the story is based loosely on Lucky and me, it's really about a boy who has superpowers that he uses to help solve crimes, but he can only decipher all the noise in his head when the dog is with him. The dog gets kidnapped as blackmail at one point, and the rest of the story becomes about getting Lucky back. It's set in Ireland."

"Wow. Why Ireland?"

"I've always had this weird obsession with all things Irish." He pointed to the two shamrocks on his abs. "Case in point. I think it's my way of trying to connect to that side of me—Randy's side—since I have no real connection with him. That sounds kind of fucked up, but it's the only explanation I have."

"What happened to Lucky?"

"Lucky died shortly after Randy left my mother. So, it was a lot happening at once."

I put my hand on his arm. "I'm sorry, Elec."

"It's okay."

Looking down at my hand sitting atop his sleeve tattoo, I thought long and hard about asking my next question. "Why does he treat you like that?"

He looked over at me. "Thank you for standing up to him last night. I wasn't that drunk. I heard everything you said, and I'll never forget it." He closed his eyes. "But I don't want to talk about him, Greta. It's a long story, and it's too complicated to get into at two-thirty in the morning."

I wasn't going to press my luck. This was more than I'd ever gotten out of him.

"Okay. We don't have to talk about it." After a long moment of silence, I asked, "Can I read your book?"

He laughed and shook his head. "Wow. You're just a million questions tonight."

"I guess I'm just excited that I'm finally getting to meet my stepbrother."

He nodded in understanding. "I don't know if I want you to read the book. No one's ever read it. I keep telling myself I'm gonna figure out how to publish it, but I never do. It's not perfect, but it's the story I'm most happy with. I'm pretty sure there are lots of mistakes I haven't caught."

"I would love to read it. And if I catch any mistakes, I can let you know. English is sort of my thing."

He smiled and rolled his eyes. "I'll think about it."

"Okay. Fair enough."

When he turned to me again, the gray of his eyes lit up in the lamplight. He made himself comfortable and relaxed into the pillow. "Tell me about your father."

He was looking at me so attentively, and it touched me that he wanted to know about him.

I sighed and stared off. "His name was Keith. He was a good man, a Boston firefighter, actually. My mom was 17 when she met him, but he was older—in his twenties—so it was really taboo. He was her one true love. We lived a simple life, but it was a good one. I was his little princess. One day, he just started complaining about a cough and within a month, he was diagnosed with advanced lung cancer. It took him from us six months later."

He placed his warm palm over my hand, which was still grasping his arm. Then, he ran his fingers through my own. His touch felt electric. I never imagined that just holding someone's hand could make me feel more than anything ever had up until that point.

"I'm sorry you had to go through that," he said.

"Me, too. He left me some letters, one for every year until I'm 30. So, on my birthday, I read them."

"He'd be proud of you. You're a good person."

I didn't really know what I'd done to deserve this glimpse into what Elec was like behind the tough act, but I loved it. At the same time, I expected it to end at any moment.

"Thanks." I caught my eyes lingering on his and abruptly turned away. He removed his hand from mine, and I felt it on my chin as he brought my face back to meet his stare again. "Don't do that."

"What?"

"You turned away from me. That's my fault. I made you feel like I didn't want you looking at me—that self-respect bullshit I fed you. Out of everything I ever said to you, that was the *biggest* lie, and I regret it the most. I'd started to let my guard down, and it freaked me out. I never had a problem with the way you look at me. My issue is the way it makes *me* feel when you look at me: things I'm not supposed to feel, things I *can't* let myself feel for you. At the same time…nothing felt worse than when you *stopped* looking at me, Greta."

He had feelings for me?

"What does it look like I'm thinking when I look at you?" I asked.

"I think you like me even though you think you're not supposed to." I smiled in silent agreement as he continued, "You're trying to figure me out constantly."

"You don't make it easy, Elec."

"Sometimes, you also look at me like you want me to kiss you again, but that you wouldn't be sure what to do if I did. That kiss…was why I got the hell out of that restaurant so fast. It started as a joke, but it sure as hell felt real to me."

My heart leaped to know he'd felt what I did that day. "Are you attracted to me?" I immediately felt stupid for having blurted it out. "I mean…I don't look anything like the girls you date. I don't

51

have big breasts and don't color my hair. I'm like the total opposite of the ones you bring home."

He chuckled. "That you definitely are." He leaned in. "What makes you think I prefer them just because I bring them home? Those girls, they're...easy...for lack of a better word, but they don't do anything for me, really. They don't try to get to know me. They just want to fuck me." He wiggled his brows. "Because I'm really good at it."

I laughed nervously. "I figured."

The tension in the air grew thicker by the second. Nothing had ever turned me on like the sexual confidence he'd exhibited in that moment.

I was beyond intrigued...and curious.

His eyes trailed the length of my body from head to toe. "In answer to your question, though, I prefer your body to theirs any day, actually."

Overwhelmed with arousal, I dug my fingers into my pillow upon hearing him say that. "Why?" The question had come out more like a sigh than a word.

His voice lowered. "You want details, huh?" His lips curved into a smile. He moved in closer to me as if he were telling me all of this as a secret. "Okay...you're petite, toned, limber and your tits...they're the perfect size and natural." He looked down at my chest. "I can see you have beautiful nipples because they're saluting me right now. It's not the first time that's happened, either."

I tucked my hands under my cheek and relaxed into the pillow as if he were reciting an erotic bedtime story. He whispered even lower, "I would love to suck on them, Greta."

So incredibly turned on by the words coming out of his mouth, I felt a trickle of wetness and throbbing between my legs. Urging him to continue, I breathed out, "What else?"

"You have an amazing ass, too. That night we went to the movies, you were wearing that little red skirt. Every time that prick would drag his hand down to your ass when we were walking, it would drive me insane. I wanted to be the one touching you."

I couldn't help it. I edged in even closer and put my hand on the scruff on his face. "Really?"

"You're really pretty, too."

Dying to taste his mouth, I ran my fingertip across his lip ring. "I thought I was pretty 'plain?'"

He shook his head slowly and caressed my cheek. He leaned into me, whispering softly over my lips. "No…just pretty."

The need to kiss him was overwhelming. "Kiss me," I sighed.

He continued to speak over my lips, his breathing labored. "It's not that I don't want to kiss you. I want that so fucking badly right now. But I just—"

I didn't wait for him to finish. I took what I wanted, what I *needed*.

He moaned into my mouth when my lips covered his. He planted each of his hands on either side of my face. Without the hot sauce from our previous encounter, I was able to just taste *him* and knew immediately that there was no going back for me. I don't know if it was my hormones or if the past several weeks were just major foreplay, but I felt completely out of control. The noises coming from the back of his throat made me even hungrier for him, and I caught them with my breath.

At one point, I rubbed my tongue gently around the cut on his lip as he closed his eyes. Then, he took over and started to kiss me harder, more demanding. I pushed my body into his and felt his erection press against me. I didn't care about any of the consequences in that moment. I just knew I never wanted this to stop and shocked myself with what came out of my mouth next.

"I want you to show me how you fuck, Elec."

He pulled away from me suddenly, looking stunned. "What did you just say?"

It was the most humiliating moment of my life.

His eyes widened, almost like he'd woken up from a dream. "Fuck. No…no. You need to understand something, Greta. That is *never* gonna happen."

Okay, *that* was actually the most humiliating moment of my life.

"Why would you say that after everything you just told me?" *God, I felt so stupid.*

He rested his head again on the headboard, looking almost tortured. "It was important to me that you know how much I want you and how beautiful I think you are—inside and out—because I feel like I've beaten down your self-esteem even though it wasn't my intention. I meant everything I just said, but the kiss should not have happened. I shouldn't even be in this fucking bed, but it just felt so good to lie here with you for a while."

"How am I different from any of those other girls you give yourself to?"

He ran both hands through his hair, messing it up then looked at me with darkened eyes. "Actually, there's a big difference. You're the only girl in the entire world that's forbidden, and fuck me if that doesn't make me want you more than anything."

CHAPTER 8

Nearly a month passed since that encounter in my bedroom.

Elec had left my bed that night shortly after he'd repeated that I was strictly off limits and that nothing could *ever* happen between us. It didn't make sense to me that he could feel so strongly about it, considering we weren't *actually* related. So, I felt that there had to be more to the story.

The worst part about what happened in my room was that Elec started to distance himself. There were no more rude texts, no more invites to play video games. When we were home at the same time, he stayed in his room, and I stayed in mine. He'd also been spending more time at the bike shop or out of the house.

I never thought I'd miss his insults and crude talk, but I would have given anything for things to at least go back to the way they were before I kissed him—and told him I wanted to fuck him.

Ugh.

I cringed whenever I thought about it. But in that moment, I was drunk off him and wanted to know what that felt like more than I'd ever wanted anything. I was ready.

Elec and I had both turned 18 in the weeks since that night. Our birthdays were just five days apart. So, I definitely felt old enough to take that step with someone. It wasn't as if I were intentionally saving myself for marriage or anything. I was a virgin simply because I'd never wanted it with anyone before...until Elec. He'd spent the past few weeks making it crystal clear that it was never going to happen between us.

But I missed him.

Then, one night after dinner, the tides changed, and I got a little piece of him back. Normally, Elec never ate at home, but this particular Wednesday night, for some reason, he decided to join us. Ever since the night I saw how badly Randy treated him, I'd all but avoided my stepfather, except for sitting down with him at dinner. My mother and I were not really on the best terms either because she continued to insist that it wasn't her place to get involved in Randy's issues with Elec.

Elec wasn't making eye contact with me at the table. He'd just look down and twirl the pasta around his fork. At one point, I'd stared out the window to gaze at the neighbor's laundry lined up and drying in the breeze. I could feel his eyes on me. It was as if he were waiting for me to turn away so that he could look at me when he thought I didn't notice. Sure enough, when I turned toward him, his head moved downward again, and he was back to playing with his vermicelli.

Randy was in rare form that night, complaining that the plain dinner of pasta and red sauce did nothing to curb his appetite. He abruptly got up and walked over to the snack closet.

"Greta, what the hell are you doing stuffing all these underpants inside a can of Pringles?" he yelled.

My mouth hung open, and I looked over at Elec. We stared at each other for a good few seconds before Elec snorted and lost it. We both simultaneously burst into laughter. Neither of us could stop.

I loved the sound of his genuine laugh.

Looking over at Randy's confused face made me crack up even harder.

When the laughter dissipated, Elec was still smiling at me and said low enough just for the two of us to hear, "I told you they weren't in my room."

Randy slammed the can on the table in front of me. I opened it and checked the inventory. "These aren't all of them."

Elec winked. "I kept a couple for me," he said seductively.

I rolled my eyes and threw one at his face. He promptly put it on his head and wore it like a beanie. Only my stepbrother would look smoking hot with a pair of underwear on his head. He continued looking at me with the wicked grin I'd longed for. It felt good to have his attention again, albeit briefly.

That night, I was just getting into my pajamas when my phone buzzed.

Can you come in here for a minute?

My heart raced as I walked down the hall. When he opened the door, he looked so incredibly sexy.

His breath smelled like mint toothpaste. "Hey," he said, flashing his beautiful white teeth, which contrasted perfectly with his tanned skin and black hair.

"Hi," I stepped inside the room and took a deep breath, noticing that the clove cigarette smell was almost completely gone.

He was wearing a black hoodie with the sleeves rolled up. It was left open over his bare chest, and his hair was still drenched from the shower. I stared at his lips where the cut had long healed. The metal of his lip ring glistened, and I hadn't ever yearned for anything more than to lick it, to feel his mouth and tongue against mine again.

Kissing me.

Licking me.

Biting me.

Change the subject.

"Why does it smell so fresh and clean in here?"

He lay back on the bed with his hands resting behind his head. I couldn't help staring at the V just below his abs and wished I could lie on top of him against his skin.

"Are you saying my room normally smells like shit?"

"Did you quit smoking?"

"I'm trying."

"Really?"

"Yeah…this weird girl who walks around commando once told me it was bad for me. So…I thought about that and finally listened."

"I'm really proud of you."

He sat up straight and looked at me. "Well, the truth is, you were right. That shit will kill me someday. A lot of aspects of my life may suck, but there are other things that make it worth living."

Something in the air seemed to shift when he said it, and an awkward silence ensued.

I cleared my throat. "Why did you need me to come in here?"

He walked over to his closet to get something. Then, I realized it was his book. He handed me the binder. "I wanted to give you this. I want you to read it."

"Seriously?"

"I don't let anyone read my shit, Greta. This is a big step for me. Whatever you do, don't show Randy. I don't want him anywhere near it."

"Okay. I promise. Thank you for trusting me with it."

"Be honest, too. I can take it."

"I will. I'll take my time with it."

***

I'd gone straight to my room that night and started reading. Minutes turned into hours. I'd told him I'd take my time with it, but the truth was, I couldn't put it down and ended up staying up the entire night to finish it.

Even though the story was told in the third person, and the boy named Liam was supposedly only loosely based on Elec, it felt like I was getting a window into his mind and soul through Liam's character.

There were too many similarities that I knew were derived from his life, particularly the fact that Liam's father was verbally abusive. The beginning of the story before Lucky came into the picture was quite sad. At the same time, it would make me cry in one part and literally laugh in the next. There were actually lots of funny parts separate from the main plot.

In one scene, Liam had a crush on the girl across the street, so he asked Lucky to go her house. His hope was that the girl would think Lucky was lost and that the dog would lead her back to Liam's house. Instead, Lucky, who was a big dog, ended up humping the girl's Pomeranian puppy out front. Liam watched from the window as she took her puppy inside and slammed the door. Lucky proceeded to take a dump on her lawn before running back home to Liam empty-handed.

But the main plot surrounded Liam's ability to sense evil via his hypersensitive hearing. The information he received was not always clear, often jumbled unless Lucky was present. At one point, Liam took information surrounding the murder of a local girl to the police. It turned out that a corrupt police officer was behind the crime. He had Lucky kidnapped so that Liam wouldn't be able to help authorities finish solving the murder. Lucky ended up escaping,

58

and the reunion scene between Liam and the dog was so touching that it had me bawling.

Everything was depicted so realistically, from the vivid descriptions of the Ireland landscape to the emotions Liam experienced. There was even a fun bonus chapter written from the dog's point of view at the very end. I had found only a few grammatical errors and jotted them down in a notebook for him.

By the end of the story, I'd felt as though I'd fallen in love with the characters, which was a testament to his writing. At the same time, I felt closer to him and was so honored that he'd given me a glimpse into his incredibly creative mind. I needed to find the right words to properly explain to him how amazing this was…how amazing *he* was.

So, the next day, I decided that I would sit under a shady tree after school and write down all of my feelings in a letter that I would give him when I returned his manuscript. I poured my heart into it and explained why I felt he was born to write and that it didn't matter if his father wasn't proud of him but that *I* was so incredibly proud of him.

***

That afternoon, I planned to drop the letter off at his room. When I got to the top of the stairs, my stomach turned when I heard a girl's voice from behind the closed door.

Giggling

Lips smacking together

Elec hadn't brought anyone home since long before the night we kissed in my bed. I thought that maybe he'd been respecting my feelings for him or that he'd changed.

I was wrong.

Knowing he was with another girl used to annoy me and make me jealous, but this time, it felt different. It just made me incredibly sad. I couldn't even bear to stay in the house, so I left the book along with the note in front of his door and ran back down the stairs, worried that his writing wasn't the only thing I'd fallen in love with.

CHAPTER 9

It upset me that he hadn't even acknowledged my letter after several days.

Victoria had also given me no choice but to finally tell her the truth about my feelings for Elec. She wouldn't stop talking about how she couldn't understand the fact that he never asked her out again after their kiss at the diner. I had no patience for it anymore and told her everything that had happened between us. She was shocked, but at least it got her to stop talking about him once and for all.

Elec continued to basically ignore me over the next week. He took on more hours at the bike shop and during the other times, stayed in his room with the door closed. He obviously knew that I'd overheard the girl in his room that day since I had left the book on the ground outside. He clearly didn't care to apologize or address what impact that might have had on my feelings.

So, when Corey Jameson asked me out on a date that week, I said yes. Corey was probably one of the sweetest guys at school. Truly, I was not physically attracted to him but needed a distraction and knew at least, we would have a good time together. He was one of the few males I'd considered a friend, although it was obvious he wanted to be more.

Friday night rolled around. I had styled my hair into waves and put on a royal blue dress I'd bought on sale at the mall, but my enthusiasm level was the same as if I were going over to Victoria's to watch a movie.

When Corey came to the door, my mother opened it and yelled upstairs, "Greta, your date is here!"

There was low music coming from Elec's room, and the door was closed. A part of me wanted him to see me leaving with Corey, but another part didn't want to deal with him.

Corey was waiting at the bottom of the stairs with flowers, and that made me feel oddly embarrassed for him. I could never picture Elec picking up a girl and handing her Gerbera daisies. Let's face it; he didn't need to.

"Hey, Corey."

"Hey, Greta. You look awesome."

"Thanks."

"Do you mind if I use your bathroom real quick before we leave?"

I hesitated to send him upstairs in the event Elec were to come out of his room. "Sure. It's upstairs. Just take a left, and it's at the end of the hall."

I waited on a stool at the counter.

"He seems totally nice," my mother said.

"He is," I said, placing the flowers into a vase.

That was the problem. I'd grown to love a little mean mixed in with my nice.

After a five-minute wait, Corey had an odd look on his face when he returned.

"Are you ready?" I asked.

"Sure," he said without making eye contact. He walked in front of me and led me to his Focus parked out front.

He was still acting strange after we got in the car and before he started the engine, he turned to me.

"I ran into your stepbrother upstairs."

I swallowed the lump in my throat. "Oh?"

"He said to give you these, that you'd left them in his room." He handed me a pair of pink lace panties, the second to last piece of underwear that Elec had been harboring.

I took them and stared out into the street in disbelief, confused as to whether I was angry or slightly amused.

When I composed myself, I turned to him. "He's just trying to mess with you…and me. It's sort of what he does. I know this sounds silly, but he took all of my underwear as a joke and hasn't given them all back. Nothing else is going on."

He sighed but still seemed a little uncomfortable. "Okay. That was just really weird."

"I know. Believe me. I'm sorry."

Corey was looking straight ahead at the road, so I took out my phone and discreetly sent Elec a text.

Greta: Why would you do that???

61

Elec: Don't get your "panties in a bunch." It was funny and you know it.

Greta: It wasn't funny to him.

Elec: You don't even like him.

Greta: How would you know that?

Elec: Because you like me.

Greta: You're full of yourself.

Elec: You wanted to be full of me too once, remember?

My jaw dropped.

Greta: Why do you always do this?

Elec: What's that?

Greta: Revert back to your inner asshole.

Elec: In her asshole, huh?

Greta: You suck!

Elec: I do…very well. I'd show you if I could.

Greta: Why are you doing this?

Elec: Because I can't fucking stop.

I wasn't going to write back. He texted again.

Elec: Come home.

Greta: What?

Elec: Come home. Hang out with me.

Greta: No!

I shut off my phone and glanced over at Corey who was still looking ahead quietly.

Elec was out of his mind. Who did he think he was, trying to prevent me from casually dating while he continued to whore himself out?

Elec had cast a shadow over the rest of the night, and while we were able to make small talk at the Mexican restaurant, I knew that Corey was totally turned off by what Elec did. The sick thing was, I wasn't even *that* mad. If I were being honest with myself, it secretly satisfied me that Elec cared enough to want to sabotage my date.

I tried to focus my attention solely on Corey and was doing a half-assed job while eating my flan dessert. All I could think about was Elec. He'd not only gotten under my skin tonight, he'd hijacked my entire mind.

My phone chimed just as we were getting ready to pay the bill.

I need you to come home.

Greta: No.

Elec: I'm not messing around this time. Something's happened.

My stomach suddenly felt unsettled.

Greta: Everything ok?

Elec: No one hurt or anything. We need to talk.

Greta: Ok.

Elec: Where are you? Will it be faster if I come get you?

Greta: No, Corey will take me home.

Elec: Ok. Don't take too long.

My heart was pounding.
What was this about?
I'd made up a story about severe stomach pains and asked Corey if he wouldn't mind driving me straight home. He wasn't too thrilled, but then again, the whole night was shot after what Elec pulled.

I couldn't get home fast enough.

Corey hadn't even waited for me to go inside before he drove off. I headed straight up the stairs and knocked on Elec's door before opening it.

He was sitting on the bed waiting for me with a troubled looked on his face. Actually, I'd never seen him look so upset. He got up from the bed and caught me off guard when he immediately pulled me into a hug. "Thank you for coming back."

His heart was beating through his chest as he held me firmly. My body yearned for him to hold me even tighter.

"What's wrong, Elec?"

He released me then led me by the hand over to the bed where we both sat down. "I have to go back to California."

All of the food I'd just consumed felt like it was coming up on me at once.

"What?" I put my hand on his knee because it felt like I was losing my balance. "Why?"

"My mother is back."

"I don't understand. She was supposed to be in England until the summer."

He looked down at the ground and hesitated before looking up at me with melancholy in his eyes. "What I'm about to tell you can't leave this room. You can't tell your mother, and you absolutely cannot tell Randy. Promise me."

"I promise."

"My mother wasn't in England. Shortly before I came here, she checked herself into a hospital for severe depression and substance abuse out in Arizona. It was supposed to be a six-month

64

program, and then she was going to stay with a friend for the remaining time until the end of my school year."

"Why didn't she tell Randy the truth?"

"My mother is a very talented painter. I know you know that. Anyway, she *was* offered an opportunity to teach in London for a year and used that as the excuse she gave Randy even though she turned it down. She's ashamed to let him know how bad things have gotten. Before she decided to check herself into the program, she'd overdosed on some sleeping pills, and I found her on the ground. I thought she was dead."

"That was the nightmare you were having."

"What?"

"The night you were yelling in your sleep, you were saying 'Mami, wake up.'"

"Yeah. That makes sense. I dream about it a lot, actually. My mother is a weak person. Ever since Randy left her, she's never been the same. I was afraid I'd lost her. She's all I have."

I squeezed his knee. "Do you really think our parents had an affair and that he left your mother for mine?"

"I know he cheated on my mother, because I hacked into his computer. He met your mother online while he was still married to mine. He'd say he was going away on business, but he was really coming to Boston to visit Sarah. I wouldn't lie to you about that."

"I believe you."

"In Sarah's defense, I'm not sure what story he fed her. He may have tried to play it off like he was separated. You know how you told me your father was your mother's one true love?"

"Yeah..."

"Well, that's what Randy was to my mother even though it may not have been reciprocal. He's a horrible father, but that didn't seem to matter to her. She's basically obsessed with him and has always based her self-worth on his actions toward her. She's obsessed with Sarah now, too. It's a sickness. There's so much more to this story, but I'm just telling you what you need to know as it relates to you and me."

"When you said I was forbidden...is it simply because I'm Sarah's daughter?"

He smiled and caressed my cheek with the back of his hand. "You look just like her. My mother thinks that her marriage ended because of Sarah. She hates your mother probably more than anyone. Deep down, I know he would have found a way to leave Mami anyway, but she's in extremely bad shape. She could never handle it if she ever found out there was something going on between me and Sarah's daughter."

"Why did she come home early?"

"She thinks she's doing better. She's not, Greta. I can hear it in her voice, but they let her check out anyway. The friend who was supposed to watch over her flaked out and isn't even in town. I'm scared for her to be alone. That's why I'm leaving tomorrow morning. My flight is already booked. Randy thinks her job fell through and could care less that I'm going back."

A teardrop fell from my cheek. "I just wasn't expecting this." I leaned against his chest as he wrapped his arm around me. We sat in silence until I looked up at him. "I'm not ready for you to leave."

"Swallowing my pride and coming to live with Randy so my mother could try to get better and not have to worry about me, was one of the hardest things I ever had to do. It was hell at first, but you were a little piece of heaven in the midst of it all. I never thought I'd go from dreading being here to dreading leaving, but that's how I feel right now. I want to stay but only because of you. I want to be able to protect you and not necessarily in a brotherly way, and that's fucked up."

I grabbed his hand. "I get it."

He wrapped his fingers inside mine and leaned in, lightly pressing his lips against my forehead. "I feel like you see me in ways that most don't. Getting you to hate me was impossible because you knew that wasn't really me. Thank you for being smart enough to see through me."

I couldn't help it. I wrapped my arms around him and breathed in the smell of his skin and cologne, wanting to burn it into memory.

He'd be gone tomorrow.

I might never see him again.

His breathing quickened then he let go of me.

I looked around at his bags and realized there was still a lot left to pack. "Do you need me to help you?"

"Please don't take this the wrong way."

I chewed my bottom lip. "Okay."

66

"What I need is for you to go back to your room. It's not because I don't want to spend time with you. It's because I don't trust myself."

"I want to stay here with you."

"With the way I'm feeling right now, I just can't be in the same room with you. I was a wreck when you went out on that date with flower boy. And that was before I found out I was leaving. Then, you come in here looking so fucking beautiful in that dress. I only have so much control."

"I don't care if something happens. I want it to."

He looked down at the ground and shook his head. "We can't let it." Elec was quiet then looked me in the eyes. "The other day, you knew I had a girl over. Nothing happened. She tried, but I couldn't get it up. It didn't feel right, and it's been that way for a long time—ever since that night in your room. You don't think I've fantasized about doing what you asked me to, knowing I'd be the first you would get to experience that with? Do you have any idea what even hearing the words 'show me how you fuck' coming out of your sweet little mouth did to me? It ruined me."

"I'd rather have one night with you than nothing at all."

"You don't mean that. If I thought you were the type of girl who did, we wouldn't be talking right now." He placed both hands on my shoulders, causing a shiver to run through me. "And for the record, I *like* that you're not that type of girl." He let out a deep breath that I felt on my chest. "Even if you say you could handle it...I'm not sure I could."

We stayed silent for several seconds with our eyes locked before I got up. "Okay. I'll leave." My eyes began to water because this felt like the end.

He could see I was starting to cry. "Please, don't cry."

"I'm sorry. I can't help it. I'm just gonna miss you."

He hugged me one last time and buried his nose in my hair. He spoke into my ear. "I'm gonna miss you, too." Our hearts were both beating fast against each other before he stepped back. "My flight doesn't leave until 10. Maybe we can get breakfast."

I walked back to my room in disbelief over how fast things could change in life. Little did I know, things with Elec would change again in the blink of an eye or should I say, in the middle of the night.

CHAPTER 10

Crushed couldn't begin to describe what it felt like having to go back to my room, knowing he wanted me in the same way I wanted him but that we would never stand a chance. It felt empty here already, and he wasn't even gone yet.

It bothered me that he'd have to return home to that situation with his mother. Not that his interactions with Randy had been anything less than awful, but at least here, I could have been there to support him. He really hadn't won in the parent department no matter how you cut it.

He'd only just begun to open up to me. I knew that if he stayed, we would have grown closer. I tried to convince myself that this was for the best because he was leaving in the summer anyway. But despite my self-talk, the ache in my chest just wouldn't go away.

I couldn't help envying all of those girls at school who'd gotten the chance to experience being with him on a physical level. Even though I connected with him in a different and better way, there was still a deep longing for what I'd missed.

My mother came in briefly to check on me and to ask if I'd heard the news about Elec leaving.

"You two seemed to be getting along better. It's a shame he wants to go back now that his mother's home. He could have certainly stayed until the school year ended."

Since my mother knew nothing about the real reason Pilar was back home, I mainly nodded my head as she spoke. I tried my best to mask the tears that up until then had been falling pretty consistently. She kissed me goodnight, and I stayed clutching the stuffed Snoopy doll that had been my right-hand man since I was three.

That was how my night was supposed to end.

***

It was only a light knock on my bedroom door. Thinking back, a "light" knock hardly seemed appropriate for what happened after I opened it.

His chest was rising and falling with heavy breaths.

"Are you okay?" I asked.

For a few seconds, Elec was staring at me as if he didn't know how he'd gotten to my door. "No."

"What's wrong?"

His eyes had a frantic hunger in them. "Fuck tomorrow."

Before I could process it, his warm hands cupped my face and brought my mouth to his. A low groan from the back of his throat vibrated down mine, and I caught it with a deep intake of breath. His chest pressed against my breasts as he pushed me back into the room. The door closed behind him.

What was happening?

His mouth was hot and wet as it devoured mine, his tongue circling the inside almost desperately. This was far more intense than the last two times we'd kissed, and I realized this was what it felt like when Elec didn't hold back. This was different and a prelude to something more.

He stopped kissing me for a moment, and his hands slid from my face down the length of my neck. He pulled my hair, bending my neck back. He sucked on the base before kissing his way back up and sighing into my mouth.

My tongue brushed back and forth over his lip ring, and he responded by gently biting my bottom lip as he moaned through his teeth.

I wanted more.

I was ready.

There wasn't a doubt in my mind; I was going to let him go all the way.

When he stopped to look at me, I took the opportunity to ask what I absolutely had to know. "What happened?"

He took my hand and led me to the bed where he sat and lifted my body on top of his so that I was straddling him. The heat of his erection pressed against my throbbing clit. He placed his head in the middle of my chest and spoke into my shirt, causing my breasts to tingle.

"You wanna know what happened to me?" he whispered in a hoarse voice. "I finally opened that letter you wrote after you read my book. That's what happened. No one's ever said those things to me before, Greta. I don't deserve it."

I ran my fingers through his hair, which felt like silk. "You do deserve it. I meant every word."

He looked up into my eyes. "The words in that letter…I'll carry them with me forever. I could never pay you back for what you just gave me. Then, I thought about how I couldn't even give you the one thing you asked me for. It made me angrier by the second as I was packing. I decided I'd rather have tonight than nothing at all, too. It's fucking selfish, but I want your first time. I want to be the first one to show you everything and to be the one you'll always remember for the rest of your life. But only if you meant it when you said that was what *you* wanted."

"I want it more than anything." I pulled him tighter into my chest.

He resisted, staring up into my eyes again. His expression was serious. "Look at me, Greta. Because I need to make sure you're really okay with the fact that this would end tomorrow. You would never be able to tell anyone. I'll give you anything and everything you want tonight as long as you truly understand all of that. You need to promise me that you could handle this."

"I can handle it. I already told you that I wanted my first time to be with you even if it's the only time. I don't want you to hold back. I want you to show me everything. I want to experience the same things all of those other girls did. I don't want you to treat me any differently."

"I won't give you exactly the same thing…but I can give you more. Okay? I can give you better. It may be one night, but I will make every second count."

This was really happening.

When my nerves suddenly got the best of me, Elec took notice and put his hands on my shoulders. "You're shaking. Maybe this isn't a good idea."

"I can't help it. I'm gonna be nervous, but it's in a good way."

I was still sitting on top of him when he looked up at me in one last moment of hesitation. I reached for his face with my hands and kissed him deeply in an attempt to prove that I was as ready as I was going to be. I looked him in the eyes one last time and said, "I want this."

He searched my eyes for several seconds then lifted me off him and stood up. Rubbing his fingertips along my neck, he moved them slowly in a scratching motion then wrapped his hand around the middle as if…he were going to choke me. But it wasn't anything like that. He just held onto my neck, rubbing it gently with his thumb. I felt myself getting wet from just the way he was looking at me, like there was nothing else in the world he wanted more than to have me.

"I love your neck. It was the first thing I wanted to kiss. It's so long and delicate."

I closed my eyes and bent my head back. He still wasn't kissing me, just lightly squeezing my neck.

Finally, he moved his hands down and slowly lifted my tank top off. His eyes were glassy as he stared at my breasts.

In a stupid moment of insecurity, I said, "They're small."

He kissed my cheek then spoke close to my ear. "Good. They'll fit inside my mouth perfectly."

His hands then gripped my sides and lowered to pull off my shorts. "Shit," he muttered and looked up at me with an impish grin when he realized I wasn't wearing any underwear. I kicked my shorts off and stood in front of him, feeling vulnerable.

He just continued to look at me for several seconds, and it was driving me nuts that he was keeping a little bit of a distance.

As his gaze traveled from head to toe, in a sense, every movement of his eyes felt like he was touching me.

He took a step forward and spoke softly just under my earlobe. "Is there anything in particular you'd like me to do or show you first?"

My body was still trembling in anticipation.

Everything.

"What are my options?"

He scratched his chin. "Rope, chain, cuffs…belt."

"Um…"

He immediately took my face in his hands. "Oh, God. You're so cute." He kissed me firmly on the lips. "There was a small part of you that wondered if I was serious. It was a joke."

"I figured. I just wasn't 100-percent sure."

"So…nothing in particular?"

"You could start by touching me, maybe taking off your clothes, too."

"You want me to take off my clothes, huh?"

"Isn't that usually how it works?"

He slowly shook his head and nipped my nose. "No."

"No?"

"*You'll* take off my clothes. But not until we play a little bit."

"Play?"

"You have no experience. I can't just get naked and start fucking you. You need to be ready for me. It's gonna hurt the first time no matter what, so we need to make sure you're as wet as possible. Sometimes, less is more at first because the more I withhold, the more you'll want it, the more ready you'll be."

Leading me over to the bed, he lay back against the headboard and pulled me into a sitting position on top of him. He was fully hard beneath me.

"*You* feel ready," I joked.

"I've been ready since the day I walked in the door, took one look at you and realized I was fucked."

"You've always wanted me like this?"

He nodded. "I did a really good job of hiding it for a while, didn't I?"

"You could say that."

He pushed me down over the hard-on bursting through his camouflage cargo shorts. "It's pretty obvious now, wouldn't you say?"

I was throbbing between my legs as I rubbed my hands over the black t-shirt that stretched against his torso. "Yes."

Like the darkening of a theater before the start of a movie, the lightness of his expression faded, indicating that things were about to begin. He wrapped his hands around my neck again. He slid them down and cupped my breasts, massaging them slowly and firmly as I bore down onto his shorts. I pressed myself into his cock to satisfy the arousal that was building in me with every movement of his hands.

He kept one hand on my breast and lifted his other one to my face, rubbing his thumb over my mouth then pushing two of his fingers inside. "Suck."

His skin tasted salty. I squeezed the muscles between my legs, so stimulated by look on his face as he watched his fingers moving in and out of my mouth.

When he pulled them out, he rubbed the wetness of my saliva over my right nipple and licked his other hand before rubbing his fingers over my left.

"They're perfect." Elec slid both hands down my torso and wrapped them around me, squeezing my ass. "So is this." He gave it a light smack and smiled. "I want to do things to this," he said as he gripped it harder.

I wanted him to kiss me so badly or put his mouth on me in some way while he touched me, but he just continued looking at me as he massaged my ass. Slipping my hands under his t-shirt, I continued to grind over his cock. "Can I take this off?"

"Okay…but just the shirt."

I lifted it over his head, causing his tousled hair to become even messier. I marveled at the contours of his cut, tanned chest. He had a small nipple ring on the left side. I'd seen him shirtless many times before but never up close with the ability to touch him.

I moved my hands over the tattoos on his arms, the word *Lucky* on his right and the full sleeve on his left and down to the shamrocks on his rippled stomach. I ran my fingers down the happy trail of hair that led into his shorts. He tightened his abs at my touch, and I felt his cock twitch under me.

"Sensitive spot?"

"It was…when you touched my abs."

I bent down and kissed his chest gently, and that intimate gesture seemed to have had an effect on him. When I backed away, he caught me off guard when he pushed me back down on him and held me there for a while. My bare chest was plastered against his heart that was beating uncontrollably fast.

"Why is your heart racing?" I asked.

"You're not the only one who's trying something new."

"What are you talking about?"

"I've never been anyone's first before."

"Really?"

"Yeah…really."

"Are you nervous?"

"I just don't want to hurt you." The way he looked at me when he said it made me realize he wasn't really talking about the physical pain. He didn't want me getting attached to him.

My chest tightened, and I was pretty sure it was a lie when I said, "You won't."

You will, but I want you anyway.

"I want to just take you so fucking badly right now, but I'm holding back because I'm scared of what this will do to you in more ways than one."

"Elec, you asked me what I wanted. What I want is for you not to hold back. We just have tonight. Please…don't hold back."

For the first time since he'd walked in the room, he kissed me with the same fervent hunger I craved, lashing me with his tongue and groaning into my mouth. He flipped me over onto my back and kneeled above me, locking me in with his arms. His disheveled hair fell over his beautiful gray eyes as he looked down at me and once again stuck two of his fingers in my mouth. I realized that if he were going to be comfortable letting go of his apprehension, I needed to step it up.

I held onto his hand and sucked on his fingers hard, taking them deeply down my throat. His eyes were half shut while he intently watched me do it as he licked his lips. Then, he reached down and spread my legs open wide.

"Beautiful," he whispered as he slipped his finger inside of me. "God, you're so wet." He moved it out of me and replaced it with two fingers the next time, pushing them into me slowly as deep as they'd go. I gasped.

"Feel good?"

"Yes."

He started to move his fingers in and out of me harder and faster. I could even hear how wet I was. Squeezing my breasts together, I bent my head back, and my body bucked. I started to lose control, moving my hips to meet his hand. He knew it when he pulled his fingers out of me suddenly. "Don't come yet," he said.

He flipped me over so that I was on top of him again and moved me back and forth over his cock. His shorts were soaked from me. At any given moment, I could have come if I let myself.

It seemed he had the ability to sense when I'd hit a breaking point. He stopped me and backed away.

"Do you feel ready now?"

"Yes. I've been ready."

"I want you to touch yourself."

I was kneeling over him as my fingers rubbed over my clit. My knees started to shake.

"What do you want, Greta?"

"I want to see you naked."

"Then, *take* what you want."

I unzipped his shorts with my free hand, and he helped me push them down. When his cock sprung forward out of his boxers, it shocked me just as much as it had when I'd walked in on him.

He smiled, knowing full well the reason behind my reaction. "Something wrong?"

"I just..."

He was stifling a laugh. "You look like you have some questions."

"Not really...I—"

"Get them out of the way now."

I got my first up-close look at the circular barbell piercing. "Will it break the condom?"

"That's never happened. I use a sturdy kind and extra large for that reason...and extra large for the other reason." He winked.

I laughed nervously, seriously not understanding how he was going to fit inside of me. "Does it hurt you?"

"It took a long time to heal but now, not in the least."

"Will it hurt me?"

"I've been told it actually enhances the pleasure."

"Wow."

"Anything else?"

"No. I'm good."

"You sure? Now's your chance to run."

I leaned down and pressed my lips to his, and we both laughed through the kiss.

I could feel the metal from the piercing as his cock slid against my stomach. I clenched the muscles between my legs with a renewed need to satisfy myself.

He lifted me off of him and placed my hand on his cock. "Touch me while you touch yourself and listen if I tell you to stop."

75

With one hand on my clit and the other on him, I did as he said. Nothing had ever turned me on more than seeing the moisture build at his tip with every stroke of my hand, to feel him hot and slick, growing even larger than before. I loved watching him watch me.

He was breathing uncontrollably. "Stop."

"I want to feel you inside of me now," I said.

"You will. There's something else I need to do first…just to make sure you're ready."

"What?"

Instead of answering me, he slid his body down under me and lifted me up. I still wasn't sure exactly what he was doing, but then it became abundantly clear when he positioned his face right underneath my crotch. I gasped when I felt it: the most amazing sensation of my life. I could have never imagined how good his hot mouth pressing against me would feel. His tongue brushed across my mound in slow but firm strokes. When he moaned, it vibrated through my core, and I let out an unintelligible sound.

"Ssh," he said against me. "We have to be quiet."

It felt impossible. "You need to stop, then."

"I don't want to. You taste too good," he said as his tongue continued to lap over me. Then, he slipped it inside of my opening while pressing his mouth harder against my clit.

Oh. My.

"I'm gonna come if you don't stop, Elec."

He sucked on my clit one last time and slowly released it from the grip of his mouth. I was pulsating between my legs, shaking and felt tears start to form in my eyes.

He slid back up from under me, took my face in his hands and smiled up at me. "Now…you're ready."

He reached into the pocket of his shorts that were on the floor and took out a condom. He ripped the package with his teeth, and the look in his eyes had me ripe with anticipation. Elec spread the rubber over his thick shaft and carefully squeezed the tip.

Positioning me under him, he kissed me deeply while his cock rubbed against my sex. I couldn't take any more and wrapped my hand around it, leading him into my entrance.

"Easy," he warned. "This is gonna hurt."

"I don't care."

"You will." He spread my knees back as far as they would go. "Hold onto my back and squeeze me, hit me, bite me…do whatever you have to do if you're in pain, but please don't scream. They can't know we're in here."

Even as wet as I was, it burned like hell when he first tried to enter me. I dug my nails into his back to curb the discomfort. I breathed through it as he stretched me. Eventually, the pain became tolerable. I'll never forget the way it felt when he was fully inside of me for the first time or the sound he made. He'd been so controlled until that moment when he shut his eyes and panted. "Greta…this…you…fuck."

With each subsequent movement, the penetration went from painfully uncomfortable to painfully incredible. He was still taking it easy, but honestly, from the look on his face, I wasn't sure if he could take much more.

He pulled out slowly then pushed back in even slower. "It's tougher to control myself than I thought. You're so tight. This feels so good; it's indescribable. I need to come, but it has to be with you."

As if on command, my muscles began to contract. "I am. Now. Oh God. Elec!" I'd yelled his name out too loudly.

He placed his hand over my mouth. "Shh…oh God. Greta…fuck…Greta," he whispered as he came, his cock pulsating inside of me. I could feel the heat of his release through the condom as his heart slammed against mine.

"That was the most incredible thing I've ever felt in my life," I said.

"Yeah." He kissed my nose. "And I haven't even fucked you yet."

CHAPTER 11

The fact that it felt empty when he'd only gotten up to go the bathroom was not a good sign about how tomorrow would feel. His leaving was only a few hours away, and I was already craving the return of his smell and his touch in the two minutes he was gone.

It was convenient to have a small half-bathroom off of my room since he might have woken up Randy and my mother if he had to go down the hall. He returned with a small washcloth and lay back down next to me.

"Open your legs." He placed it between them and held it there. "Does that feel good?"

"Yeah, it does. Thanks."

I really wasn't in that much pain, but the warmth of the cloth was soothing.

"Does it hurt?"

"No. It's really not bad at all. I'd be okay to try it again."

"We will. I want you to rest up a little first."

The room was dark except for the light coming from the bathroom. Over the next hour, he got up a few times to replace the cloth with a warmer one. He'd just lie next to me, holding it between my legs. We were both still completely naked, and it surprised me that it no longer phased me because he'd made me feel completely comfortable in my own skin. I almost wished he wasn't being so caring and sweet toward me.

We talked a lot in that hour: about his writing, about my pondering becoming a teacher, about our plans for next year. He would be attending a community college near his house in Sunnyvale. He'd live at home to keep an eye on Pilar and planned to get a job on the side.

Elec would talk about anything openly, except the subject of his history with Randy. That was still off-limits the one time I tried to bring it up.

The red digital numbers of the alarm clock taunted me. It was now three-am. My heart was starting to palpitate, and I felt almost panicky. There wasn't much time left. He must have read my mind because he'd suddenly turned me onto my back so that he was leaning over me.

"Don't go there," he said over my lips.

"Where?"

"Wherever your mind is right now."

"It's hard not to."

"I know. What can I do to make it better?"

"Make me forget."

He stared at me long and hard before I felt his hand wrap gently around my neck.

That seemed to be his thing. I loved it.

"I know you said it before. But do you really want me to show you how *I* do it?"

"Yes."

"You don't want me to hold anything back?"

"Don't go easy on me this time, Elec. Please."

He looked at me for what seemed like a full minute then said, "Turn around."

Just that command alone had caused wetness to build between my legs.

It gave me chills when I felt his strong hand slide down the length of my back. Then, with both hands, he firmly squeezed the cheeks of my ass before lowering his mouth and biting it gently...and then again and again.

He whispered against my skin. "I love your ass." His words caused my muscles to tighten in anticipation.

I let out a deep sigh when his hot mouth landed between my legs from behind me. The sensation of his going down on me from that angle was almost too much to handle. I was throbbing as he licked and sucked harder as if I were his last meal. The sounds he was making were driving me crazy.

"God, you taste so good. I could do this all night," he groaned into me.

I'd yelled out loudly at one point, and he fisted my hair to bring my face back to his. "Shh. You're gonna get us in trouble," he said before sliding his tongue into my mouth and kissing me with the taste of my own arousal.

His kiss then moved down the length of my back, and he suddenly stopped. "Fuck, I can't take it anymore. We need to move to the floor because this bed will make too much noise."

I threw a few pillows down without delay and got down on my hands and knees.

He was quiet. When I turned my head around, his eyes were fixed on me as he stroked his engorged cock.

"You on all fours like this...nothing has ever turned me on more in my entire life."

Watching him pleasuring himself while looking at me had been *my* biggest turn on.

When I turned back around, I heard the rip of the condom packet and looked back one last time to watch him sheath himself.

"Relax," he said as he slid one hand up my back and wrapped it around the base of my neck. I'd grown to love the erotic feel of his signature light chokehold. After an initial burn, his cock sank into me with ease, and I knew right away that this experience was going to be different from the first time.

"Tell me if at any point, it becomes too much."

I knew that no matter what it felt like, that would never happen.

Every thrust was more intense than the last. He let out a deep breath with each one that I could feel on my back as he continued to hold onto my neck. He was completely in a zone, having finally let go of all apprehension.

This was Elec fucking me.

I wanted it to continue, to see where it would go. "Fuck me harder."

That had caused him to grab my hips as he pounded into me faster. It felt impossible not to scream because it felt too good. In a weird way, having to refrain from making any noise bottled up the pleasure inside me and intensified it. I started to match the rhythm of his movements with my body, and that seemed to put him over the edge.

"Touch yourself, Greta."

I massaged my swollen clit as he slowed down to encourage my climax. I could feel him even deeper inside me now. He gently pushed my torso down so that my ass was lifted higher into the air.

The penetration at that angle was so intense, so deep that I could feel the brink of my orgasm.

"Do you feel that?" he whispered.

"Yes. Yes. It's incredible like this."

"I've never been this deep inside anyone before. It's never felt like this for me," he panted. "Never."

"Oh God…Elec…"

"I want you to come first, and then I want to come all over your back."

Hearing him say that had set me off. My mouth pressed against the carpet to mask the sound as my orgasm pulsed through me.

When he sensed that I was coming down from it, he pounded into me faster. He pulled out and ripped the condom off then I felt warm liquid shoot out all over my back. That wasn't something I'd originally thought I'd enjoy…but I *loved* it.

"I'll be right back," he said, running to the bathroom to get a towel. After he cleaned me off, he lifted me off the ground and onto the bed.

The red digital numbers on the clock continued to make me extremely nervous. It was now four in the morning. We lay there facing each other, our lips inches apart.

He brushed his thumb along my cheek. "Are you okay?"

"Yeah." I smiled. "That was crazy."

"That's what happens when you ask me not to hold anything back. Was it too much for you?"

"No. It was what I expected."

"You expected that…grand finale?"

"No…uh…that was definitely a surprise." I laughed.

"I hadn't ever done that before. I wanted to try something new, too."

"Really?"

"I wish we had more time. I want to do everything with you."

"Me, too."

I wished we had forever.

***

Exhaustion from our activities must have gotten the best of me because I didn't even remember falling asleep.

It was five in the morning, and the sun was starting to rise when I awoke to Elec lying on top of me, lightly kissing my neck. He was fully hard and had a condom on. His breathing was erratic as he continued to kiss my neck and suck on my breasts.

Already wet and ready for him, I had woken up even more aroused than I had been all night.

He kissed down to my stomach and back up then I felt him pushing inside of me. His thrusts were slow but intense. His eyes were closed, and he looked pained. An influx of emotions overwhelmed me suddenly as the reality of what had happened last night and what was about to happen today hit me.

The clock taunted me again. We were running out of time.

My heart felt like it was breaking a little more every time he entered me. He started to kiss me, and his mouth never left mine as he continued to push deeper into me in slow, controlled movements. This time felt different than the other two. It felt like he was trying to tell me with his body what he couldn't with his words.

It felt like he was making love to me.

If there were any doubt about that, it was erased the minute he stopped kissing me and placed his face close to mine with his eyes open as he fucked me slowly. He never stopped looking into my eyes after that. It was as if he didn't want to miss a moment of it because he knew it was the last. This time, it wasn't about showing me anything. He was taking something he wanted to keep for himself.

The reflection of my own expression in his gray eyes told my side of the story. I had definitely lied. I had lied to him and to myself in saying I could handle this. It had only been a few hours, but it felt like a lifetime of attachment had built up in this room overnight, and it was about to be ripped apart.

His body shuddered as his orgasm suddenly shook through him. His eyes never left mine as he opened his mouth in a silent scream. My muscles clenched in climax as I watched him. He continued pumping into me slowly until there was nothing left of his orgasm.

His voice was hoarse. "I'm sorry," he whispered.

"It's okay," I said, not even knowing exactly what he was referring to. Was it for coming before I had? Was it for his scheduled abandonment? Was it because he saw the look in my eyes and knew what I was really feeling? Either way, it didn't change the fact that he was leaving.

Elec stayed with his head on my chest until his breathing calmed down.

When he returned from disposing the condom, I set the clock for seven. He leaned his cheek against my breast, closed his eyes and held me for the last time until we fell asleep.

***

When the alarm went off, I jumped up to find that the bed was empty. My heart started to race.

He'd left without saying goodbye.

The sun was now pouring through my window, adding to the rude awakening. I buried my head in my hands and cried. This was my own fault. I knew this would happen and had let it. My shoulders shook as tears seeped through the grooves separating my fingers. The soreness between my legs, which didn't seem noticeable last night in the midst of my sex-induced fog, was now suddenly prominent.

My body flinched when I felt a hand on my back.

I turned around to find Elec standing above me, his eyes dark and empty. "You promised you could handle this, Greta." He repeated almost inaudibly, "You fucking promised."

My mouth trembled. "I thought you left without saying goodbye."

"I went back to my room so that Randy and Sarah wouldn't catch me in here when they got up. They both already left. I just finished packing my stuff."

I sniffled and stood up. "Oh."

"I wouldn't have done that to you…left without saying goodbye…especially after what happened between us."

I wiped my eyes. "What's the difference? It doesn't change the outcome."

"No, it doesn't. I don't know what to say except that last night…it meant something to me. I want you to know that. I'll never

83

forget what you gave me. I'll never forget any of this. But, you *knew* it was going to end."

"I didn't know it was going to feel like *this*."

His hands were in his pockets, and he looked down at the ground then up at me. "Fuck. Neither, did I." When he leaned in to hug me, I backed away.

"No...please. I don't want you to touch me. That's only going to make this worse."

I couldn't even speak as more tears fell. I shook my head in disbelief over how badly I'd lost my composure.

I cleared my throat. "What time do you have to leave?"

"A cab is coming any minute. It's gonna take at least an hour to get to the airport in traffic."

A fresh teardrop fell down my cheek. "Damn it," I said, wiping it away.

"I'll be right back," he said.

He left to take his luggage downstairs. By the time he'd returned to where I was standing in the same spot in my room, a car horn beeped outside.

"Shit. Hang on," he said, running back out of the room.

I looked out the window and eventually saw Elec putting his suitcases into the back. When the trunk slammed shut, I could have sworn I felt it in my heart.

Elec said something to the driver and came back upstairs. I was still looking out the window blankly when his footsteps crept up behind me.

"I told him to wait. I'm not leaving until you look at me."

I turned around. He must have seen the despair written all over my face.

His eyes looked watery. "Fuck. I don't want to leave you like this."

"It's okay. It's not gonna get any easier in the next minute. You'll miss your flight. Go."

Ignoring my earlier request not to be touched, he took hold of my face and looked deeply into my eyes. "I know this is hard for you to understand. I haven't opened up to you about my relationship with Randy. Without your knowing everything and without your understanding what my mother is really like, it's not going to make sense. Just know that if I could stay with you, I would." He gave me

84

a chaste kiss on the lips and continued, "I know that despite my warning, you gave me a piece of your heart anyway last night. And even though I tried to stop it, I gave you a piece of mine. I know you could feel that happening this morning. I want you to keep it with you tucked away. And when you decide to give the rest of yours to another guy someday, please make sure it's someone who deserves you."

Elec gave me one last desperate kiss. My eyes were stinging. When he pushed back, I gripped his jacket, tempted to never to let go. He waited until my hands left him to turn around and walk away.

Just like that, he'd exited my life as fast as he'd entered it.

I stood at the window and wished I hadn't when he looked up at me one last time before entering the cab with the piece of my heart he knew he'd taken with him. As for the rest of my heart left behind, it was shattered.

***

Later that night, my phone chimed. It was a text from Elec with a link.

On the plane, I figured out if you scramble the letters of Greta, you get GREAT. Greta=Great. You're amazing, actually. Don't ever forget that. This song will always remind me of you.

It took me a few hours before I had the courage to click on the link. The name of the song was *All I Wanted* by Paramore. It was about wanting someone you couldn't have and wanting to relive the short time spent together from the beginning.

I replayed the song over and over again in a torturous cycle that included inhaling his scent that lingered on his shirt that I was still wearing and on my bed sheets.

Elec would only contact me one other time over the next seven years.

On a random night almost one year after he'd left Boston, I was out with Victoria. I had just been thinking about him when a text came in and shook me to my core.

I still dream about your neck. I still think about you every day. For some reason, I just needed you to know that tonight. Please don't write back.

I didn't.

Despite the tears that fell so easily upon reading it, I didn't. He hadn't contacted me in so long, and I figured maybe he was just drunk. Even if he weren't, it wouldn't have changed anything. I understood that now. Actually, I'd become an expert at burying all of my feelings for Elec. His being so far away made that possible. The couple of times I disappointed myself by giving in to curiosity and checking online, he wasn't even on social media.

Randy had also stopped going out to California now that Elec was an adult.

Even after several years, my heart still ached whenever I'd allow myself to think about our one night together. So, I did my best not to go there—out of sight, out of mind, right? That motto is just a temporary fix—until you're forced to come face to face with what you've been running from. That's when the mental walls you've built to hide behind come crashing down in one hard blow.

PART TWO

CHAPTER 12

"Randy's dead."

At first, it seemed like it could have been a dream. It was the middle of the night, and I'd had too much to drink while out with friends in Greenwich Village the evening before. When the phone rang at 3 A.M., my heart began to pound in dread, and to hear those words right off the bat had nearly stopped it altogether.

"Mom?"

She choked through sobs. "Randy's dead, Greta. He had a heart attack. I'm at Mass General. They couldn't save him."

"Mom, breathe. Please."

My mother was crying uncontrollably, causing me to feel helpless because there was nothing I could do about it from my apartment in New York.

She and Randy's marriage had remained intact over the years, although in recent months, they'd been having a rocky time. Randy had never displayed toward my mother the same disrespect he'd shown Elec, but he'd always had an unpredictable temper with highs and lows and was difficult to live with.

The truth was, my mother had lost her soul mate when my father died all those years ago. Her marriage to Randy had always been one of convenience and stability. Even with his modest income as a car salesman, he provided for us well. Mom never worked and wasn't the type who could handle being alone. Randy had been the first person to come along in the years after Dad passed away. I'd always gotten the impression that Randy was far more enamored with her than she was with him. Still, losing him was going to turn her life upside down. With my living far away, he'd been her whole world, not to mention, this was the second husband she'd now lost prematurely. I didn't know how she was going to handle it.

I started to shake. "Oh my God." I took a deep breath in an attempt to compose myself. "I'm so sorry. I'm *so* sorry, Mom."

"He was dead before we even got to the hospital."

I got up and immediately rolled my small suitcase from the closet. "Listen, I'm going to see where I can rent a car at this hour.

I'll try to be there by morning. Keep in touch by phone and let me know when you get home. Is someone with you?"

She sniffled. "Greg and Clara."

That had made me feel better. Greg was one of Randy's oldest friends who happened to relocate with his wife to the suburbs of Boston a few years back after a job transfer.

When I was able to find a rental car place that was open, I hit the highway about five in the morning.

On the four-hour drive to Boston, my mind became littered with thoughts about what Randy's death would mean. Would I need to quit my job in the city and move back to Boston for Mom? She'd have to work for the first time in her life to support herself. How much time would I need to take off from work? And then, it hit me.

Elec.

Elec.

Oh my God. Elec.

Did he know about Randy? Would he come to Boston for the service?

Would I have to face him?

My hand anxiously gripped the steering wheel tighter as my other hand switched the music on the radio over and over unable to find anything that could drown out the noise in my head.

Even after seven years and a failed engagement to another man, my one true heartbreak had remained at the hands of my stepbrother. Now, my heart broke for him again in a different way because not only had my mother lost her husband, but Elec had just lost his father.

Randy was too young to die. Granted, his relationship with Elec was horrible, but the fact that they'd never made amends saddened me. Nothing stirred up my emotions like thoughts of Elec did. Even moving away from Mom and Randy never really changed that for me.

Two years after graduating from community college in Boston, I transferred to a small college just outside of Manhattan where I graduated with a liberal arts degree. Right out of school, I took an administrative position in the city. I've lived in New York for the past three years, and it was there that I met Tim.

We were together for two years. Tim worked in software sales and traveled a lot. We lived together for the last year of our relationship until his job wanted to transfer him to a European sales position. He'd accepted it without discussing it with me, and when I refused to move with him, we ended up breaking up. The move had pushed me to make a decision I would have made eventually anyway. He was a good guy, but overall, the passion I'd longed for was missing. Even in the beginning of our relationship, there was never the adrenaline and butterflies that I'd experienced in my short time with Elec. When I accepted Tim's proposal, I'd hoped things would change and that I'd grow to love him like he deserved. That never happened.

I'd had two other boyfriends before Tim, and it was the same situation. I'd compared my feelings for them to my crazy attraction to Elec. Even though I knew Elec was gone from my life, I couldn't seem to help comparing everyone to him, both sexually and intellectually. Even though it may not have shown on the surface, Elec was deep. There were many layers to him, and his writing exhibited that. There was so much I never got to know or unravel. But I knew I wanted to find someone with those same qualities. One thing my time with Elec also taught me was that sexual desire and fulfillment were just as important to me as an emotional connection.

My other boyfriends were nice guys, but they were average Joes. And it was sad, but I preferred to be alone than to give myself to someone with whom there was no spark. I hoped that someday I would have real chemistry again with someone.

The *Welcome to Massachusetts* sign made me anxious. There was so much that was unknown about what the next few days would bring. I'd have to help my mother with funeral arrangements, and it would surely trigger flashbacks to the horrible time when we had to do the same thing for my father.

When I pulled into our driveway, Randy's Nissan was parked on the left, and the sight of it made me shudder. I used my key to let myself in and found my mother staring blankly at a cup of tea in the kitchen with no lights on. She hadn't even noticed me walking into the room.

"Mom?"

My mother looked up at me, her eyes red and swollen. I ran to her and embraced her.

The dirty dishes from Mom and Randy's dinner last night were still in the sink, bringing to light what a sudden and unexpected blow this was, how life could change in an instant.

"I'm here now. I'm here. You just let me know what you need me to do. It'll be okay. I'll help you through it. You'll be okay."

She spoke into her teacup. "He just woke up in the middle of the night complaining of pains and collapsed before the paramedics got here."

I rubbed her back. "I'm so sorry."

"Thank God you're here, Greta."

"Where is...you know...where is he now?"

"They took him to the funeral home. Clara is making all of the arrangements for me. She and Greg have been wonderful. I couldn't bear to do it...not again."

I hugged her tighter. "I know."

That night, I slept next to my mother so that she didn't have to be alone. It felt surreal sleeping where Randy had slept just last night, and now, he was gone.

***

The next day was a blur: people dropping off casseroles and flowers, my mother retreating to her room to cry, Victoria stopping in to pay her respects. We'd grown apart in the years since I moved, but we always made a point to see each other when I came home even if it was just for coffee.

So, when Mom took a nap late that afternoon, Victoria and I walked down to the Dunkin Donuts on the corner. It was a small piece of normal in an otherwise surreal time.

"How long can you take off work?" she asked.

"I just called them this morning. They gave me a day for bereavement then I took the rest of the week off as vacation. I may take Mom back to the city with me until she can figure things out."

"Has anyone talked to Elec?"

Just the mention of his name had caused what felt like a knot in my stomach.

"Greg and Clara are handling contacting people. I'm sure they called him. He and Randy have been estranged according to my mother, and I'm not sure if he would even come."

"What are you going to do if he does?"

I nervously bit into my vanilla crème donut. "What *can* I do?"

Victoria knew about my night with Elec. I'd told her bits and pieces but kept a lot of the specifics to myself. Some of it was too intimate to share, and I didn't want to devalue what that experience had meant to me. Even though it was only one night, it had shaped me in many ways and set the bar for future expectations.

She sipped her iced coffee. "So, I guess we'll just have to wait and see…"

"My mother is my priority. I can't lose sleep over whether Elec is coming."

It was all I could think about.

That night, Greg and Clara had me and my mother over for dinner. They insisted I get her out of the house since I'd told them she spent most of the day crying in her room while random people dropped off food.

During dinner, Mom was quiet and barely touched her chicken and dumplings. She drank copious amounts of Zinfandel wine instead.

The wake was scheduled for the day after tomorrow. The pit in my stomach was growing by the second.

I just needed to know.

I finally asked, "Have you contacted Elec?" I swallowed the lump in my throat in anticipation of Clara's response.

"Yes. I spoke to him today. He was despondent when I told him, and it wasn't clear whether he would be coming."

Just knowing that she'd spoken to him had made my heart beat even faster. "Where is he?"

"He's still living in California near Pilar."

"Did you have his phone number?"

She looked over at her husband and said hesitantly, "Um…Greg's kept in touch with him. We know he and Randy had a horrible relationship. Greg had tried to intervene some years back. Elec and he sort of bonded in the process. Randy actually never really knew about that."

I looked over at Greg as if he were holding all in the information in the world that mattered to me. "What is he doing now?" My voice was shaky.

"He graduated from college, got his social work license. He's working with disadvantaged youth. The last time we spoke was probably about six months ago."

"Really..."

Wow.

That was more information than I'd gotten in years. It made me both happy and sad at the same time to know that he was doing well—sad only because I didn't know him anymore and hadn't ever met the man that he'd become.

I cleared my throat. "So, you don't know if he'll be here?"

"No. He wouldn't say," Clara said. "I think he was in shock. I gave him all of the details so that he'd have them."

My heart tightened in agony at the thought of what might have been going through Elec's mind wherever he was at that very moment.

***

The smell of lilies made me sick. Everyone seemed to be sending the Stargazer kind that stunk the most. I offered to drive a bunch of the arrangements that had been sent to the house over to Thomas' Funeral home.

The service would be starting at four, but before then, we were supposed to be going over to Greg and Clara's again for a light lunch.

My mother accompanied me as we laid out the flowers in the corners of the room surrounding the spot where the coffin would go. We also dropped off pictures of Randy and us from over the years. It made me sad that there wasn't one photo of Randy and Elec.

The funeral home smelled liked a mix of musty wood and air freshener. I wasn't looking forward to coming back later and having to see Randy's body or my mother's reaction.

On the drive back to Greg and Clara's, I held my mother's hand. She was doing better than expected, although I was fairly certain she'd taken some Xanax to take the edge off.

When we got to the house, I was relieved that there were no cars that I didn't recognize out front. That meant it would just be the four of us for lunch.

My relief turned to panic almost immediately when I entered the house and spotted a black suitcase outside of the closet in the foyer.

Clara hugged my mother as I looked around anxiously.

Too nervous to ask the question I wanted to, I stood in silence as my chest tightened. Then, finally, I took a deep breath in and out and asked, "Whose suitcase?"

"Elec is here, Greta. He's upstairs."

My heart started to pound furiously, and I felt like I couldn't breathe. I suddenly needed air. "Excuse me," I said, walking out the back door and into their yard.

Unprepared to face him, I stared over at the red tulips in the flower garden. A part of me truly didn't think he'd be here because of his volatile relationship with Randy, although the dread I'd been carrying around the past couple of days was proof that another part of me was readying for it.

I didn't know what I was going to say to him.

The cool spring air blew my hair around, and I looked up at the sky as if to shun the universe for dropping this bomb on me. Perhaps, I got my response because thunder rumbled in the distance.

Call it intuition or instinct, something made me turn around and look up at the French doors on the second floor balcony that overlooked the garden where I was standing.

From behind the glass, I saw him.

Elec.

He stood looking down at me with a white towel wrapped around his waist. I always imagined what he might look like after seven years, but even my wildest dreams couldn't have conjured up what I was actually met with.

His messy black hair had now been replaced by longish sexy waves that curled around his ears. He was wearing glasses.

He looked even sexier in glasses.

Even from here, I could see the piercing gray of his eyes through them.

His inked body was bigger, even more built than before.

He lifted a cigarette to his mouth and even amidst the shock of seeing him, disappointment set in that he was smoking again.

Elec blew out the smoke as his eyes stayed fixed on mine. He wasn't smiling. He just looked at me intently. His powerful stare alone had put all of my senses on high alert, throwing my body out of whack.

My head was pounding, my eyes were teary, my ears were beating, my mouth was watering, my nipples were hard, my hands were trembling, my knees were shaking and my heart...I couldn't describe what was going on inside my chest.

Before I could process any of this, a woman with blonde hair came up from behind him and wrapped her arms around his waist.

CHAPTER 13

Once I finally built up the courage to go inside, I sat at the dining room table and downed the water at my place setting. My mouth was still dry. It felt like the room was spinning.

"Are you okay?" my mother asked.

I should have been asking *her* that. I nodded, grabbing her water, too and drinking it all. Needing to be strong for her, I couldn't allow myself to lose my shit today.

They hadn't come downstairs yet.

After the mystery woman appeared behind Elec through the glass, he'd immediately turned around and disappeared from sight. It took me a few minutes to move from my spot in the garden.

He had a girlfriend...or a wife.

Even though this should have crossed my mind as a likely possibility after seven years, it wasn't something that entered into the equation when I imagined seeing him again.

The sound of two sets of footsteps descending the stairs in unison caused me to stiffen and sit straighter in my chair.

Thump.

Thump.

Thump.

When they entered the dining room, my body went into fight or flight mode as adrenaline pumped through me.

Maybe I should have stood up or said something, but I just stayed glued to my chair.

My mother walked over to Elec and pulled him into a hug. "Elec, it's so good to see you. I'm so sorry about your father. I know you and he had a rough time, but he loved you. He did."

Elec's body was rigid, but he didn't back away from her. He simply said, "I'm sorry for *you*."

As he reluctantly let my mother hug him, his eyes darted over to me and stayed there. I couldn't tell what he was thinking, but I was pretty sure it was along the same lines of what was running through my own head.

This reunion was never supposed to happen.

After Mom let go of him, Elec's companion went over to hug her. "Mrs. O'Rourke, I'm Chelsea, Elec's girlfriend. I'm so sorry for your loss."

"Call me Sarah. Thank you, sweetheart. Nice to meet you."

"I'm sorry it had to be under these circumstances," she said as she rubbed my mother's back.

My eyes landed on her French-manicured nails. She was petite, and her body shape was similar to mine. Her long blonde hair cascaded down her back in beachy waves. She was gorgeous.

Of course, she was.

My insides felt like they were twisting.

Elec slowly walked toward me. "Greta…"

The sound of my name rolling off his tongue had momentarily taken me back seven years in an instant.

"Elec." I got up from my chair. "I…I'm so sorry…about Randy," I stuttered, and my lips started to tremble. It felt like all of the breath left my body when he stood in front of me, and I inhaled the old familiar smell of clove cigarettes and cologne. So much time had gone by, but emotionally, it still felt like yesterday.

Like yesterday.

The only difference was that the person who left my bedroom that day was still essentially a boy, and the person before me now was clearly a man.

I looked up at him and marveled at how he'd grown even more handsome. My favorite characteristics were still there but with some changes. His gray eyes still glowed, but now it was through those black-framed glasses. He still wore his lip ring, but had a little more facial hair now. A black pinstriped shirt that was rolled up at the sleeves hugged his chest, which was now bigger, even more defined.

He just stayed looking at me. I finally reached out to hug him and felt his warm hand on my back. My heart was beating so fast, it felt like it might stop altogether. One thing that apparently hadn't changed was the way my body instantly reacted to his touch. Just as I closed my eyes, I heard a voice from behind him.

"You must be Sarah's daughter. You two look like twins."

I separated from him suddenly and held out my clammy hand. "Yes…hi, I'm Greta."

She didn't take it. Instead, she smiled sympathetically and hugged me. "I'm Chelsea. It's nice to meet you. I'm sorry about your stepfather." Her hair smelled as I expected it would, a clean, delicate scent to match her apparently sweet personality.

"Thank you," I said.

The tension in the air was palpable as the three of us just stood there in awkward silence.

Clara walked in carrying a pot roast that she'd garnished with asparagus spears on an oval plate. I used the opportunity to escape from the situation and offered to help her bring in the rest of the items, leaving Elec and Chelsea standing there.

My nervous hands fumbled with the silverware Clara tasked me with gathering from the drawer in the kitchen. I closed my eyes and took a deep breath before reentering the dining room.

Greg was talking while I walked around distributing the flatware. A case of the butterfingers got me good as forks and spoons kept slipping out of my trepidatious hands.

With nothing left to do, I then sat down across from where Elec and Chelsea were sitting. My eyes stayed glued to the reflection of my face on my plate.

"So, how did you kids meet?" he asked them.

I glanced up.

Chelsea smiled and looked adoringly over at Elec. "We both work at the youth center. I head up the after school program, and Elec is a counselor. We started off as friends. I really admired how good he was with the kids. They all love him." She placed her hand on his. "Now, I do, too."

I could see from the corner of my eye that she leaned in and kissed him. The black dress I was wearing suddenly felt like it was suffocating me.

"That's very sweet," Clara said.

"Elec, how is Pilar taking this?" Greg asked.

"She's not doing well," he said abruptly.

I looked up upon hearing him speak. He hadn't spoken the entire time since saying my name.

Chelsea squeezed his hand. "We tried to get her to come, but she didn't think she could handle it."

We.

She was close to his mother.

98

This was definitely serious.

"Well, it's better off then that she stayed back," Clara said.

Probably uncomfortable at the mention of Pilar, my mother took a long sip of her wine. She knew she was the number one reason for Pilar not showing up today.

Chelsea turned to me. "Where do you live, Greta?"

"I live in New York City, actually. I just came into town a couple of days ago."

"That must be exciting. I've always wanted to visit." She turned to Elec. "Maybe we could visit her sometime? We'd have a place to stay."

He nodded his head once, looking extremely uncomfortable as he played with his food. At one point, I could feel his eyes on me. When I turned to look at him to confirm it, our eyes met for a quick second before he shifted his gaze back down to his plate.

"Elec never told me he had a stepsister," Chelsea said.

He never mentioned me.

My mother spoke up for the first time. "Elec only lived with us for a short time back when they were teenagers." She looked at me. "The two of you didn't get along too well back then."

Mom knew nothing about what really happened between Elec and me. So, from her perspective, that statement was an accurate one.

Elec's deep raspy voice cut right through me. "Is that true, Greta?"

I dropped my fork. "Is what true?"

"That we didn't get along?"

Surely, the hidden meaning in his question was meant for only me to understand. I wasn't sure why he was taunting me in the midst of what was already an uncomfortable situation.

"We had our moments."

His eyes seared into mine, and his voice lowered. "Yeah, we did."

Suddenly, I was burning up.

His mouth spread into a smile. "What was it you used to call me?"

"What do you mean?"

"'Stepbrother dearest,' was it? Because of my glowing personality?" He turned to Chelsea. "I was a miserable fuck back then."

A miserable "fuck." He didn't mean it that way, but I couldn't help where my head went with that.

"How did you know about that nickname?" I asked.

He smirked.

I smiled. "Oh, right. You used to eavesdrop on me."

"Sounds like those were some fun times," Chelsea said as she looked innocently back and forth between Elec and me.

"They were," he said, glaring at me with a look that was hardly innocent.

***

Chelsea and I helped Clara bring the dishes into the kitchen. In forty minutes, we were scheduled to be at the funeral home for the viewing hours.

Her voice startled me. "What do you do, Greta?"

I didn't feel comfortable getting into the details of my job right now, so I kept my response generic. "I work in an administrative position in the city, just mindless stuff, really."

She smiled, and I felt like a jerk for liking that she had some laugh lines and the beginnings of crows feet around her eyes.

I was stretching here.

"Sometimes, mindless can be good. Working with kids is fulfilling but exhausting. There's never a dull moment."

We both glanced out through the sliding glass door. Elec was standing in the garden alone, deep in thought with his hands in his pockets.

"I'm really worried about him," she said as she looked out at him. "Can I ask you something?"

This conversation was making me uncomfortable. "Sure."

"He won't talk about his father. Did something bad happen between them?"

Her question caught me off guard. It wasn't my place to talk to her about Randy and Elec's relationship. I knew almost nothing myself.

"They used to argue a lot, and Randy could be very disrespectful toward Elec, but honestly, I still don't know what caused it all."

That was all she was going to get from me.

"I'm just worried that he's bottling stuff up. His father just died, and he's hardly shown any emotion. I mean, if my father died, I'd be a mess."

I know.

She went on, "I'm afraid it's going to all hit him at once. He's not okay. He's not sleeping. It's bothering him, but he won't talk about it or allow himself to cry."

My heart ached hearing her say that, because I was worried about him, too.

"Have you tried talking to him?" I asked.

"Yes. He just says he doesn't want to talk about it. He almost didn't come here for the service. I knew he'd regret it, so I pushed and pushed and finally, he gave in."

Wow. He really wasn't going to come.

"I'm glad you did."

"I really love him, Greta."

I had no doubt that she did and while hearing her say that had made my stomach hurt, the more logical side of me was happy that Elec had found someone who cared about him like that. I didn't know what to say. I couldn't exactly tell her I might have felt the same way.

I cared about him, too.

Maybe that made no sense after so long, but my feelings for him were just as strong today as they were seven years ago. And just like before, I'd have to harbor them.

She put her hand on my arm. "Will you do me a favor?"

"Okay..."

"Will you go out there...see if you can get him to talk about it?"

"Um..."

"Please? I don't know who else to ask. I don't think he's going to be prepared for everything tonight."

I looked back out at Elec and his strong stature as he stood in the garden. This could have been my only opportunity to talk to him alone, so I agreed.

101

"Okay."

She hugged me. "Thank you. I owe you one."

In that case, I'll take Elec. I couldn't help my thoughts, which were out of control.

That embrace had made me realize that it was absolutely possible to genuinely like someone that you were insanely jealous of.

I took a deep breath and made my way through the sliding glass doors. The sky was turning gray as if it were about to open up into a thunderstorm.

It was not the appropriate time to notice how incredible his ass looked through the fitted black dress pants he was wearing, but nevertheless, I did. A breeze blew around the sexy black waves of his hair.

I cleared my throat to announce myself.

He didn't turn but knew it was me.

"What are you doing out here, Greta?"

"Chelsea asked me to come talk to you."

He shrugged his shoulders, his laugh full of sarcasm. "Oh, really."

"Yes."

"Were you two comparing notes?"

"That's not funny."

He finally turned around to look at me, blowing out the last of the smoke from his cigarette before promptly throwing it on the ground and crushing it with his foot. "You think she would have sent you out here to talk to me if she knew the last time before today that you and I were together, we were fucking like rabbits?"

Although it shocked me, hearing him acknowledging that sent a shiver through my body. "Did you have to put it like that?"

"It's the truth, isn't it? She would freak the fuck out if she knew."

"Well, I'm not going to be the one to tell her, so you don't have to worry. I would never do that."

My eye started to twitch.

He lifted his brow. "Why are you winking at me?"

"I'm not...my eye is twitching because—"

"Because you're nervous. I know. You used to do that when I first met you. Glad to see we've come full circle."

"I guess some things never really change, do they? It's been seven years, but it seems just like—"

"Like yesterday." He repeated, "It seems like just yesterday, and that's fucked up. This whole situation is."

"It was never supposed to happen."

His gaze fell to my neck and then back up to my eyes. "Where is he?"

"Who?"

"Your fiancé."

"I'm not engaged. I was…but not anymore. How did you know I was engaged?"

He looked dumbfounded then stared down at the ground for the longest time before dodging my question. "What happened?"

"It's kind of a long story, but I was the one that ended it. He moved to Europe for a job. It just wasn't meant to be."

"Are you with anyone now?"

"No." I changed the subject off of me. "Chelsea is really nice."

"She's wonderful; one of the best things that's ever happened to me, actually."

Punched in the gut.

"She's really worried about you, because you haven't shown any emotion. She asked me if I knew what the story was between you and Randy. I didn't know what to say because there is so much I still don't even know."

"You know more than she does, and that wasn't my choice. The bottom line is, he was a crappy father and now, he's dead. Seriously, that's all my mind can process right now. This hasn't even hit me yet."

"It was such a shock."

"My mother is taking it really hard," he said.

"How was she doing before this?"

"Better than she was back then, but not 100-percent. The verdict is still out, though, on what Randy's death is gonna do to her mental state."

The wind suddenly intensified, and misty raindrops started to fall. I looked up at the sky then down at my watch. "We have to leave in a few minutes."

"Go back inside. Tell her I'll be in there in a minute," he said.

I ignored him and stayed standing there. I felt like a failure. I'd gotten nowhere with him.

Fuck. My eyes were starting to water.

"What are you doing?" he snapped.

"Chelsea's not the only one who's worried about you."

"She's the only one that has a *right* to be. *You* don't need to be worrying about me. I'm none of your concern."

It had stung harder than anything he had ever said to me.

In that moment, he'd violently thrown back and stomped on whatever piece of my heart I'd given him all those years ago. It disappointed me that I'd idealized him all this time, compared all my boyfriends to him, put him up on a pedestal when clearly he didn't care about my feelings.

"You know what? If I didn't feel so sorry for what you're going through right now, I'd tell you to kiss my ass," I said.

"And if I wanted to be a dick, I'd say you were asking me to kiss your ass because you remembered how much you fucking loved it when I did." He brushed past me. "Take care of your mother tonight."

The past couple of hours had been an emotional roller coaster of shock, sadness, jealousy and now…anger. Pure anger. The tears started to pour down my face in a stream that matched the intensity of the raindrops now steadily falling after he left me speechless in the garden.

***

"I didn't know Randy had a son."

I couldn't count the number of times someone visiting us in the receiving line had said it. It made me feel really bad for Elec despite his crushing me earlier.

The smell of flowers mixed with the perfume of a dozen random women was suffocating.

Most of the people who showed up to the wake were either Randy's work friends from the car dealership or neighbors. The line curled around the corner, and it was a little unsettling to see people having easy conversations, sometimes laughing as they waited to

104

visit the coffin. It was like a cocktail party without the alcohol, and it was pissing me off.

I stood next to my mother who'd broken down completely after seeing her husband's lifeless body for the first time since the heart attack. I rubbed her back and replaced her tissues and did whatever I could to help her hold it together long enough to make it through until the end.

Chelsea had convinced Elec to stand in the family lineup despite his initial resistance. I think he was just too worn out to fight it.

The makeup caked onto Randy's face made it look stiff and almost unrecognizable. It was devastating to see him lying there and brought back flashbacks of when my father died.

Elec wouldn't go up to the casket or even look at it for that matter. He just stood there, stoic and robotically shaking hands while Chelsea responded on his behalf as people repeated the same phrase.

"I'm sorry for your loss."

"I'm sorry for your loss."

"I'm sorry for your loss."

Elec looked like he was about to break, and I felt like I was the only one who knew it.

I had to go to the bathroom at one point, so I let my mother know I'd be right back. I hadn't been able to find it and eventually made my way downstairs to an empty seating area. It smelled a little musty, but it was a relief to escape the noise of the crowd.

Upon entering the quiet of the lower level, I finally saw the sign for the bathroom at the other end of the room.

When I came out, the hairs on my body stiffened at the sight of Elec alone on one of the couches. He leaned into his knees with both of his palms plastered to each side of his head. When he lowered his hands, he was still looking down. His ears were red, and his back was rising and falling from the heaviness of his breathing.

This was a private moment, and I was inadvertently intruding on it.

Perhaps it was the breakdown I'd seen coming earlier by the look on his face upstairs. Nevertheless, I didn't want him to see me. The problem was I had to pass him in order to get to the stairs.

Despite his upsetting me earlier, the need to comfort him was overwhelming, but I knew after what he'd said to me, that it wasn't my place.

So, I walked slowly past him.

When I got to the hallway where the stairs were located, the sound of his voice startled me. "Wait."

I stopped in my tracks and turned around. "I need to get back upstairs to Mom."

"Give me a few minutes."

I brushed the white lint off the black material of my dress and walked toward him, taking a seat next to him on the couch. The warmth of his body with his leg pressed against mine was not lost on me.

"Are you okay?" I asked.

He looked at me and shook his head no.

Squelching the urge to hug him, I placed my hands firmly on my lap.

It's not your place.

Then, every part of me felt it when he put his hand on my knee. That one touch undid any progress I'd made in the hours since our altercation in the garden.

"What I said to you earlier…I'm sorry," he said.

"Which part?"

"All of it. I don't know how to handle this…Randy…you…none of it. It all seems surreal. On the plane here, I prayed that by some miracle you wouldn't show up."

"Why?"

"Because this situation is hard enough."

"I didn't think I'd ever see you again. I certainly didn't expect it to be this hard, to feel like this after seven years, Elec."

"Like what?"

"Like no time's passed. For me, it's because I've held onto it all. In my mind, I've never let you go, and it's affected my relationships and my life. It was manageable before, though...before this. Anyway, I really shouldn't be getting into it. It doesn't matter anymore. You love Chelsea."

"I do," he said abruptly.

Hearing him confirm it so vehemently had caused my eyes to unexpectedly well up. "She's a good person. But seeing you with someone else after the way we left things is still really hard for me. Seeing you in pain is even harder."

I had completely thrown up my words and said exactly what was on my mind because once again, I wasn't sure if it would be the last time we'd be alone together. It was important that he knew how I felt. I shook my head repeatedly. "I'm sorry. I shouldn't have said all that."

The people upstairs sounded like they were a million miles away. You could have heard a pin drop where we were all alone.

I was looking down when his hand startled me as it landed on my cheek. He slowly slid it down and wrapped it around my neck.

"Greta..." he breathed out with a level of emotion I'd only seen from him one other time before—seven years ago.

I closed my eyes and realized that for a moment we were back in that place. I was with the old Elec—my Elec. This was something I never thought I'd get to feel again. He kept his hand on my throat and lightly squeezed it. It was innocent, but there was a fine line being drawn with every second that passed. His thumb brushed back and forth over my neck slowly. The feel of his rough, calloused fingers warmed my entire body. I didn't understand what was happening, and I wasn't sure if he did, either. I prayed that no one came downstairs because the second he snapped out of it, my Elec would be gone.

"I hurt you," he said, his fingers still locked around my skin.

"It's okay," I whispered. My eyes were still closed.

Elec quickly moved his hand off of me when we heard footsteps.

"There you are," Chelsea said as she walked toward where we sat on the couch. "I don't blame you two for wanting a breather. This night has been exhausting."

I immediately got up and offered her probably the fakest smile I'd ever conjured up in my life. My heart was still racing from what I'd just experienced.

"The priest is getting ready to lead a prayer. I wanted to make sure you didn't miss it," she said to him. "Are you feeling okay to head back upstairs?"

"Yeah...uh...I'm fine," he said. "Let's go."

He gave me a quick look that was hard to read before turning around toward the stairs with Chelsea. I followed them and watched as he placed his hand on the small of her back, the same hand that had just been wrapped around my neck a minute ago.

***

After the wake, Greg and Clara invited a few people back to their house for tea and pastry. My mother felt obligated to go, which meant I needed to stay with her and drive her home.

Mom and I were the last to leave the funeral home, so by the time we got to the house, the dining room table was full of people. The house smelled like freshly made coffee and the blueberry scones Clara had just taken out of the oven.

I wished I could have just gone home and slept, though. Tomorrow would be another long day with the funeral. I didn't even know when Elec was leaving to go back to California and assumed he wouldn't be staying much longer than tomorrow.

Elec and Chelsea were nowhere to be found. Even though it was none of my business, I couldn't help wondering where they were and what they were doing.

Just as soon as I'd had the thought, Chelsea appeared in the living room, carrying a scone on a paper plate. She had changed out of her black dress and into some casual shorts and a t-shirt. Her hair was tied into a loose ponytail, and she appeared younger without any makeup.

"Hey, Greta. Can I join you?" She sat next to me before I even responded.

"Sure." I scooted over on the loveseat.

"I'm glad you came back here," she said. "Greg and Clara's house is really nice, isn't it? I'm so glad we're staying here instead of a hotel."

"It is."

"I hope to own a house someday, but with our salaries at the youth center, it'll be a while before that happens. Our apartment back home is really small."

Our apartment.

"How long have you lived together?"

"Just a few months. We've been together almost a year. Elec was hesitant to move further away from his mother, but he eventually gave in. Pilar wasn't well for a long time. You know that, right?"

"Yes. I knew she had issues."

"Well, the past year has been a lot better. She actually has a boyfriend now...but when she found out Randy died, she took it really hard, so we're worried she'll have a relapse."

"Where's Elec now?"

"He's just upstairs."

"How is he doing?"

"Actually...he's acting really strange tonight."

"What do you mean?"

She looked around to make sure no one was listening to our conversation. "Okay...well, we left the wake a little early and came back here. He..."

"He what?"

She leaned in and whispered, "He wanted to have sex."

I nearly regurgitated my tea.

Why in God's name was she telling me this?

I coughed. "Is that unusual?"

"No, I mean...he has a huge sexual appetite, but this was different."

Huge sexual appetite...

I did my best to play it casual and pretend I wasn't sick to my stomach over this conversation, which I was pretty sure would traumatize me. "Different?"

"We got back here, and he immediately dragged me upstairs and started ripping my clothes off. It was like he was doing it to bury his feelings, to forget about tonight. And I understood that. But then, once we started, he couldn't finish. The look in his eyes...it was like his mind was somewhere else. Then, he just ran to the bathroom, slammed the door, and I heard the shower running."

"Did he say anything after?"

"No. Nothing."

"It must have had something to do with everything that happened tonight," I said.

And by that, I don't mean him wrapping his hand around my neck, Chelsea.

"I can't leave him like this," she said.

"What do you mean leave him?"

"He didn't tell you? I can't stay for the funeral."

"Why?"

"My flight leaves at nine in the morning. My sister is getting married tomorrow night. I know…a Friday night wedding, right? I guess having it on a weeknight cut the cost of the venue in half. But it still sucks for the rest of us who have to work or have lives. I'm her maid of honor. The timing couldn't be worse."

She was leaving.

"When is Elec going back?"

"His flight is Saturday night."

"Oh."

She crossed her legs and took a bite of the scone. "Was he always this complex? I mean, when he was younger?"

"From the brief time I knew him, I would say so…yes. His writing books is a good example of that."

She tilted her head. "His writing…books?"

She didn't know?

"Oh…uh…just something he toyed around with. I shouldn't have brought it up. It's irrelevant."

"Wow, I need to ask him about that. I can't believe I didn't know he liked to write. Books about what?"

How could he not have told her?

I started to panic. "Just fiction. Don't say I told you." I shook my head, urging her to drop it. "I shouldn't have said anything."

His voice was cold. "No. You shouldn't have."

We both turned at the same time to find Elec standing in front of us.

Shit.

The icy stare he gave me was all the indictor I needed that I'd made a big mistake. But it was too late. Now, he was the one that had to do damage control.

Chelsea patted the seat next to her. "Come here, baby. Why would you not tell me you used to write? That's so cool."

"It's not really a big deal. It was just a hobby I had when I was a teenager."

It wasn't a hobby; it was a passion.

Why aren't you writing anymore?

"I can't believe you never told me," she said.

He brushed it off. "Well, now you know."

I was waiting for him to look at me so that I could at least mouth a silent apology, but he never gave me the opportunity.

Clara walked into the room. "Elec, can I get you anything?" she asked.

"Something strong."

"You got it."

She returned with three shot glasses filled with some kind of amber-colored liquor. Elec downed the first two immediately.

Chelsea whispered to me. "See? Promise you'll keep an eye on him for me, okay?"

Elec slammed the last shot glass down after finishing its contents. "She doesn't need to keep an eye on me," he spewed.

"You know how badly I feel about leaving you alone."

"You shouldn't. I'll be fine. I'll be home before you wake up on Sunday morning."

He'd be gone again before I knew it.

She leaned her head on his shoulder. Elec had changed into jeans, and his feet were bare. That triggered a flashback to the night he initially opened up to me in my bedroom when I noticed for the first time how beautiful his feet were bare. I willed the thought away because when Chelsea had asked me to keep an eye on him, I hardly think she meant ogling him.

My mother walked into the living room. "Honey, I think I need to get home and rest up for tomorrow."

"Okay, we'll get going." I couldn't get off that couch fast enough.

Chelsea stood up. "Greta, I won't see you again. I can't tell you how good it was to meet you. I hope we'll meet again."

"Likewise." I lied.

As I hugged her, I looked behind her shoulder at Elec and mouthed, "I'm sorry," hoping he'd forgive me for letting the cat out of the bag about his writing. He just looked at me with an unreadable expression. While I couldn't understand why he never mentioned it to her if they were so serious, that didn't matter. I'd once again overstepped my boundaries when it came to him. Despite whatever that was between us downstairs at the funeral home, I had no real place in his life anymore. I made a vow then and there to keep my distance from him tomorrow unless he sought me out.

He doesn't need me. He has her. That would be my mantra.

111

She hugged my mother. "Sarah, please accept my sincerest condolences again. I'm so sorry that I have to be in California for my sister's wedding tomorrow."

"Thank you," my mother said. I could tell she was exhausted.

Chelsea whispered into my ear. "Thank you for letting me vent about that stuff earlier, too."

"Anytime."

Thank you for traumatizing me.

In another life, this girl could have been my best friend. I could just tell she was the kind of person you could call at any hour of the night to vent about all your problems. She was *that* nice, and I was *that* evil for the amount of relief I'd felt knowing that she'd be leaving on a jet plane tomorrow morning.

Now, the only hurdle would be getting through the next twenty-four hours. Then, Elec would be on a plane, too and out of my life again.

Right?

It didn't quite turn out to be that simple.

CHAPTER 14

It was a beautiful day despite the somber mood. The birds were chirping, the sun was shining, and I'd actually managed to sleep. But this wasn't your ordinary beautiful spring morning in Boston. Today, my mother would have to bury a husband for the second time in her life, and Elec would have to bury his father.

I hadn't realized until Chelsea told me she was leaving last night how much anxiety her presence had caused. Even though I'd have to face Elec again, today didn't feel half as horrible as yesterday.

When I walked into my mother's room, she was sitting on the bed holding a picture of Randy and her on their wedding day. She had been wearing a simple white suit for their ceremony at Boston City Hall. They seemed really happy together back then.

"He had a lot of demons, but he loved me," she said. "That was probably the only thing I was certain of when it came to him."

I wrapped my arm around her and took the picture frame from her grasp. "I remember that day like it was yesterday."

"This marriage…it was like a fresh start for him, but he was never able to resolve his past or his anger over it. He never opened up to me about it, and I never pushed it."

Sounds familiar.

She continued, "I didn't really want to know everything, I guess. After the pain of losing your father, I just wanted something easy. It was a bit selfish of me." She started to cry. "I'd been prying lately, and it caused a lot of tension. I felt ashamed for never getting involved in the situation with Elec. I was living in a bubble."

"Well, neither of them made it easy to figure out how to help," I said.

She wiped her eyes and looked at me. "I'm sorry you had to go through that."

"Me? Go through what?"

"Seeing Elec with her…with Chelsea."

"What do you mean?"

"I know, Greta."

"What do you think you know?"

"I know what happened between you and him the night before he left for California."

I put the picture I'd been holding down on the bed to prevent it from accidentally smashing to the ground in the midst of my shock. "What?"

"I'd gotten up early that day. Elec didn't know I saw him leaving your room to go back to his. Then, later that afternoon, after I came home from running errands, I went to check on you, but you had gone to the store. I found a condom wrapper in your room, and there was a little blood on your sheets. The week after he left, you were so depressed. I wanted to tell you I knew. I wanted to be there for you but didn't want to embarrass you or get anyone in trouble with Randy. He would have blown a gasket. I kept telling myself that you were eighteen, and if you wanted me to know, you would have told me."

"Wow. I just can't believe you knew all this time."

"He was your first…"

"Yes."

She held my hand. "I'm sorry I wasn't there for you."

"It's okay. Like you said, it was better that you kept it quiet."

"Was it…just sex…or was it more?"

"It was a lot more to me. I think he felt the same way at the time. But that doesn't matter now."

"He seems pretty settled with that girl."

"Yeah. They live together."

"He's not married, though."

I squinted my eyes. "What is that supposed to mean?"

"Just that if there's anything left unsaid between the two of you, this might be your last opportunity to get it out in the open. With Randy gone, we'll likely never see Elec again after today."

Even though I knew that was the case, it really hit home when she said it.

"Thanks for the advice, but I'm pretty sure that ship has sailed."

A tear fell down my cheek despite my attempt to seem unaffected.

"Clearly, for you it hasn't."

***

114

I could smell that he was right behind me. Even before that, my body could feel him there. The windows in the church were open, and a brisk wind blew the scent of cologne and clove cigarettes right into me. It was strangely comforting. The only other scent was the burning of candles that surrounded the altar and the occasional whiff of the lilies that had been transported here from the funeral home.

My mother and I were sitting in the front pew. I turned around to find Elec sitting next to Greg and Clara. They had arrived just a few minutes after us. Dressed in a fitted black satiny button-down shirt with no tie, he was looking down. Either he didn't catch me watching him for those few seconds, or he pretended not to notice.

There weren't half as many people here as there were at the wake. It was quiet except for the distant sounds of traffic and the echo of shoes as people walked down the long aisle to their seats.

An organist started playing *On Eagle's Wings*, and the music prompted my mother's tears to flow heavier.

The priest said the eulogy, which was generic and impersonal. When he referred to Randy as a "loving father," every muscle in my body tightened. Technically, if Randy and Elec had a normal relationship, his son might have gotten up to speak. I couldn't imagine what Elec would actually say in reality if he had the opportunity. Instead, he was quiet the entire service. He wasn't crying. He wasn't looking up. He was just…there, which I suppose was better than not showing up at all. I had to give him credit for that.

The service went by quickly and at the end, the priest gave out the address of the cemetery and announced that the family would like to invite everyone for a meal at a local restaurant following the burial.

I watched as Elec, Greg and a few other men who were Randy's friends served as pallbearers and carried the coffin out of the church. Elec continued to show no emotion.

My mother opted not to use a limo, so we drove together in my rental car and followed the hearse. Greg, Clara and Elec were in the car behind us.

When we got to the graveyard, we gathered around the massive dirt hole that had been dug into the ground right in front of a granite headstone with *O'Rourke* carved into the front. The question of whether my mother would be buried in this same plot or with my father crossed my mind.

Elec emerged from the car and walked over to where I had been standing and looking down into the ditch. He was staring down into it just as I was. When he turned to me, the look in his eyes was one of panic.

It's funny how fast you can set aside your pride when you truly sense that someone you care about needs help. I reached out for his hand. He didn't resist.

"I can't do this," he said.

"What?"

"What if they want me to help lower the casket into the ground? I can't do it."

"It's okay, Elec. You don't have to do anything you don't want to. I don't think that's something they expect you to do anyway."

He was just nodding and blinking but not saying anything. He swallowed anxiously. Then, he let go of my hand, turned around and weaved through the people who were starting to arrive. He kept walking down the road farther and farther away from the burial site.

Without thinking it through, I jogged in my heels to catch up with him.

"Elec…wait!"

When he stopped, his breathing was heavier than mine even though I'd been running. If I thought he was having a breakdown last night at the funeral home, I was wrong. I was pretty sure *this* was the moment where he was actually coming undone.

"There's just something about this part of it all that makes it final for me. I can't watch them putting him in the ground, let alone having a hand in it."

"It's okay. You don't have to."

"I don't think he'd even want me here, Greta. Either way, I can't witness it."

"Elec, that's a perfectly normal reaction. We don't need to go back. I'll stay here with you."

He just kept shaking his head no and stared out away from me. He was deep in thought.

A black crow landed near us, and I wondered what that symbolized.

After several seconds of silence, he started to talk. "It was during one of our worst fights, probably about a year before I met you. Randy had said he'd rather be dead and buried than to have to live to see what a fuck up I'd turn out to be." He looked down at his shoes and shook his head repeatedly. "I said something back to him along the lines of, 'well, then, I'll be smiling the entire time they're lowering you into the ground.'" He let out a deep breath as if he were holding it the entire time he'd been speaking.

I was starting to cry. "Elec…"

He spoke in a whisper looking up at the sky and said, "I didn't mean it." You could barely hear him, and I realized that was because he was talking to Randy in that moment.

He looked at me with his hand on his chest. "I need to get out of here. I can't be here. I'm losing it. I feel like I can't breathe."

He suddenly started walking fast, and I followed him.

"Okay. Where? Where do you want to go? The airport?"

"No…no. You have your car, right?"

"Yeah."

"Just get me the fuck out of here."

I nodded my head as he followed me down the gravel road to the parking area. A crowd was still gathered around Randy's grave several feet away. I fumbled with my keys, unlocked the car and Elec got in, slamming the door.

I immediately started the engine and pulled out of the lot, heading toward the exit.

"Where do you want to go?"

"Wherever the fuck the polar opposite of this nightmare is. Just drive for a while."

Elec was leaning his head back on the seat rest with his eyes closed. His chest was rising and falling as he loosened the top three buttons of his shirt. When we hit a red light, I sent a text to my mother.

Everything is fine. Elec had something like a panic attack and I'm driving him around. Make sure Greg gives you a ride to

117

the restaurant and let him know Elec is with me. Not sure if we'll miss the meal.

I didn't expect her to respond since the service was still going on but hoped she'd check her phone once she noticed we were gone.

He grunted. "Fuck."

"What?"

"My cigarettes are in Greg's car. I really need one."

"We can stop and get some."

He held up his hand. "No. Don't stop. Just drive."

So, that's what I did. For two hours straight, I drove on the highway. It was the middle of the day, so traffic was light. Elec was quiet the entire time, mostly looking out the window.

I had to stop at some point; otherwise, we'd be heading out of state. Sure enough, fifteen minutes later, the *Welcome to Connecticut* sign greeted me. He'd told me to take him to the polar opposite of a graveyard, to make him forget. I suddenly had a brilliant idea and knew exactly where we could go.

"Just about another twenty minutes then we're gonna stop somewhere, okay?"

He turned to me and spoke for the first time in hours. "Thank you."

I wanted to reach for his hand but resisted. A few minutes later, it looked like he'd fallen asleep. I remembered Chelsea saying he hadn't been getting any sleep since finding out Randy died.

My phone rang, and I picked it up.

"Hey, Mom."

"Greta, we've been worried. The meal is over. Is everything okay?"

"Everything is fine. We're still driving. We're gonna stop soon. Don't worry, okay? I'm sorry I had to leave you."

"I'm alright. The worst is over. I'm with Greg and Clara for the night. Just take care of Elec. He shouldn't be alone."

"Okay. Thanks for understanding, Mom. I love you."

"I love you, too."

We were approaching our destination, so I nudged Elec. "Wake up. We're here."

He rubbed his eyes and looked over at me as we continued down the long driveway.

"Are you taking me to visit the magical Wizard of Oz?"

He was right. The approach to the building kind of reminded me of the yellow brick road with the massive castle at the end.

"No, silly. It's a casino."

"We escaped from a funeral so that you could take me gambling? What the fuck?"

When I turned to look at his face, I expected to see a confused expression, but instead, he was giving me that rare genuine smile that I'd only seen a few times—the one that told me he was just messing with me. It was the same look that always made my heart flutter.

Then, he started laughing hysterically into his hands. I think he was delirious.

"You think it's distasteful?"

He wiped his eyes. "No, I think it's fucking brilliant!"

When I pulled into a parking spot, he was still laughing.

"Well, you told me to take you to the polar opposite of a graveyard, Elec."

"Yeah, I was thinking maybe a Zen Japanese restaurant or I don't know…a beach?"

"You want to leave?"

"Hell no. I would have never thought of it myself, but shit, if there's one place where you can drown your sorrows, this would be it." He gazed out the window then turned to me with a look that gave me chills. "So, help me drown my sorrows, Greta."

***

The influx of cigarette smoke when we entered the building had nearly choked me.

I hacked. "You're not gonna have a problem finding your cancer sticks in this place. In fact, everyone might as well be smoking here. The second hand is just as bad at this quantity."

"Try to have fun, sis." He shook me jokingly. My body's reaction to his strong hands on my shoulders wasn't surprising. If he kept touching me like that, this was going to be a long day.

"Please don't call me that."

119

"What would you prefer I call you here? No one knows us. We can make up names. We're both dressed in all black. We look like mafia high rollers."

"Anything but *sis*," I shouted through the dinging sounds of the hundreds of slot machines as we entered one of the casinos.

"What do you like to play?" I asked.

"I want to hit one of the tables," he said. "What about you?"

"I just do the penny slots."

"The penny slots? You're going wild today, huh?"

"Don't laugh."

"You don't go to a casino like this to play the slots, especially the penny ones."

"I don't know how to play any of the tables."

"I can show you, but first we need drinks." He winked. "Always liquor before you poker."

It took me a second. *Always lick her before you poke her.*

I rolled my eyes. "God, some things never change. At least you're back to making dirty jokes. That means I did something right today."

"Seriously, this idea…" He looked around. "Coming here…it was perfect."

After we bought some chips, I followed Elec to a room with dimmed lighting where people were playing table games. There was a bar in the corner.

"What are they playing?" I asked.

"Craps. It's a dice game. What do you want to drink?"

"I'll have a rum and Coke."

"Okay, I'll be right back. Don't go winning anything without me," he said, walking backwards with a smile.

The grin on his face made me truly happy even though I knew all of this was only a temporary diversion from the pain he was experiencing earlier.

As I waited for Elec to return with our drinks, I made my way over to one of the tables and stood just behind the players who were standing. A red-faced inebriated man with a Southern accent and a cowboy hat smiled at me before returning his eyes to the game.

Not understanding how the game was played, I daydreamed and stared at the table until everyone started clapping. When the drunk guy found out he'd won, he turned around and grabbed me by the waist.

"You, pretty lady, are my good luck charm. I haven't had one win tonight until you showed up out of nowhere. I'm not letting you out of my sight."

His breath reeked of beer, and sweat soaked through his shirt.

I smiled at him because it all seemed pretty innocent. That is, until he whacked me on the ass…really hard.

When I turned to walk away, Elec was approaching with two drinks in his hand. He was no longer smiling.

"Tell me I did not just see that fucking slob smack you on the ass." He didn't wait for my answer. "Hold these," he said.

He grabbed the guy by the neck. "Who the fuck do you think you are putting your hands on her like that?"

The man held up his hands. "I didn't know she was with someone. She was helping me out."

"It looked like you were helping yourself." Elec dragged him by the neck over to me. "Apologize to her right now."

"Look man—"

Elec squeezed his neck harder. "Apologize."

"I'm sorry," the man choked out.

Elec was still irate and wouldn't take his eyes off the guy.

I gestured with the drinks in my hand. "Come on, Elec. Please let's just go."

I breathed a sigh of relief when he took his drink from me and started walking away.

The man called out from behind us. "You're lucky you came when you did. I was just about to ask her to blow on my dice."

Elec flipped back around and charged toward the man, but I ran in front of him blocking his aim. In the process, he bumped into me, and both drinks spilled all over my dress.

"Elec, no! We can't get kicked out of here. Please. I'm begging you."

Despite the maniacal look in his eyes, by some miracle, Elec backed down. I think he knew if he took another step forward, it would have meant the end of our night. I was glad he realized that the guy wasn't worth it.

"You can thank her that you still have a face," Elec said before following me out of the room.

We walked in silence toward the exit until he took one look at my dress when we reentered the bright lighting.

"Shit, Greta. You're a mess."

"A hot mess." I laughed.

"Let's go. I'm buying you a new outfit."

"It's fine. I'm just a little wet."

Good God, Greta. Choose words wisely.

"No, it's not fine. That was my fault."

"It'll dry. Tell you what, if you win something tonight, you can spend it all on a new outfit for me at one of these expensive shops. That's the only way I'm letting you spend any money on me."

"I better get to work then, because you smell like a bar dumpster."

"Why, thank you."

"First, let's get you another adult beverage. Come on."

I stuck with Elec while he ordered our drinks at a different bar. "You want to come watch me play poker, or do you prefer playing your old lady slots?"

"I'd love to watch you play."

He looked over at the poker tables to survey the scene. "On second thought, I won't be able to concentrate. It's all men over there right now. Those guys are gonna be all over you, and I really don't feel like getting into another fight tonight. Why don't we split up for a little bit. You go play your pennies, and I'll come find you once I've played a couple of rounds."

I pointed to the slots diagonally across the room. "I'll be over there, then."

As I walked away, I thought about how I should have asked him why it bothered him so much if guys hit on me. I was the single one after all. Didn't he say it wasn't my place to care about him? So, why did he care about that if he's with Chelsea? I had to endure watching his girlfriend all over him right in front of me, so why shouldn't he have to endure some guy flirting with me?

I wanted to text him that question but wasn't sure if he had the same phone number from seven years ago. I decided I'd text the old number in my phone anyway to get it off my chest, and if it was no longer his number, then so be it.

Why does it matter to you anymore if other guys hit on me?
You're not supposed to care.

After a few minutes, there was no reply. It wasn't his number anymore. Well, it still felt good to type those words out.

I chose a *Lucky Sevens* machine and situated myself next to an old woman whose hair was pretty much blue because it had so much rinse in it.

She smiled over at me. Her lipstick was the brightest florescent pink, and she had a smear of it on her front teeth.

I pulled the lever repeatedly not even paying attention to whether or not I was winning anything.

Her voice startled me. "You look like you have something on your mind."

"I do?"

"Who is he, and what did he do?"

I'd never see this woman again after today. Maybe I should just let it all out.

"You want the long version or the short version?"

"I'm ninety, and the dinner buffet opens in five minutes. Give me the short version."

"Okay. I'm here with my stepbrother. Seven years ago, we slept together right before he moved away."

"Taboo…I like it. Go on."

I laughed. "Okay…well, he was the first and last guy I ever really cared about. I never thought I'd see him again. His father died this week, and he came back for the funeral. He wasn't alone. He brought a girl he supposedly loves. I know she loves him. She's a good person. She had to go back to California early. Somehow, I ended up at this casino with him. He leaves tomorrow."

A single teardrop fell down my face.

"It looks to me like you still care about him."

"I do."

"Well, then you have twenty-four hours."

"No, I don't plan to screw things up for him."

"Is he married?"

"No."

123

"Then, you have twenty-four hours." She looked at her watch and leaned on her walker to stand herself up. She gave me her hand. "I'm Evelyn."

"Hi, Evelyn. I'm Greta."

"Greta…fate gave you an opportunity. Don't fuck it up," she said before she scooted away on the walker.

Over the next several minutes, I kept thinking about what she said while mindlessly pulling the lever on the penny slot machine. Even if Elec weren't with Chelsea, the fact remained that he never felt we could be together because of Pilar. I didn't know if things had changed in that regard now.

My phone buzzed. It was Elec.

I know I'm not supposed to care. But when it comes to you, what I'm supposed to be feeling has never seemed to matter.

In that moment, I'd made a decision. I wasn't going to be the one to initiate anything between Elec and me, but I would keep an open mind. I wouldn't rule anything out. I would have hope. Because before I knew it, I'd be 90 and waiting for the dinner buffet. When that time came, I didn't want to have any regrets.

CHAPTER 15

The lights started flashing on my machine, and it was dinging like crazy. A bunch of number sevens were lined up in a nice neat row. The number of credits displayed kept going and going.

I looked around to find all eyes in the nearby vicinity were on me.

People started clapping.

My heart was racing.

Holy crap. I won.

I won!

What did I win?

I still didn't know. I couldn't figure the machine out. It gave the number of credits but no dollar amount. When everything finally stopped, I ejected my ticket and took it to the cashier's booth. "I think I won, but I couldn't figure out how much?"

"Do you want to cash out?"

"Uh...yeah."

The person seemed less than enthused to assist me.

"How much did I win?"

"One-thousand."

"One-thousand pennies?"

"No, one-thousand dollars."

I covered my mouth and spoke into my palm. "Oh my God!"

"Do you want it in fifties or hundreds?"

"Um...hundreds."

She handed me a wad of cash, and I smelled it before running off to find Elec.

As I made my way through the bright lights and chaos with the money burning a hole in my purse, I finally located him at one of the poker tables. He was deep in thought, scratching his chin and didn't know I was watching him. His shirt was loosened even further, and his sleeves were rolled up. His hair looked like he'd been running his hands through it in frustration. His tongue slid back and forth across the lip ring as he concentrated. There was something so painfully sexy about the contrast between his new bespectacled look and the tattoos all over his arms.

Finally, he smacked his cards down and mouthed, "Fuck." He checked his phone and got up from the table. He walked toward me and finally noticed me smiling at him from the corner.

"I lost my shirt—200 dollars. I was up for a while then that last game fucked me over. How did you make out?"

I stuck my hand in my bag and lifted out the cash. "Oh—you know—the lame penny machine."

"Are you kidding me?"

"A thousand dollars!" I said, waving it in his face and jumping up and down.

"Shit, Greta! Congratulations!"

When he pulled me into a quick but firm hug, I quickly closed my eyes because it felt so good to be in his arms again. Every nerve in my body came alive in that brief moment.

I kept hearing Evelyn's voice in my head.

You have twenty-four hours.

It was less than that now. A funny visual of Evelyn with a gun to my head entered my mind.

I put the money back in my purse. "Let's go out to dinner to celebrate."

As we walked the corridors looking for a restaurant, his phone rang. We stopped in our tracks.

"Hey, baby." He quickly glanced over at me when he'd said it, and I instinctively turned away.

With my heart in my mouth, I walked a few feet away, still listening to every word.

"I'm glad you made it okay."

"I had a little bit of a freak out at the burial, actually. Greta drove me around for a while until I calmed down. We ended up at a casino in Connecticut. That's where we are."

"I will."

"Me too."

"Have fun. Tell everyone I said 'hi.'"

"Love you, too."

Love you, too.

Well, that was a reality check. And why was I upset that he told her the truth as if this trip were supposed to be some secret rendezvous? In that moment, I realized I was delusional. Sure, his feelings after seeing me may have been a little conflicted, but he loved her, not me. Plain and simple. His heart was in a different place than mine was, and I needed to accept that.

He walked over to me. "Hey."

"Hey."

"That was Chelsea. She says hello and to thank you for helping me out today."

I flashed a fake smile. "Hello and you're welcome."

"Have you figured out what you're in the mood for?"

Admitting the true answer to that question would have put me back at square one.

Seeing as though the rum and Coke I'd had earlier had gone right through me, I said, "I'm heading to the bathroom. You decide what you feel like."

I took the opportunity to freshen up even though I still smelled like the alcohol that spilled on my dress earlier. I guess I could have afforded to buy myself a new dress now.

When I emerged from the bathroom, Elec was looking down at his phone. When he looked up, his face appeared pale.

"Are you alright?"

His hand was trembling, and he wouldn't answer me. "Elec?"

"I just got this text. It's from an unknown number."

He handed me the phone.

I was confused. "22?"

"Look what time it says the message came in."

"2:22. That's weird, but why does it bother you?"

"Randy's birthday is February 22nd."

Chills ran through me. "You think the message is from Randy?"

His eyes stayed fixed on the phone. "I don't know what to think."

"It might just be a coincidence. Why would he just send you the number 22?"

"I don't normally believe in that shit. I have no idea. It just weirded me out."

"I can understand why."

Elec was preoccupied all throughout our meal at the steakhouse. I knew he was obsessing over the text. To be honest, it really freaked me out as well.

Reentering the bright lights of the casino after dinner did nothing to lighten Elec's mood. At one point, I'd gone to get us a couple of drinks.

When I returned to where he was sitting, my heart felt like it fell to my stomach. He was wiping tears from his eyes. It shocked me to see my hardened stepbrother crying out in the open.

It was proof that we can't always choose the moment the reality of a loss hits us. Sometimes, it's predictable, and other times, it happens in the place you'd least expect. He hadn't cried at the wake or the burial but had chosen this moment here in this crowded casino to let go.

"Don't look at me, Greta."

Ignoring his plea for privacy, I put the drinks down and slid my seat closer to his. I pulled him toward me and held him into my chest. He didn't resist. The moisture from his tears seeped through the top of my dress. His fingernails dug into my back as if he were holding onto me for dear life. The harder he cried, the more I wanted to comfort him and the tighter I held onto him.

No one seemed to notice us in our corner of the room, although it wouldn't have mattered to me if they had.

His shaking seemed to calm down, and eventually, he was just breathing onto my chest.

"I hate this," he said. "I shouldn't be crying for him. Why am I crying for him?"

"Because you loved him."

His voice was trembling again. "He hated me."

"He hated whatever he saw in you that reminded him of himself. He didn't hate you. He couldn't have. He just didn't know how to be a father."

"There's a lot I haven't told you. The screwed up thing is, after all the shit we went through, I still wanted to make him proud of me someday, wanted him to love me."

"I know you did."

He continued to lean on me. At one point, he looked up, and his gray eyes were laced with red. "Where would I be tonight without you?"

"I'm glad I got to be the one with you tonight."

"I've never cried in front of anyone before. Not once."

"There's a first time for everything."

"There's a bad joke in there somewhere. You know that, right?"

We both laughed. I imagined how good it must have felt for him to laugh. For me, laughter never felt better than when it followed a good cry.

"You make me feel things, Greta. You always have. When I'm around you, whether it's good or bad...I feel *everything.* Sometimes, I don't handle it too well, and I fight it by acting like an asshole. I don't know what it is about you, but I feel like you see the real me. The second I saw you again for the first time at Greg's when you were standing in that garden...it was like I couldn't hide behind myself anymore." He rubbed my cheek with his thumb. "I know it was hard for you to see me with Chelsea. I know you still care about me. I can feel it even when you're pretending you've stopped."

"This has been hard, but it was worth it to be able to see you again."

"I don't want to cry anymore tonight."

"I don't want you to cry anymore, either. But if you feel like you have to, don't be afraid to. It's good to let it out."

He was staring at my lips. I was staring at his. The past few minutes had weakened me. I wanted to kiss him. I knew I couldn't, but the need was so intense I had to get up from my seat.

I was feeling like I was going to burst—both physically and emotionally. We were sitting diagonally across from the roulette wheel. It was the only non-slot game I understood how to play. I needed to take my impulsivity out on something and had an idea.

When you're gambling with your heart, taking a chance with money seems like nothing. I headed for the roulette table and threw a bunch of bills from my stash down on one number.

"Straight up," I said.

The casino worker looked at me like I was crazy.

Elec had come up from behind me. "What are you doing?"

He hadn't seen which bet was mine. My heart was beating faster with every turn of the wheel, and everything thereafter seemed to happen in slow motion.

Elec's hands were on my shoulders as our eyes stayed glued to the wheel.

The wheel stopped.

The worker's eyes bugged out of his head.

Someone handed me a drink that wasn't mine.

More alcohol spilled on me.

People were clapping, cheering, whistling.

"22 is the winner!"

"That's me. I won!"

Elec lifted me up into the air, spinning us both around.

When he put me down, he looked at me in shock. "You bet 22? You fucking bet it *all* on 22! Do you have any idea how much money you just won?"

I turned to the man behind the table.

"How much did I just win?"

"19-thousand dollars."

"Holy shit, Greta." Elec took my face in his hands, shook my cheeks and repeated, "Holy shit." It seemed like he was going to give me a celebratory kiss, but he stopped short.

I'd just won a crapload of money but that didn't seem to matter as much as getting to share this moment with him. Nothing beat the feeling of his hands cupping my face, of seeing his eyes smiling back at mine, of being able to turn his misery toward the number 22 into something positive. If this money could have bought more time with him, I would have given every red cent of it away.

Elec and I walked over to the cashier's booth in a daze. While I went to collect the money, he stood back a ways talking to a few of the people who were at the table when I won.

I opted to take a check for the majority but asked for one thousand in cash. They'd also given me a complimentary room key for the casino hotel. That had caught me off guard, and I wasn't sure if I should even mention it to Elec.

By the time I walked back over to him, he was standing alone with a huge smile on his face.

I handed him the ten crisp hundred-dollar bills. "I want you have this."

His smile faded, and he tried to hand the cash back to me. "I'm not taking any money from you."

"If it weren't for you, I wouldn't have even played 22. I chose it for you."

"No way." He shoved it in my face. "Take it."

I wouldn't budge. "That's only a fraction of the winnings. I have a check for all the rest. I'm gonna put in the bank to help my Mom out. If you don't take this cash, I'll bet it all."

"Don't do that. There's no way you'd get lucky a third time tonight."

I crossed my arms. "I'm not taking it back. So, either you take it, or I'm gambling with it."

He sighed. "I'll tell you what. I'll take the money, but we're spending it together tonight. We'll have the time of our lives with it."

"Okay." My mouth spread into a smile. "I can live with that."

He glanced at the card I was holding. "What's that?"

"Oh, uh…they also gave me a complimentary room key. I guess they want me to stick around a while and dump all of my winnings back into the casino. I'm not gonna use it. We're heading back to Boston later, right?"

"Neither of us is really in condition to drive tonight."

"You want to stay overnight? We can't sleep in the same room."

"I wasn't suggesting that, Greta. I'll get my own room."

Of course. Now, I felt stupid for even assuming that was what he meant.

"Right. Okay. If you think that's a good idea, we can stay."

"The truth is, I'm not ready for this night to end. I don't want to face reality again until I absolutely have to. My flight isn't until tomorrow night. If we leave in the morning, we'll have plenty of time."

I rubbed his arm. "Okay." I followed him out of the game room. "Where are we going first?"

"To buy you a new outfit. I get to pick it out. We're going clubbing later. You can't wear that."

"Clubbing?"

"Yeah. They have a nightclub downstairs."

"Should I be worried? Exactly what do you consider clubbing attire?"

He looked at my outfit. "Something that doesn't make you look like an 85-year-old Greek woman in mourning."

I straightened my dress. "What are you trying to say?"

"Make that an 85-year-old *drunk* Greek woman since you smell like a bucket of booze."

"Thanks to you."

"Let's go spend some money."

CHAPTER 16

"How about this one?" I lifted a canary yellow chiffon mini-dress off the rack.

"You'll look like a banana."

I chose another one. "This?"

Elec shook his head. "No."

He picked up a burgundy satin and sequin number that draped over the tattoos on his arm as he showed it to me. "This is hot. This is it."

At first, I thought it was too much but agreed to try it on.

Out of the three dresses I'd taken into the fitting room, the one he picked fit my body the best. It actually made me look like I had boobs, and the short style accentuated my legs. I had to give him credit. The sequins were a little loud, but then again, we were dressing for *da club*.

The dress fit me so well, in fact, that it didn't want to come off. The zipper was stuck, and I couldn't pull the dress over my head. I was starting to sweat because I couldn't reach it to diagnose the problem.

"You alright in there?" Elec asked.

"Uh…can you see if there's a salesperson that can help me?"

"What's the problem?"

"I can't get the dress off."

"Well, you did finish off my steak and yours at dinner…"

"The zipper is stuck!"

He laughed. "I can help you."

"No! I'd just be more comfortable if—"

The curtain slid open suddenly, and he stepped inside. "Come here."

The warmth of his body was tangible in the small confines of the space. He slid all of my hair to the front and pulled at the material that was stuck. My breathing quickened with every second that his hands worked the zipper at the top of my back.

The image in my head of him ripping the dress off and wrapping my legs around him wasn't helping.

"You weren't kidding," he said as he fiddled with it." After about a minute, I heard him say, "Got it."

"Thank you."

He slowly lowered it a few inches then stopped. "All set." But his hands lingered on my shoulders. I'd been looking down, and when I looked up, he was staring into my eyes from behind me in the mirror.

I turned around abruptly. Our faces were close, and his eyes dropped to my mouth and stayed there. This time he didn't try to hide the fact that he seemed mesmerized by my lips.

He closed his eyes briefly as if to fend off the urge to kiss me. It troubled me that if he had tried, I knew without a doubt that I couldn't have resisted. I would have kissed him with everything in me. That lack of self-control scared me.

It was impossible to see anything beyond him at that moment, not Chelsea, not the consequences. The memory of his mouth all over me, of him deep inside my body was overwhelming me.

My mind could be talked down, but my body knew better. It knew that it had within its grasp, the one thing it craved every day for the past seven years.

No one had ever been able to measure up or replace him.

Elec had wrecked me.

He may have been Chelsea's now, but my body still believed that it belonged to him whether he knew it or not, whether that was right or wrong.

He was hers.

I was his.

It. Was. Fucked. Up.

The store attendant came by. "Is everything okay in there?"

"Yes!" I shouted.

No. No, it's not.

***

Nothing had happened.

Elec exited the dressing room as soon as the attendant interrupted our moment.

We ended up picking out some clothes in the men's section for him to wear that night.

We then went to the hotel lobby to book his room. He insisted on paying for that with his credit card and not the stash of money.

We each retreated to our separate rooms to shower and had planned to meet in a half-hour to head to Roxy's nightclub.

As the water poured down on me, it felt good to wash the alcohol and perspiration off my body. Even though this seemed like the longest day of my life, the thought of it coming to an end terrified me.

Needless to say, my shower was of the coldest variety. Despite the temperature, the need to relieve the tension that had been building between my legs all day was overwhelming. I slid myself down to the ground of the bathtub at one point, letting the water pummel me while I massaged my clit to thoughts of him.

Elec's face between my legs, his lip ring scraping my clit while he licked me ravenously...

His pierced cock down my throat...

The feel of him deep inside of me...

His eyes glued to mine while he came...

I climaxed almost violently.

My back was still pressed to the cold ceramic floor of the tub when I heard the knock.

Shit! Either I'd lost track of time, or he was early.

"Just a minute!"

I wiped down as fast as I could. I slipped the burgundy dress on, quickly ran a brush through my wet hair and opened the door.

"Wow." After a long pause, he added, "You definitely can't pass for an old lady in mourning anymore."

"What do I look like now?"

"You look flushed, actually. Are you feeling alright?"

Having to face the person you'd been masturbating to in your head just seconds earlier was not something I could say had ever happened to me before.

"I'm fine."

"You sure?"

I pursed my lips trying not to look guilty. "Yep."

135

He was dressed to kill in the dark jeans and a fitted navy shirt he bought downstairs in the men's section. The more casual look had transformed him back into the Elec I remembered. His hair was still wet, and the way it was parted accentuated his eyes.

Those fucking glasses.

"It felt so good to take a shower," he said.

"I know what you mean."

Mine felt particularly good.

"Do you need to dry your hair?"

"Yeah. Just give me a minute."

I went to the bathroom and ran the blow dryer through it as swiftly as I could and then put it into a quick updo.

When I reentered the room, Elec had turned on ESPN and was lying flat on the bed with his hands resting behind his head. His shirt had ridden up, teasing me with a glimpse of one of the shamrock tattoos on his abs. It became clear to me that pleasuring myself in the shower had done nothing to resolve my "issues." The sooner we could get out of this room, the better.

"I'm ready."

He hopped up and turned the television off. I followed him out as the door clicked behind us.

"You clean up nice," he said as we entered the elevator. "I like your hair up like that."

"You do?"

"Yeah. It's how you were wearing it the night when I first met you."

"I'm surprised you remembered that."

A feeling of nostalgia came over me when I thought about waiting for him at the window that first night. I had no idea what kind of adventure I was in for with Elec.

"You were so innocent at first. You were just trying to be sweet to me, and I was such a prick."

"You were. But I grew to like that about you."

"When I wasn't making you cry?"

"I had my moments of taking you too seriously, but overall, your jabs were fun. I don't look back on any of it negatively."

"You *were* a little bit of a masochist. That sort of screwed up my evil plan pretty early on."

"Well, you weren't exactly as mean as you wanted me to believe you were."

"And it turned out you weren't that innocent."

Our sexual tension-filled trip down memory lane came to an end as soon as we arrived at the line into Roxy's. We entered the confines of the dark nightclub, and Elec disappeared into the flashing strobe lights to fetch us some drinks.

The bass of the music vibrated through me as I rocked back and forth trying to get into the mood while I waited.

When he returned with his beer and my drink, I couldn't take the first sip fast enough. My throat felt frozen from the crushed ice of the daiquiri. We stood on the second level, looking down at the swarms of people on the dance floor as we sipped our drinks. Alcohol was going to be my best friend tonight. I didn't want to get totally sloshed but hoped that it would help me forget about tomorrow.

A good buzz was starting to develop just as I felt Elec's firm grip on my wrist.

"Come on." His fingertips grazed the small of my back as he led me down the stairs.

I should have expected that he might drag me on to the dance floor. What I absolutely couldn't have predicted was how phenomenal of a dancer he was.

The eyes of several of the women in the club followed his every move as I discovered for the first time that my stepbrother could dance his ass off.

Who knew?

Although, should it really have surprised me that someone who could fuck like Elec could also move his body just as well in other ways?

I felt for those women. We all had one thing in common. We all wanted a piece of him, and none of us would be getting any.

Seriously. His movements were like those of a stripper, but this was even more of a tease because you knew he wouldn't be taking his clothes off.

It was truly like an erotic show: the way he moved his hips, the way his ass swayed to the music, the way his tongue glided slowly along his lip ring as he got lost in the rhythm.

Imagine you're watching *Magic Mike*, and the DVD gets stuck on repeat right before the first strip scene starts. That was watching Elec dance.

I moved my body to the music alongside him, but he never put his hands on me while we were dancing together.

At one point, his hot breath tickled my ear as he leaned into me. "I'm gonna find a bathroom. Stay here where I can locate you."

After Elec left me alone, a man wearing a pink collared shirt started to dance with me. He began to speak loudly through the music as he asked me questions to which I gave him one-word answers.

A few minutes later, I felt an arm wrap around my waist from behind. The addicting smell of Elec's skin identified him right away, so I didn't resist when he pulled me back. After I turned around to face him, his eyes peered into mine with a warning look. He couldn't say anything about my dancing with the man because that would have been inappropriate given his own situation. He had no right to stop me from dancing with someone. Yet, he knew he could get away with it because of the tunnel vision effect he had on me.

A flashback of Elec's texts to me the night of my date with Corey all those years ago came to mind.

"You don't even like him."
"How would you know that?"
"Because you like me."

Once Elec got me far enough away from the guy, he let go of me. We were back to dancing to the fast-paced music and after another round of drinks, it became even easier to get lost in the mood. In the span of an hour, we never stopped dancing. Even though we weren't touching, Elec's eyes were fixed on mine a lot. The room was starting to sway a little, and that was an indicator that perhaps it was time to stop imbibing.

Suddenly, the music changed to the first slow song of the night. An alarm went off in my mind. This couldn't happen. I nudged my head for him to follow me off the dance floor. I started to walk off and felt his hand on mine. I stopped and turned to him.

Still holding my hand, he mouthed, "Dance with me."

Even though I knew this was going to be the moment that completely undid me, I nodded my head and reluctantly let him pull me into him. He let out a deep breath the moment I landed in the warmth of his arms.

Closing my eyes, I rested my head on his chest and conceded to the pain that had been building inside me since the moment I first saw him with Chelsea. With each pounding beat of his heart, another of my old wounds would burst open, destroying all of the self-protective mechanisms I'd tried to implement over these past couple of days.

If I hadn't moved from my position, I might have been able to get through the song. But I was a glutton for punishment and needed to know if the look on his face matched the intensity of his heartbeat.

My cheek slowly slid away from his chest. As I lifted my head upwards to look at him, he lowered his head slowly at almost exactly the same time as if he'd been waiting for me to look at him.

The desire in eyes was blatant. I breathed in to catch each heavy breath that escaped his lips. If I couldn't kiss him, I wanted to at least taste every breath.

Then, he touched his forehead to mine.

It was a simple and seemingly innocent gesture, but couple that moment with the climactic part of the song, and that was it for me.

To save myself from falling further into this, I intentionally replayed his words to Chelsea in my head. *I love you, too.*

This. Was. My. Breaking. Point.

I ripped myself away from him and ran off of the dance floor.

I could hear him calling after me. "Greta, wait!"

Tears were pouring down my face as I weaved through the heat of the club, bumping into sweaty drunk people as I tried to find the exit. Someone's drink spilled on me in the process. I didn't care. I just needed to get out of there.

He'd lost me through the crowd.

Having escaped the darkness of the club, the lights of the casino lobby were a welcome contrast.

I ran to the elevators and pressed the up button, hoping to get to my room as fast as possible. The doors started to close right before I saw a tattooed arm slide inside, prompting them to open.

His breathing was erratic. The doors closed.

"What the fuck, Greta? Why did you run from me like that?"

139

"I just need to go back to my room."

"Not like this."

He pressed the stop button, causing the elevator to come to a jolting halt.

"What are you doing?"

"This isn't how I wanted our night to end. I crossed a line. I know that. I got lost in the moment with you, and I'm so fucking sorry. But it wasn't going to go any further because I won't cheat on Chelsea. I couldn't do that to her."

"I'm not as strong as you are, then. You can't dance with me like that, look at me like that, touch me like that if we can't do anything about it. And for the record, I wouldn't *want* you to cheat on her!"

"What *do* you want?"

"I don't want you to say one thing and act in a way that contradicts it. We don't have much time left together. I want you to talk to me. That night at the wake…you wrapped your hand around my neck. It felt like for a moment you were back in that place where we left off. That's sort of how I feel around you all of the time. Then, later that night, Chelsea told me what happened after you got home."

He squinted. "Exactly what did she tell you?"

"Were you thinking about me? Is that why you couldn't perform that night?"

Understandably, he looked shocked that I knew. I still didn't understand why Chelsea shared that with me.

Because she trusted me, and she shouldn't have.

I regretted saying anything, but it was too late.

He stayed silent, glaring at me, but he looked like he wanted to say something.

"I want you to tell me the truth," I said.

The look on his face turned angry, like he'd lost some battle of self-control within himself. "You want the truth? I was fucking my girlfriend and could see nothing but you. That's the truth." He took a few steps toward me, and I stepped backwards as he continued, "I got into the shower that night, and the only way I could finish the job was to imagine coming all over your beautiful neck. *That's* the truth."

I leaned against the elevator wall as he locked his arms on each side of me and continued, "You want more? I was going to ask her to marry me tonight at her sister's wedding. I was supposed to be engaged right at this very moment, but instead, I'm in an elevator fighting the urge to back you up against this wall and fuck you so hard that I'll have to carry you back to your room."

My heart was beating out of control, and it was unclear which part of what he'd just said shocked me more.

He dropped his arms and lowered his voice. "Everything I thought I knew has been turned upside down in the past forty-eight hours. I'm questioning everything, and I don't fucking know what to do. That's. The. Truth."

He released the stop button, and the elevator continued rising up to our floor—the 22nd floor.

He was going to ask her to marry him.

It was still sinking in. What a rude awakening as to exactly how far out of my league I'd been all of this time.

The elevator doors slid open, and as we walked down the hall, I simply said, "I don't want to talk anymore. I need to be alone."

He didn't protest as I retreated to my room without saying anything further. It saddened me that our night had been cut short, but it finally became crystal clear that any more time spent with him would be dangerous. He was leaving on a plane tomorrow, and there simply wasn't enough time to resolve all of these feelings.

Since I hadn't bought any pajamas, I wrapped myself in a sheet and lay down. Devastated from the proposal bombshell he'd dropped and still painfully aroused by what he'd said to me after, I knew that sleep was not in my future tonight.

A half-hour passed. It felt like déjà vu as the red digital numbers of the alarm clock taunted me.

My text alert sounded at 2 A.M.

If I knock on your door tonight, don't let me in.

141

CHAPTER 17

He was trying to do the right thing, and I respected the hell out of him for it. As powerful as temptation could be, I meant it when I told him I would never want him to cheat on her. At the same time, if I hadn't gone to my room, I'm not sure that we could have avoided something happening. Tonight proved that whatever connection existed in the past between us was very much still alive and powerful. That was why it was best that we spent the rest of the night apart.

I was tossing and turning, still conflicted about leaving him alone. Even though what happened in the elevator had tainted the rest of the night, I needed to remind myself how this day started; he was still mourning his father. He really shouldn't have been by himself tonight. Not to mention, we were wasting precious time because once he returned to California, I'd probably never see or hear from him again.

He was going to marry her.

Rustling in my sheets, I couldn't take the insomnia anymore. The fact that the room was freezing didn't help. I got up to shut off the air conditioner and grabbed my phone before returning to the bed.

Are you awake?

Elec: I was just about to order this amazing juicer. If I order right now, they'll even throw in a bonus mini chopper all for just 19.99.

Greta: Can we talk? On the phone?

Not even three seconds went by before my phone rang.

"Hi."
He whispered, "Hi."
"I'm sorry," we both said in unison.
"Jinx," he said.

"You go first," I said.

"I'm sorry for what I said to you in the elevator. I lost control."

"You were being honest."

"That doesn't make it right. I'm sorry for the way it came out. You bring out the worst in me."

"I'm touched."

"Fuck. That came out wrong."

I laughed. "I think I know what you're trying to say."

"Thank God you could always read between the lines with me."

"How about we not rehash anything that was said in that elevator. I just want to talk."

I could hear him moving around in the bed. He was probably gearing up for whatever conversation we were about to have.

He let out a deep breath into the phone. "Okay. What do you want to talk about?"

"I have some questions. I don't know if this is my last opportunity to ask them."

"Alright."

"Did you stop writing?"

"No. I didn't."

"How come you didn't tell Chelsea that you write?"

"Because from the time that I met her, I've only been working on one project, and it's not something I really feel like I can share with her."

"What is it?"

"It's autobiographical."

"You've been writing your life story?"

"Yeah." He sighed. "Yeah, I have."

"Does anyone know?"

"No. Just you."

"Is it therapeutic?"

"Sometimes. Other times, it's hard to relive certain things that happened, but it just felt like I needed to do it."

"If she doesn't know about it, when do you write?"

"Late at night when she's asleep."

"Are you gonna tell her?"

143

"I don't know. There are things in there that would upset her."

"Like what do you—"

"My turn to ask a question," he interrupted.

"Okay."

"What happened with the guy you were engaged to?"

"How did you know I was engaged anyway?"

"Answer me first."

"His name was Tim. We lived together for a little while in New York. He was a good person, and I wanted to love him, but I didn't. The fact that I wouldn't consider moving to Europe for him when his job transferred him there proved that. Really, there's not much more to it than that. Now, will you tell me how you knew?"

"Randy told me."

"I thought you were estranged."

"We still spoke from time to time. I asked him about you once, and he gave me the news. I assumed that meant you were happy."

"I wasn't."

"I'm sorry to hear that."

"Did you have any other girlfriends besides Chelsea?"

"Chelsea's my first serious relationship. I screwed around a lot before that."

"I see."

"I didn't mean…you. You weren't part of the screwing around. What happened with us was different."

"I know what you meant." After a block of silence, I said, "I want you to be happy, Elec. If she makes you happy, I'm happy for you. You told me she was the best thing that ever happened to you. That's great."

"I didn't say that," he said curtly.

"Yes, you did."

"I said she was *one* of the best things. So were you. Just in another time."

Another time—a time that's passed.

You get the picture now, Greta?

"Thank you," I said.

"Don't thank me. I took your fucking virginity and left. I don't deserve your thanks."

"You did what you felt you had to do."

"It was still wrong. It was selfish."

"I still wouldn't change anything about that night if that makes you feel better."

He let out a deep sigh. "You seriously mean that?"

"Yes."

"I don't regret one thing that happened that night either, only what happened after."

I closed my eyes. We were both silent for a long time. I think the day had finally caught up with both of us physically.

"You still there?" I asked.

"I'm still here."

I let those words sink in, knowing that tomorrow he wouldn't be. I needed to get at least a couple hours of sleep before the two-hour drive back to Boston in the morning.

I needed to let him go.

Let him go.

"I'm going to try to get some sleep," I said.

"Stay on the phone with me, Greta. Close your eyes. Try to sleep. Just stay on the phone."

I pulled the comforter over myself.

"Elec?"

"Yeah…"

"You were the best thing that ever happened to *me*. I hope someday I can say you were *one of* the best, but for now, it's only you."

I closed my eyes.

***

Elec met me at the hotel registration desk where we both checked out.

We had each showered but were wearing the same clothes we'd worn to the club the night before. The scruff on his chin appeared to have grown out overnight and even though his eyes were weary, he still looked painfully hot in his club attire at 10 in the morning.

His words from last night rang out in my head. *"I'm fighting the urge to back you up against this wall and fuck you so hard that I'll have to carry you back to your room."*

We stopped at the casino Starbucks, and as we were waiting for our coffees, I could feel him staring at me. I'd been intentionally trying not to look at him because I was sure he'd be able to see the sadness in my eyes.

We ended up taking our breakfast on the road. The ride home was eerily quiet. It was like the calm after the storm. The whirlwind of the previous day had given way to a numb and helpless feeling this morning.

Light rock played on the radio station as I kept my eyes on the road. What felt like the weight of a million unsaid words loomed over us as we remained silent.

He said one thing the entire ride. "Will you drive me to the airport?"

"Sure," I said without looking at him.

Clara was originally going to drive him, and I wasn't sure how I felt about the change of plans, which would prolong the agony.

We pulled into Greg and Clara's. Elec ran in to gather his belongings while I waited in the car. Since we had a little extra time, the plan was to go to my mother's house and check on her before we headed to the airport.

He'd left his phone on the seat and a text came through. The screen was lit, and I couldn't help peeking down at it. It was from Chelsea.

I'm going to wait up. I can't wait until you're home. Have a safe flight. Love you.

I regretted looking at it because it solidified that this was really the end.

Before I could wallow in self-pity, Elec approached carrying a large black travel bag. He got in, looked down at his phone and sent a quick text as I put the car in reverse and backed out of the driveway.

Mom wasn't home when we got to the house. When I texted her, she said she'd gone for a walk.

146

It certainly wasn't my intention to find myself alone with Elec in the house that held all of our memories together.

He leaned against the counter. "Hey, you got any of your ice cream lying around? I've been jonesing it for seven years."

I've been jonesing you for seven years.

"You might just be in luck," I said, opening the freezer.

Ironically, thinking I was going to need it, I'd made a batch with my old ice cream maker the night before the funeral and put it in the freezer. Of course, I never came home to have it.

I scooped it out into one bowl and took two spoons out of the drawer. We always shared the bowl and for old times' sake, I kept to that tradition.

"You put extra snickers in it."

I smiled. "I did."

He closed his eyes and moaned upon taking the first bite. "There is nothing better than your fucking ass cream. I've missed it."

I've missed this.

Being in this kitchen and sharing the ice cream with him made it really feel like yesterday more than any other moment up until now. I wished we could go back to that time for just one more day. He'd be right upstairs and not heading home to her. We'd play our video game. It was so simple then.

Then, memories of the night he made love to me started to flash through my mind at a tremendous pace. *Not so simple.* His leaving was starting to really hit me all of a sudden. The silence wasn't working for me anymore, and I tried to make light conversation to mask my melancholy.

"What did Greg and Clara have to say?"

"They were asking where we went. I told them."

"Did they think it was bizarre?"

"I could tell Greg was a little concerned."

"Why would he be concerned?"

He pulled the spoon slowly from his mouth and looked down in hesitation. "He knows."

"Knows what?"

"About us."

I put my spoon down and wiped the corners of my mouth. "How?"

"I confided in him a few years back. I knew he wouldn't tell Randy."

"Why would you tell him?"

"Because I felt like I needed to talk about it. I didn't have anyone else I could trust."

"It's just…you told me not to tell anyone, and I didn't for a long time until I finally told Victoria years later."

"Greg is the only person I told."

"I just didn't think—"

He raised the tone of his voice. "You didn't think what happened between us affected me in the same way it affected you. I know. Because I led you to believe that."

"I guess it doesn't matter anymore," I said under my breath so low that I didn't think he heard me.

Elec scowled as he took the empty bowl to the sink, washed it and put it in the strainer.

He looked back at me. "You'll always matter to me, Greta. Always."

I just nodded, refusing to shed a tear but feeling completely broken inside. This was different from the last time we said goodbye. Back then, even though I was an emotional wreck, I was young and suspected that my feelings might have been infatuation and that I would grow out of it.

Unfortunately, this time with the advantage of experience and hindsight, I knew without a shadow of a doubt that I was hopelessly in love with him.

***

The drive to Logan Airport seemed like it only took a few minutes. A pink hue lit up the sky, appropriate symbolism for sending Elec off into the sunset. Unprepared for how to say goodbye, I opted not to say anything at all during the ride, and neither did he.

As we exited the car at the curb just outside the entrance to his terminal, the wind was powerful amidst the deafening sound of jets taking off.

Clutching my own arms protectively, I stood across from him. I didn't know what to say or do and couldn't even look him in the eye. Now was not the time to completely freeze up, but that was exactly what was happening to me.

I looked up at the sky, down at the ground, over at the luggage handlers…anywhere but at Elec. I knew as soon as I looked into his eyes, I would lose it.

His tone was gruff. "Look at me."

I shook my head and refused as the first teardrop fell. I wiped my eye and continued to look away from him. I couldn't believe this was happening to me right now.

When I finally looked into his eyes, I was shocked to see them watering, too.

"It's okay," I said. "Go. Please. Text me if you want. It's just…I can't do a long goodbye…not with you."

"Okay," he simply said.

I leaned in and gave him a quick kiss on the cheek before rushing back to the car and slamming the door.

He reluctantly picked up his bag and walked away toward the entrance.

When I saw the automatic doors finally close behind him, I leaned my head against the steering wheel. My shoulders shook as I let the tears I'd been struggling to hide fall freely. It was only a matter of time before someone told me to leave since this was only a temporary drop off area. I just couldn't seem to move.

Sure enough, someone knocked on my window.

"I'm going. I'm going," I said without even looking up. As I was about to start my car, the person knocked again.

I looked to my right to find Elec standing there.

I frantically wiped my tears and got out of the car, walking around to him. "Did you forget something?"

He dropped his bag and nodded yes. He startled me when he suddenly took my face in his hands and kissed my lips tenderly. It felt like I was melting in his arms. My tongue instinctively tried to enter his mouth, but he didn't open for me. He just kept his lips pressed hard against mine as he breathed erratically. This was a different kind of a kiss, not one that leads to something, but a hard, painful one.

It was a goodbye kiss.

I pulled back. "Get out of here. You're gonna miss your flight."

He wouldn't take his hands off of my face. "I never got over hurting you the first time, but hurting you twice…believe me when I say this was the last thing I ever wanted to see happen in my lifetime."

"Why did you come back just now?"

"I turned around and saw you crying. What kind of a heartless asshole would leave you like that?"

"Well, you weren't supposed to see that. You really should have kept walking because now you're making it worse."

"I didn't want that to be my last visual."

"If you really love her, you shouldn't have kissed me."

I hadn't meant to yell it.

"I do love her." He looked up at the sky then back at me with anguished eyes. "You want to know the truth? I fucking love you, too. I don't think I realized how much until I saw you again."

He loved me?

I laughed angrily. "You love us both? That's messed up, Elec."

"You've always told me you wanted honesty. I just gave it to you. I'm sorry if the truth is a fucked up mess."

"Well, she has the home court advantage. You'll forget about me again soon enough. That will simplify things." I walked back around to the driver's side.

"Greta…don't leave like this."

"I'm not the one leaving."

I closed the door, turned the ignition and drove away. I only looked in the rearview mirror once and saw Elec standing in the same spot. Maybe my reaction was unfair, but if he was being honest with his feelings, then so was I.

All I could think about on the drive home was how life could be cruel. The "one that got away" was supposed to *stay* away, not come back and leave you all over again.

When I pulled into my driveway, I noticed an envelope on the passenger seat. It was the one thousand dollars cash I'd given him. That meant any money we'd spent last night was his. There was a note inside.

I just didn't want you to gamble it. I could never repay you for everything you've given me, let alone take money from you.

Two months after Elec returned to California, I was finally getting back to a regular routine in New York.

My mother had come to stay with me for the first month after Randy's death but decided that she wasn't happy living away from Boston. With Greg and Clara looking out for her and my visiting every other weekend, she was adjusting as well as could be to her new normal.

Elec and I hadn't contacted each other at all. It was a little bit of a let down to not have received even a text, especially after how we left things, but I wasn't going to be the first to make contact. For all I knew, I'd never hear from him again.

Thoughts of him still consumed me everyday. I'd wonder if he had asked Chelsea to marry him. I'd wonder whether he was thinking of me. I'd wonder what would have happened if I hadn't gone to my own room the last night we were together. So, even though I was back to my home base, my mind was constantly elsewhere.

My life in Manhattan was pretty predictable. I worked long days at the office and got home around eight each night. If I didn't go out for drinks with my co-workers, I'd spend the weeknights reading until I fell asleep with my kindle on my face.

On Friday nights, my neighbor Sully and I would have dinner and drinks at Charlie's, the pub underneath my apartment. Most women in their mid-twenties would spend their Friday nights with a boyfriend or a group of women their own age. Instead, I chose to spend it with a 70-year-old transvestite.

Sully was a petite Asian man who dressed as a woman and in fact, I assumed he *was* a woman until one night a pair of spandex revealed some disproportionately massive junk. I sometimes thought of Sully as a *he*, other times, as a *she*. It didn't make a difference because by the time I figured "it" out, I'd already fallen in love with her as a person, and it didn't matter what gender she was.

Sully was never married, had no kids and was extremely protective of me. Any time a guy would walk into Charlie's, I'd turn to Sully and say jokingly, "What about him?"

The answer was always the same. "Not good enough for my Greta…but I'd do him." Then, we'd just have a good laugh.

I'd always been hesitant to talk to Sully about Elec because I was seriously afraid she'd want to hunt him down and kick his ass. One particular Friday night, though, after one too many margaritas, I finally divulged the entire story from start to finish.

"Now, I understand," Sully said.

"Understand what?"

"Why you're here with me every Friday night and not on a date with some man, why you've been unable to open your heart to anyone. It belongs to someone else."

"It used to. Now, it's just broken. How do I fix it?"

"Sometimes, we can't."

Sully stared off, and I suspected she was speaking from experience.

"The trick is to force yourself to open it even though it's broken. A broken heart is still a beating one. And there are many men who I'm sure would like an opportunity to try to fix yours if you'd let them." She continued, "I'll tell you one thing, though."

"What?"

"This…Alec?"

"Elec…with an e."

"Elec. He's lucky I won't set foot on a plane. I'd set his balls on fire."

"I knew you'd feel this way. That's why I was afraid to tell you."

"And I don't know who this Kelsey is…"

"Chelsea…"

"Whatever. There is no way she's better than my Greta, more beautiful or with a bigger heart. He's a fool."

"Thank you."

"Someday, he'll realize he made a big mistake. He'll show up here, you'll be long gone, and the only bitch greeting him will be me."

***

That weekend, I felt better for the first time since Elec left. Even though it didn't really change anything, Sully's words of encouragement had helped bring me out of my funk a little.

On Sunday, I'd finally gotten around to replacing my winter clothes with summer outfits. I'd always put off the wardrobe changeover until it was almost too late when half the summer was already over. I spent the entire day doing laundry, purging items to donate and neatly organizing my drawers. The weather was dry and warm, and the windows in my apartment stayed open.

I decided I deserved a glass of Moscato wine after my long day of housework. I sat on the balcony and stared out at the street below. There was a gentle summer breeze as the sun started to go down; it was such a perfect evening.

I closed my eyes and listened to the sounds of the neighborhood: traffic, people yelling, children playing in the small courtyard across from me. The smell of barbecuing meat trickled over to me from an adjacent balcony. It reminded me that I hadn't eaten anything all day, which explained why the wine had already hit me so fast.

I told myself that I loved my independence: being able to do whatever I wanted, go wherever I wanted, eat whatever and whenever I wanted, but deep down, I longed to share my life with someone.

My thoughts always seemed to travel back to him no matter how hard I tried. What I didn't expect on this quiet summer night was reciprocation.

When my text alert sounded, I didn't immediately check it. I was sure it was Sully inviting me over to watch something on television or my mother checking in.

My heart started beating out of control when I saw his name. I didn't have the courage to immediately read the text because no matter what, I knew it was going to disrupt the calm mood of this night. I didn't know why I was so scared. It wasn't like things with Elec could have gotten any worse, unless of course he was contacting me to formally announce his engagement, which would have devastated me.

I breathed in, finished off my wine in one long gulp then counted to ten before looking down at the message.

I want you to read it.

153

CHAPTER 18

One simple sentence, and any small progress I'd made this weekend in trying to forget him went down the tubes. My hand was shaking as I pondered a response.

He wanted me to read the autobiography he was working on. Why now? Of all the things he could have said, this was the last thing I expected.

The thought of finding out everything I'd always wondered about was absolutely exciting and terrifying all at once—mostly terrifying. Even though I was certain there were parts that would upset me, I already knew what my reply to him would be. How could I have said no?

I would love to read it.

Elec: I know this is out of left field, especially after how we left things.

His response had been immediate as if he were waiting for my answer.

Greta: I certainly wasn't expecting this.

Elec: I don't trust anyone else to read it. I need it to be you.

Greta: How will you send it to me?

Elec: I can email it to you tonight.

Tonight? I knew then and there that I'd definitely be calling out of work tomorrow. There was no way I would be able to stop reading once I started. What was I getting myself into?

Greta: Okay.

Elec: It's not finished, but it's pretty long.

Greta: *I'll check my email in a bit for it.*

Elec: *Thank you.*

Greta: *You're welcome.*

I poured the rest of the bottle into my glass and couldn't inhale the night air deeply enough. The smell of the neighbor's previously appetizing barbecue was now making me sick.

I climbed off the balcony and into my bedroom through the window. Opening my laptop, I anxiously typed in my email password too fast, having to try it several times before it went through correctly.

There in bold right at the top was a new email from Elec O'Rourke. The subject simply was *My Book*. There was no message in the body of the email, just a Word document attached. I immediately converted it to another format so that I could read it on my kindle.

I knew that this story was going to devastate me. There were going to be revelations that would explain Randy and Elec's behavior toward each other.

What I wasn't expecting was to be completely gutted by the very first sentence.

***

Prologue: The Apple Doesn't Fall Far

I am my brother's bastard child.
Confused yet?
Imagine how I felt when that bomb was dropped on me.
From the time I was fourteen, though, that revelation has defined me.
My miserable childhood would have made a hell of a lot more sense if I had become privy to that minor detail sooner.
The secret was never supposed to come out. The plan was to have me believe that the man who degraded me for as long as I could comprehend words was my father.

155

When he left my mother for another woman, Mami would eventually have a nervous breakdown and spill the truth one night about how I actually came to be. Once she'd divulged all of the sickening details, I couldn't figure out who was worse: the man I always believed was my father or the sperm donor I never had a chance to meet.

The fucked up story of my life actually began over 25 years ago in Ecuador. That was where a U.S. businessman who emigrated from Ireland, Patrick O'Rourke, spotted a beautiful teenage girl selling her artwork on the street.

Her name was Pilar Solis. Patrick always had a penchant for art and beautiful women, so he was instantly mesmerized. With her exotic beauty and extreme talent, she was unlike anyone he'd ever come across.

But she was young, and he was leaving soon. That didn't stop him from going after what he wanted.

Patrick was a higher-up at a U.S. coffee powerhouse. They'd tasked him with overseeing the purchase of some crops outside of Quito.

The only thing Patrick had been overseeing was Pilar.

He'd visit her street cart every morning and bought a painting each day until eventually, he'd purchased them all. Pilar's paintings were a main source of income for her large, impoverished family. All of the images depicted intricate stained-glass windows painted from memory.

Patrick became obsessed—more with the girl than her art. His trip was supposed to have only lasted three weeks, but he extended it to six.

Unbeknownst to Pilar, Patrick wasn't going home unless he could take her with him.

Even though she was under 18, he located her parents and began to court her with their approval. He'd given them money and purchased gifts for every member of the Solis family.

He spoke to her father about the possibility of taking her back to the U.S. with him where he could take her under his wing, put her through school and help her build a real art career. The family was desperate for one of their own to have that kind of opportunity. They eventually agreed to let her go to America with Patrick.

Pilar was captivated and scared of the older man all at once. She felt an obligation to go along with him despite her trepidation. He was handsome, charismatic and controlling.

After moving Pilar to the states, Patrick kept to his word. He married her when she turned 18 to facilitate her being able to stay in the U.S., enrolled her in art school in addition to English classes and used his connections to get her artwork into some Bay area galleries. The one catch went without saying: Pilar was his. He owned her.

What she didn't realize was that Patrick had a family—an estranged ex-wife who'd just moved back into town with their son.

One afternoon, Pilar was painting in the room Patrick built for that very purpose. A strapping young man wearing nothing but jeans who looked about her age appeared at the doorway. Pilar had no idea who he was, just that her body instantly reacted to him. He was a younger, more handsome version of her husband. She was shocked to find out that Patrick had a son and that he would be staying at the house for the summer.

Every afternoon while Patrick was at work, his son, Randy, would sit and watch Pilar paint. It started out as something innocent. She'd tell him stories about Ecuador, he'd introduce her to the latest music and American pop culture—things Patrick couldn't relate to at 20 years their senior.

Soon, Pilar found herself completely smitten and in love for the first time in her life. Randy, who always felt that Patrick abandoned him, held no allegiance to his father. When Pilar admitted that her feelings for her husband were platonic, Randy didn't hesitate to take full advantage.

One day, he'd crossed the line and kissed her. From that point on, there was no going back. Their afternoon encounters went from innocent conversations to sordid rendezvous. Eventually, they'd started to talk about a secret future. The plan was to carry on their affair until Randy finished college and was no longer financially dependent on Patrick. Then, they'd both run off together.

In the meantime, Randy moved permanently into Patrick's house to be closer to her and pretended to have girlfriends to throw his father off. Randy and Pilar were always extremely careful until the one time they weren't and miscalculated Patrick's return date from a business trip to Costa Rica.

That was the day Patrick walked in on his young wife fucking his son in their bed. That was also the moment that set off the chain of events that led to my existence.

An enraged Patrick locked Pilar in a closet while he beat the shit out of Randy before kicking him out of the house. Patrick then allegedly raped my mother in the same bed he'd found her in with his son. By the time Randy broke through the window, it was too late.

Exactly what happened next is not completely clear because the details given to me have always been sketchy. The only thing I know with absolute certainty is that Patrick never left that bedroom alive.

Mami says he fell and accidentally hit the back of his head in the middle of a struggle with Randy. I suspect that Randy might have killed him, but she would never admit to that if it were true. I knew she'd protect Randy until the day she died despite his betrayal of their marriage.

The police never suspected anything and bought the story about Patrick falling and hitting his head.

Because he'd lived lavishly and had been putting Randy and Pilar through school, Patrick had no money to leave them. Randy had to drop out of college and ditch his dreams to take odd jobs.

It was a really bad time for Pilar to find out she was pregnant. She knew it couldn't have been Randy's since they'd always been extremely careful with protection.

The baby was Patrick's.

Randy loved her and blamed himself for the situation they were in.

He begged her to get an abortion, but she refused.

He knew he could never grow to love the product of the night his father raped Pilar.

He was right. He couldn't, but he would raise me as his own anyway and would spend the rest of his life taking everything out on me.

That was how Randy became my father, and how I became my brother's bastard child.

***

158

That was only the prologue, and already it felt like an earthquake had barreled through my head. I couldn't believe what I just read.

My mind and body were now in the midst of a war because while my heart needed a long rest before continuing on, my brain had an urgent need to turn the page. Once I'd started reading, the pages wouldn't stop turning all night long.

I'd made it through the first half of the book by dawn. Reading about the verbal abuse Elec suffered at the hands of Randy was extremely painful. As a boy, Elec would hide in his room and get lost in books to escape reality. Randy would sometimes punish him for no reason and take the books away. One of those times, Elec started jotting a story down on paper and discovered that writing was an even more satisfying escape. He could control the destinies of his characters, whereas he had no control over the life he was forced to live in Randy's home.

As a child, he never knew the real reason behind Randy's hatred. Pilar's protection of Randy was unacceptable, and I wanted to strangle her through the pages. The only good thing she ever did was go against Randy's wishes in buying Elec a dog. Lucky became Elec's solace and best friend.

Elec also recounted the time when he found out about Randy's infidelity. He hacked into his father's computer and discovered the online affair with my mother. Elec felt guilty because he was the one who broke the news to Pilar. Randy moved out soon after.

Pilar's subsequent breakdown opened up a whole new set of challenges. She became dependent on Elec in the same way she'd always relied on Randy. That, coupled with Elec discovering the truth about Patrick, and then the death of Lucky caused a downward spiral.

He started to smoke and drink to cope with the stress, developed an addiction to tattoos as a form of self-expression and became sexually promiscuous. He'd lost his virginity at 15 to a female tattoo artist after he'd convinced her he was 18.

It was really hard for me to get through certain parts of the book, but his brutal honesty was admirable.

I read straight through until arriving at the one point where I absolutely had to stop before continuing.

159

It was the chapter about me.

***

Chapter 15: Greta

Vengeance.

That was the only thing that was going to get me through having to spend the better part of the next year living with Randy and his new family while Mami "went away."

The only consolation was going to be the satisfaction that would come from making their lives miserable.

He was going to pay for putting my mother in the looney bin and for leaving me to pick up the pieces.

I'd already decided that I hated her—the daughter. I'd never met her, but I imagined the worst based on her name alone, which ironically rhymed with vendetta.

Greta.

I thought it was an ugly name.

I was betting she had a face to match.

The second I stepped off that plane, the smog and funky smell of Boston were a big giant "fuck you." I'd heard that song before about the dirty water here, and that didn't surprise me after taking one look around.

When we first pulled up to the house, I refused to get out of Randy's car, but it was cold, and I was freezing my ball sac off, so I finally gave in and dragged my feet inside.

My stepsister stood in the living room waiting for me with a huge smile on her face. My eyes immediately landed on her neck.

Fuck. Me.

Remember that bet about the face matching the name? Well, apparently, I'd lost that bet to my dick. Greta wasn't ugly...at all.

This development was a minor hiccup in my plan, and I was determined not to let it slow me down.

I reminded myself to keep a serious face.

Her long strawberry-blond hair was tied up into a ponytail that swung back and forth as she moved toward me.

"I'm Greta. Nice to meet you," she said

She smelled good enough to eat.

I corrected the thought in my head: good enough to eat and SPIT HER OUT. Don't lose focus.

Her hand was still suspended in the air as she waited for me to take it. I didn't even want to touch her. That would further throw me off track. I eventually took her hand, squeezing it too tightly. I wasn't expecting it to be so goddamn soft and delicate like a bird's foot or some shit. It trembled a little. I was making her nervous. Good. This was a good start.

"You look different...than I pictured," she said.

What was that supposed to mean?

"And you look pretty...plain," I retorted.

You should've seen her face. She thought I was being nice for a split second. I nipped that in the bud when I added the word "plain." Then, her pretty smile dipped down into a frown. That should've made me happy, but I didn't like it at all.

In reality, she was anything but plain. Her body was exactly my type: petite with small curves. Her perfectly round little ass stretched through a pair of gray yoga pants. It was no surprise that she did yoga with a tight body like that.

And her neck...I couldn't explain what it was, but it was the first thing I noticed about her. I had to urge to kiss it, bite it, wrap my hand around it. It was fucking weird.

"Would you like me to show you to your room?" she asked.

She was still trying to be sweet. I needed to get out of there before I cracked, so I ignored her and headed for the stairs. After a brief encounter with Sarah, who I always referred to as stepmonster, I finally made it to my room.

After Randy came in to give me shit for a good half-hour, I chain-smoked and played some music to drown out the noise in my head.

Then, I went to the bathroom to take a hot shower.

I squirted some girly pomegranate body wash into my hand. There was a pink loofah sponge hanging off a suction cup on the tile wall. I bet that was what she used to clean her pretty little ass. I grabbed it and washed my body with it before putting it back. The pomegranate crap wasn't really enough to do the job, so I used some men's body wash to finish.

The bathroom filled with steam. I got out, and as I was wiping my body down, the door opened.

Greta.

Now was my chance to prove that I wasn't all bark and no bite.

I let the towel drop to the ground to shock her. The idea was that she'd run out so fast that she'd barely see anything.

Instead, she stood there with her eyes glued to my cock ring. What the fuck?

She wasn't even trying to turn away as her gaze traveled slowly upward to my chest. Finally, after what seemed like an eternity, it was like she woke up and realized what she was doing. She turned away and apologized.

But by that time, I was starting to have fun with it, so I stopped her from leaving.

"You act like you've never seen a guy naked before."

"Actually, I haven't."

She was kidding, right?

"How disappointing for you. It's gonna be really hard for the next guy to measure up."

"Cocky much?"

"You tell me. Don't I deserve to be?"

"God...you're acting like—"

"A giant dick?"

Heh heh. That shut her up.

Then, came more staring.

Now, this was just getting uncomfortable.

"There's really nowhere to go from here, so unless you're planning on doing something, you should probably leave and let me finish getting dressed."

She finally left.

I hoped to God she was kidding. If she'd never seen a guy naked before then what I'd just done was really fucked up.

***

A couple of days later, I'd overheard her telling her friend that she thought I was hot—"so fucking hot"—to be exact. Honestly, even though I knew I had some kind of effect on her, I wasn't exactly sure if it was physical attraction. So, hearing that was a little bit of a game changer. The good: I knew I could use it to my benefit. The bad: I was unbelievably attracted to her, too and needed to make sure she didn't know it.

Living at the house seemed to get a little easier each day. Although I would never have admitted it, I wasn't exactly miserable anymore—far from it.

I took joy in doing little things to mess with her, like stealing all of her underwear and her vibrator. Okay, maybe that wasn't such a little thing. Overall, though, I started to realize that the motivation behind my actions wasn't what I originally intended.

Getting back at Randy was barely an afterthought anymore. Now, I was messing with Greta simply to get her attention.

In a matter of days, I'd all but forgotten about my "evil plan."

One afternoon, though, shit got real when I intentionally brought a girl from school to Kilt Café where Greta worked. I'll admit; I had no problem getting girls and had been with a few of the hottest ones at school within the first month. But they all bored me. Everything bored me—except getting a rise out of my stepsister.

Greta never bored me.

The first thing I'd think about when I'd wake up in the morning was how I was going to ruffle her feathers next.

That day at the café was no exception, but it was a turning point—one I couldn't turn back from.

Greta was waiting on our table, and I'd been intentionally giving her a difficult time. She ended up trying to get back at me by pouring a shitload of hot sauce into my soup. When I figured it out, I gulped the entire thing down to spite her. Even though it burned like hell, I didn't let it show. I was so impressed with her that I could have kissed her.

So, I did.

Under the guise of retaliation, I used the soup as an excuse to corner her in a dark corridor and do what I'd wanted to for weeks. I'll never forget the noise she made when I first grabbed her and claimed her wet little mouth with mine. It was like she was starving for it. I could have kissed her all damn day, but this was supposed to appear like it was about the hot sauce and not the kiss. So, I reluctantly ripped myself away and went back to the table.

I was hard as hell, and that wasn't good. I told my date to meet me outside so she wouldn't notice.

I had to make it seem like what just happened didn't affect me and needed to quickly reinforce the idea that it was a joke. I'd been carrying around a pair of Greta's underwear with me for days just waiting for the perfect opportunity to taunt her with them. So, I left her the thong as part of her tip with a note that suggested she change into them because she was probably a little wet.

I wished I could have seen her reaction.

***

We were starting to spend more time together. She'd come to my room and play videogames, and I'd sneak glances at her neck when she wasn't watching me.

I'd replay the kiss in my head constantly, sometimes even when I was with other girls.

Greta and I would be eating ice cream together, and the urge to lick it off the corner of her mouth was enormous.

I could feel myself falling for her in more ways than one, and I didn't like it.

Not only was I attracted to her, but she was the first girl whose company I actually enjoyed.

I needed to keep myself in check, though, since taking it any further with her was not an option. So, I kept bringing girls home and pretended not to have feelings for Greta.

It was working out alright until I found out she was going on a date with a guy from school: Bentley. He was bad news. Her friend ended up asking me to join them on a double date, and I took the opportunity so that I could keep an eye on things.

The date had been torture. Having to hide my jealousy, I was forced to sit back and watch while this asshole put his hands on her. At the same time, Greta's friend, Victoria, was all over me, and there was zero interest on my part. I just wanted to get Greta home safely, but the night turned into way more than I bargained for. Before it was over, I'd nearly put Bentley in the hospital after he'd confessed that he'd made a bet with Greta's ex that he could devirginize her. I went ballistic. Never in my life had I felt the need to protect someone like I wanted to protect her.

164

The next day, Greta would return the favor in a big way.

Randy had barged into my room and went on one of his abusive rants. She'd overheard and stuck up for me in a way that no one ever had. Even though I pretended to be too drunk to remember it, I clung to every word until she kicked him out of the room.

Thinking back, I'm pretty sure that was the moment I fell in love with her.

***

That same weekend, our parents went away. It was bad timing because my feelings for her were at an all-time high. I'd made up a story about going out on a date just so I didn't have to be alone with her.

That night, she'd woken me up in the middle of a dream. I'd been having one of my nightmares about the night Mami almost killed herself.

I tried to lighten the mood because I must have looked like a crazy person. I said something to her like, "How do I know you're not trying to take advantage of me in the middle of the night?"

It was a joke.

She started to cry.

Shit.

I'd hit a new low.

All of the antics I'd been pulling to mask my true feelings had taken a toll on her. I had to stop, but without the insults and jokes to hide behind, those feelings would become obvious.

When she fled to her room, I knew sleep wasn't going to be possible until I'd at least made her smile again. I had an idea and grabbed her dildo I'd been hiding and took it to her room. I started to tickle her with it.

Eventually, she gave into the laughter. We spent the rest of the night lying in her bed talking. That was the first time I'd really opened up and made the mistake of admitting my attraction to her.

She tried to kiss me, and I relented. It felt so good to taste her mouth again and to not have to pretend that it wasn't real. I grabbed her face and took control of it. I told myself that nothing bad would happen as long as I could draw the line at kissing. I'd almost had myself convinced when she floored me with words that would ruin me.

"I want you to show me how you fuck, Elec."

I freaked out and pushed her off of me. It was the hardest thing I ever had to do, but it was necessary. I explained to her that we could never let things go that far.

I tried really hard after that to distance myself. Still, those words rang out in my head at night, in the shower, pretty much all day. I lost interest in other girls and preferred jerking off to explicit thoughts of fulfilling Greta's request in ways she could have never imagined.

***

Weeks went by, and I became desperate to connect with her in some way again. I decided I'd let her read my book. After she finished it, she'd written me a note that she sealed in an envelope. Afraid to see what it said, I put off opening it.

Then, came the night when everything changed.

Greta had gone out on a date. I knew the particular guy was harmless, so I wasn't worried about her this time. I was worried about me. Even though I couldn't have Greta, I didn't want anyone else to have her, either.

I watched him from the window as he walked to the door with flowers. What a twat waffle. I had to do something. When he came upstairs to use the bathroom, I accosted him in the hallway. I gave him a pair of her underwear and told him Greta had left them in my room. It was a dick move, but I was desperate.

It pissed me off even more when she left with him. When she texted me from the car, I asked her to come home. She thought I was kidding. I wasn't. I'd just lost my willpower for a second.

Soon after, the phone rang, and I was sure it was Greta.

Dread set in after I realized it was my mother.

She called me to say she was back in California, that she'd been released from rehab. I panicked because she shouldn't have been alone in her state of mind. I didn't know what to do because I knew I had to go back right away now.

I didn't want to leave Greta.

But I had to go.

I texted her to come home from her date, that something had happened. Thankfully, that time she listened.

I knew I had to tell her the truth about why I was leaving. When she came to my room, she looked so beautiful in a blue dress that hugged her tiny waist. I wanted to take her in my arms and never let her go.

I told her as much as I could about Mami that night because she needed to know that it wasn't my choice to leave.

Everything was happening so fast. I told her to go back to her room because I couldn't trust myself. After much coaxing, she finally listened. It really was my intention to do the right thing and stay away from her that night.

I was alone and missing her already even though she was just in the next room. I decided to open her letter, expecting to find some grammatical corrections and small critiques about my book.

She said things in that letter that no one had ever said to me in my entire life, things I needed to hear: that I was talented, that I inspired her to follow her own dreams, that she respected me, that she cared about me, that she couldn't wait to read more, that she fell in love with my writing, that she was so proud of me, that she believed in me.

Greta made me feel things I never had before. She made me feel loved.

I loved this girl, and I couldn't do anything about it.

Without thinking it through, I knocked on her door and decided to give her what she'd asked me for.

I could go into details about all of the things that Greta and I did that night, but to be honest, it's not something I feel comfortable writing about because of how much it meant to me. She trusted me enough to give me something that no one else will ever get. That night was sacred to me, and I hope she realizes that.

The one thing I will say is that I will never forget a certain look on her face. Her eyes had been closed, and it was the way she opened them and looked at me the very first moment I was fully inside of her.

To this day, I still haven't forgiven myself for leaving her the next morning. I'd never felt so attached to anyone. She had fully given herself to me. She was mine, and I threw her away. I let guilt and some deep-rooted need to protect my mother in order to justify my existence win over my own happiness.

I don't think Greta ever realized that I loved her long before that night.

As I write this, what she definitely doesn't know is that a few years later, I came back for her, but it was too late.

CHAPTER 19

He'd come back for me?

My hand covered my chest as if it were going to keep my heart from leaping out of it.

It was now mid-morning, and the hustle and bustle of the daily grind could be heard from my window. The sun was pouring into the apartment. I'd already called out of work earlier because I needed to finish this book today.

Tonight was a 30th birthday celebration for a co-worker at a downtown nightclub, and I wasn't sure if I'd even be able to put it down long enough to go.

I walked to the kitchen to have some water and forced down a granola bar. The energy would be much needed to get through this next part.

He'd come back for me?

I curled back into the couch, took a deep breath and turned the page.

***

You have to treat addiction to a person the same way you would a drug problem. If I couldn't be all in with Greta, then I couldn't have any contact with her at all because that would have caused me to spiral out of control.

Even calling or texting wasn't going to be possible. It seemed harsh, but I wouldn't have been able to handle even the sound of her voice if we couldn't be together.

That didn't mean that I wasn't pining for her every single day. That first year was hell.

Mami was no better than before I'd gone to Boston. She kept interrogating me for information about Randy and Sarah, stalking Sarah's facebook page and accusing me of being a traitor after I admitted that my stepmother wasn't all that bad once you got to know her. I couldn't even mention Greta's name because I didn't want my mother to look her up or suspect anything. Mami was back on sleeping pills, and I had to watch her like a hawk.

I was right in my assumption that she could have never handled even the thought of my being with Greta at that time. It was a sad irony: Mami was obsessed with Sarah, and unbeknownst to her, I'd become obsessed with Sarah's daughter. We were quite the fucked up pair.

Not a day went by without my having a thought about Greta with another guy. It made me crazy. I was so far away and powerless. Ironically, there was a side of me that wished at the very least, I were able to protect her as my sister even if we weren't together. Sick, right? But what if someone hurt her? I wouldn't even know about it and couldn't beat him down. And forget about the thought of her fucking another guy. I'd actually punched a hole once in my bedroom wall just thinking about that.

Then, one night, I lost control and texted her that I missed her. I asked her not to respond. She didn't, and it made me feel worse. I'd vowed never to repeat that mistake.

My life had gone back to exactly what it was before I moved to Boston: smoking, drinking and fucking girls I didn't care about. It was empty. The only difference from before was that now, somewhere deep beneath the filth was this longing for more…for her. She'd given me a taste of the type of human connection my life had been missing all along.

I expected the gnawing feeling in my chest to go away over time, but it never did; it only intensified. I think that was because deep down, I also sensed that wherever she was, Greta was thinking of me, feeling the same way. I somehow felt it, and it ate away at me for years.

***

Two years later, Mami's mental state had finally improved after she met a guy. He was her first boyfriend since Randy left her. George was Lebanese and owned the convenience store down the street from us. He was over the house all of the time and would always bring pita bread, hummus and olives. For the first time ever, her obsession with Randy seemed to have waned.

George was a great guy, but the happier she was with him, the more bitter I became. I'd given up the one girl I ever cared about because I thought it would devastate my mother beyond repair. Now, she was happy, and I was still miserable. And Greta was gone.

I'd felt like I made the biggest mistake of my life.

I needed to talk to someone about it because my anger was eating away at me day by day. I had never mentioned what happened with Greta to a single soul. The only person I could trust was Randy's friend, Greg, who'd become like a second father to me.

He gave me some inside information that day during our phone call: Greta had apparently recently moved to New York. He even had her address from their Christmas card list. Greg tried to convince me to fly out there and tell her how I felt. I didn't think she would want to see me even if she still cared about me. I hurt her so badly that I didn't understand how she could ever forgive me. Greg felt that going to see her in person would make a bigger impression. Despite my fears, I booked a ticket the next day, which happened to be New Years Eve.

I told Mami I was going to visit a friend I'd met years ago to celebrate the holiday in the city. I wouldn't tell her about Greta unless this worked out.

The six-hour plane ride was the most nerve-wracking experience of my life. I just wanted to get there. I just wanted to hold her again. I didn't know what I'd say or what I was going to do when I laid eyes on her. I didn't know if she was even with someone. I was going in blind.

This was the first time in my life that I ever put myself first and followed my heart.

I hoped it wasn't too late because I really wanted the opportunity to tell her all of the things I should have told her three years ago. She never even knew I loved her the night she'd given me her virginity.

If the plane ride took an eternity, the subway ride to her apartment complex seemed even more frustratingly long. As the train swayed, every single memory of her flashed through my head like a movie. I couldn't help but smile as I thought about some of the shit I pulled on her and what a good sport she was. She made me happy. Mostly, my mind drifted to that final night when she'd given me full ownership of her body. The train stopped; there was a slight delay. Getting to her soon felt urgent now.

I needed to get to her.

When I finally made it to her building, I double-checked the address I'd jotted down on a small piece of paper. Her last name, Hansen, was written in pen next to apartment 7b on the listing inside the main entrance.

There was no answer. I nixed the idea of calling or texting her because I worried she'd say she didn't want to meet with me before I had a chance to see her. I came all the way here. I needed to at least see her face.

The restaurant downstairs served as the perfect waiting spot before trying her door again in another hour.

I knocked on that door every hour on the hour from four in the afternoon until nine at night. Each time, there was no answer, and I'd just go back to Charlie's Pub and wait.

The time was 9:15. I'd never forget the moment I got my wish.

I got to see her.

But it wasn't the way I wanted it to happen.

Greta.

She was wearing a thick off-white parka as she came strolling into Charlie's. She wasn't alone. A guy—who looked a hell of a lot more put together than me—had his arm wrapped around her.

The greasy food in my stomach started to come up on me.

She was laughing as they took a seat in the middle of the restaurant. She looked happy. She didn't notice me because her back was facing me as I sat in a corner booth.

Her hair was tied up in a twist. I watched as she unwound the lavender scarf she'd been wearing, revealing the back of her beautiful neck—the neck I was supposed to be kissing tonight after I told her how much I loved her.

The guy leaned in and kissed her gently on the face.

A voice inside of me screamed, "Don't touch her!"

His lips mouthed the words, "I love you."

What was I supposed to do? Go over there and say, "Oh hello, I'm Greta's stepbrother. I fucked the shit out of her once and left the very next day. She seems happy with you, and you probably actually deserve her, but I was hoping you could step aside and let me take over from here."

172

A half-hour went by. I watched the waiter bring them their food. I watched them eat. I watched the guy reach over a dozen more times to kiss her. I'd close my eyes and listen to the sound of her sweet laughter. I didn't know why I stayed. I just couldn't get myself to leave her. I knew it was likely the last time I'd ever see her.

10:15: Greta got up from her seat and let him place her coat over her shoulders. She never once looked in my direction. I hadn't considered what I would have done if she noticed me. I was too numb to move or even think clearly.

I watched her every second until the door closed behind them.

That night, I wandered the city and eventually ended up with the masses in Times Square watching the ball drop. Amidst the confetti, noisemakers and cheering, I wondered how I'd even gotten there because I was still in a daze since leaving the restaurant.

A random middle-aged woman grabbed me and hugged me when the clock struck midnight. She couldn't have known it, but I'd never needed a hug in my life more than that moment.

I boarded a plane back to California the next morning.

A few months later, Randy had called the house for the first time in almost a year. I casually asked about Greta, and he told me she'd gotten engaged. That was the last time I ever mentioned her name.

It took me almost three years before I could really move on with someone else.

***

I had to stop. I threw my kindle across the room. My eyes were so filled with tears that the words were becoming blurry toward the end.

I closed my eyes tightly to see if I could recall anything that could have clued me into the fact that Elec was there. *He was there.* How could I not have known he was right behind me?

He'd come for me.

It still hadn't fully sunk in.

I remembered that night.

I remembered Tim and I were still in the honeymoon stage of our relationship. Things were going well.

173

I remembered even though it was New Years Eve, we'd been out all day shopping for a new computer for me.

I remembered we stopped at my apartment to drop it off and then headed into Charlie's for a late dinner before going to Times Square to watch the ball drop.

I remembered when the clock struck 12, Tim warmed me from the cold with his kisses.

I remembered wondering why in the midst of this magical night with a man who was seemingly perfect and who truly cared about me, all I wanted was Elec. All I had been able to think about was Elec: where he was at that very moment, whether he was watching the festivities on TV, whether he was thinking of me, too.

All the while, Elec was right there.

Fate had screwed us over.

***

In the next couple of chapters, he wrote about finding a career path that was meaningful, and how he came to settle on social work. He felt a responsibility to help others, particularly children who'd come from broken homes like he had.

I rushed through the following chapters detailing how he'd met Chelsea. It was the only part of the book I'd felt the need to speed through. The gist was that he met her at the youth center, they'd hung out a lot after work as friends. He was apprehensive about getting involved with her because he knew she was the type of girl who wanted a serious relationship. He wasn't sure he was ready for that. Over time, she'd made him forget about me, made him laugh, and he grew to love and care about her. She was his first serious relationship, and he planned to propose to her...until—

***

It felt like my world came crashing down on that day.

Things were going better than they'd ever had in my entire life. My job was stable and fulfilling. Chelsea and I had moved in together, and I was planning to ask her to marry me at her sister's wedding coming up in just a few days. A one-carat white gold solitaire had been stashed away for weeks.

Mami was doing a lot better. She'd been on a roll with new art projects. While she'd broken up with George a year ago and had a major relapse, she was now dating a new guy named Steve who'd once again taken some of her focus off of Randy. So, life was as good as it was gonna get—until a phone call from Clara changed everything.

"I'm so sorry to have to tell you this, Elec. Randy had a heart attack and died." Those were the first words that came out of her mouth. Initially, my reaction was the same as if she were calling to tell me what day of the week it was.

Randy was dead.

It didn't matter how many times I'd repeated it in my head that day; it wouldn't sink in.

Chelsea had somehow convinced me to go back for the service despite my better judgment. Randy wouldn't have wanted me there. I was still in shock and too desensitized to fight her pushing guilt on me. She didn't know what kind of relationship Randy and I had. From her perspective, there was no excuse for my not attending. It was easier for me to just give in than have to tell her everything. I also knew that Mami couldn't handle going. She wanted me to go in her place to represent the two of us. So, before I knew it, I was on a plane with Chelsea heading to Boston.

The stagnant air on the plane was suffocating. Chelsea kept holding my hand as I blasted the volume of my music. I'd almost managed to calm down when a flash of Greta's face induced further panic. Not only was I going to have to deal with Randy's death, but she would probably be there too with her husband.

Fuck.

I knew this was going to be the worst couple of days of my life.

When we got to Greg and Clara's house, I was really on edge. Chelsea and I took a shower together in the guest bathroom, but it hadn't done anything to pacify my nervous state. Before we'd left California, I'd picked up a case of the imported clove cigarettes I used to smoke. I took one out and lit it as I sat on the bed while Chelsea was still in the bathroom getting dressed. I was disappointed in myself for relapsing into smoking again, but it felt like the only thing holding me together at that point.

I had no motivation to get dressed and go downstairs. I lit another cigarette, inhaled deeply and walked over to the French doors that led to a balcony overlooking the backyard. The sky was overcast.

Looking down was a colossal mistake.

My fists tightened in a fighting response to the fact that my heart was beating so rapidly.

I wasn't supposed to ever see her again like this. A part of me that died was coming back to life when it shouldn't have. I didn't know how to handle it.

Greta's back was turned. She was staring out into the garden and must have just found out I was here. She was probably trying to plan her escape so she didn't have to face me, or maybe she was just as angry at this predicament as I was. The fact that she was standing all alone out there told me that my being here was affecting her.

"Greta," I whispered to myself.

It was like she heard me because she turned around. Suddenly, a tidal wave of emotions that I'd tried to bury since that night in New York came flooding out. I wasn't prepared to see her face looking up at me.

I took another long drag.

I also wasn't prepared for how angry this moment would make me. With one look into her eyes, I was starting to feel everything: the realization of Randy's death, the painful reminder of my unresolved feelings for her, the jealousy and crushing disappointment of that night in New York, the twitch of my traitorous cock.

The level of rage building inside of me was an unpleasant surprise.

I was so confused.

I never wanted to see you again, Greta.

It's so fucking good to see you again, Greta.

I felt like she could see right through me in that moment, and I didn't like it. We just stayed looking at each other for probably an entire minute. Her previously dumbfounded expression darkened as soon as I felt Chelsea's hands wrap around me.

I instinctively turned around and moved back, pushing Chelsea away from the window. I think I was trying to protect Greta's feelings in that moment but didn't know why I bothered.

What the fuck did she expect me to do, sit around and pine for her alone while she married Mr. Wonderful? Still, I knew seeing Chelsea appear out of nowhere like that must have been a shock.

"Are you okay?" Chelsea asked. She hadn't seen Greta.

"Yeah," I said dismissively.

Needing to be alone, I walked to the bathroom and shut the door to gear up before I had to face the music.

***

She was sitting at the far corner of the dining room table when we got downstairs. She wouldn't look at me.

I hate when you do that, Greta.

Sarah got up and hugged me. I gave her some brief greeting, told her I was sorry about Randy, but the entire time I was thinking about what the fuck I was going to say to Greta. I glanced over at her, and now, she was looking at me. I stood back as Chelsea hugged Sarah and gave her condolences.

I needed to bite the bullet.

I walked over to her and barely got her name out. "Greta."

She hopped up nervously like my saying her name had lit a fire under her ass. She stuttered a little. "I...I'm so sorry...about Randy."

Her lips trembled. She was discombobulated—a mess, I told myself. I didn't want to admit that she was even more beautiful than I remembered, that new highlights in her hair brought out the gold in the hazel tone of her eyes, that I'd missed the three small freckles on her nose, that the way her black dress hugged her breasts reminded me of things I needed to forget now.

I couldn't move, just stood there taking her in. The familiar scent of her hair was intoxicating.

My body flinched when she reached out to hug me. I had really tried not to feel anything, but here in her arms was the epicenter of it all. Her heart was beating against my chest, and mine immediately responded by matching the rhythm. Our hearts were communicating in a way that our egos wouldn't allow with words. The heartbeat is the purest form of honesty.

I put my hand on her back and could feel the strap of her bra. Before I could even process what that did to me, Chelsea's voice

177

snapped me out of it as Greta ripped herself away from me. The space between us felt infinitely vast.

I couldn't believe this was really happening: my past colliding with my present. The one that got away was face to face with the one who got me over it.

Greta's left hand was bare; there was no diamond. Where was her fiancé or husband? Where the fuck was he?

Engrossed in my thoughts, I didn't even hear what they were saying to each other.

Clara saved the day when she walked in with food, and Greta went to help her.

Greta reentered the dining room and started placing the silverware down around us. She was so tense, and pieces kept slipping and clinking around as she fumbled with them. I wanted to joke and ask her when she started practicing playing percussion with spoons. I didn't.

When she finally sat down, Greg asked, "So, how did you kids meet?"

Greta looked up from her plate for the first time as Chelsea explained how we met at the youth center. When Chelsea leaned in to kiss me, I felt Greta watching it, and the mood became very uncomfortable.

The subject changed to my mother, and Greta was back to pretending she was engrossed in her plate.

My body stiffened again when Chelsea asked her a question. "Where do you live, Greta?"

"I live in New York City, actually. I just came into town a couple of days ago."

"I" came into town, not "we."

I wished I had a camera to capture the look on Greta's face when Chelsea suggested we visit her in New York.

The mood got quiet again, and I'd snuck some glances in when she wasn't looking. When she caught me, I shifted my attention back to my plate.

"Elec never told me he had a stepsister," Chelsea said.

I wasn't sure whom the statement was directed toward, but I wasn't touching that subject with a ten-foot pole. Greta still refused to look at me.

Sarah spoke up. *"Elec only lived with us for a short time back when they were teenagers."* She looked at Greta. *"The two of you didn't get along too well back then."*

For some reason, the uncomfortable look on Greta's face got under my skin. She was still looking down and not acknowledging her mother's statement, not acknowledging me. An unexplainable need for her to acknowledge to me, to acknowledge what we had, overtook my better judgment. I reverted back to my old ways for a moment and started to taunt her to get her attention.

"Is that true, Greta?"

She looked frazzled. *"Is what true?"*

I lifted my brow. *"That we didn't get along."*

Her jaw tightened, and her eyes never left mine as they silently warned me not to push it.

Finally, she said, *"We had our moments."*

My voice lowered to a gentler tone. *"Yeah, we did."*

Her face was turning red. I'd pushed it. I tried to do damage control by lightening the mood. *"What was it you used to call me?"*

"What do you mean?"

" 'Stepbrother dearest,' was it? Because of my glowing personality?" I turned to Chelsea. *"I was a miserable fuck back then."*

I was for a while...until Greta made me want to be a better person.

"How did you know about that nickname?" Greta asked.

I laughed to myself, remembering how I used to snoop in on her phone calls to her friend.

It was good to finally see her crack a smile as she said, *"Oh, right. You used to eavesdrop on me."*

Chelsea was looking back and forth at us. *"Sounds like those were some fun times."*

I wouldn't take my eyes off Greta. I wanted her to know that those days were some of the best of my life.

"They were," I said.

***

The only good thing about focusing on my unresolved feelings for Greta was that it took my mind off of Randy.

179

When I escaped to be alone in the backyard after dinner, though, the fact that he was gone started to hit me.

He and I would never have a chance to make amends now. It was interesting how making amends never seemed to matter when he was alive, but in his death, it was haunting me. At the very least, I'd wanted to prove him wrong, make something of myself. Now, he was somewhere in another dimension possibly coming face to face with Patrick.

Thinking about it without distraction for too long fucked with my mind. I grabbed a cigarette and tried to just meditate. It didn't work because my emotions had only gone from sad to angry.

I heard the glass door sliding open and footsteps behind me. Don't ask me how I knew it was her.

"What are you doing out here, Greta?"

"Chelsea asked me to come talk to you."

What the fuck were they talking for? It just rubbed me the wrong way. Chelsea could not find out about what happened between Greta and me. I let out a sarcastic laugh. "Oh, really."

"Yes."

"Were you two comparing notes?"

"That's not funny."

It wasn't, but my classic protective mechanism of acting like a bastard in times of stress had come out in full force. It was too late. And dammit, I wanted her to acknowledge us.

I put my cigarette out. "You think she would have sent you out here to talk to me if she knew the last time before today that you and I were together, we were fucking like rabbits?"

The color drained from her face. "Did you have to put it like that?"

"It's the truth, isn't it? She would freak the fuck out if she knew."

"Well, I'm not going to be the one to tell her, so you don't have to worry. I would never do that."

Greta's eye started to twitch, which proved I was having an effect on her. Old habits die hard. I was addicted now.

"Why are you winking at me?"

"I'm not...my eye is twitching because—"

"Because you're nervous. I know. You used to do that when I first met you. Glad to see we've come full circle."

"I guess some things never really change, do they? It's been seven years, but it seem just like—"

"Like yesterday," I interrupted. "It seems like just yesterday, and that's fucked up. This whole situation is."

"It was never supposed to happen."

My eyes somehow landed on her neck, and I couldn't pry them away. I knew she noticed it. I felt possessive all of a sudden, something I knew I had no right to feel. I still needed to know what the fuck was going on.

"Where is he?"

"Who?"

"Your fiancé."

"I'm not engaged. I was…but not anymore. How did you know I was engaged?"

I had to look down. I couldn't let her see the effect hearing this news had on me. "What happened?"

"It's kind of a long story, but I was the one who ended it. He moved to Europe for a job. It just wasn't meant to be."

"Are you with anyone now?"

"No."

Fuck.

She continued, "Chelsea is really nice."

"She's wonderful; one of the best things that's ever happened to me, actually."

She was. I loved Chelsea; I did. I could never hurt her. I needed to convince both Greta and myself that Chelsea was it for me. It was still fucked up that hearing Greta say there was no other man had now riled me up.

Greta quickly changed the subject to Randy and my mother.

It was starting to rain, so I used that as an excuse to tell her to go inside.

She wouldn't leave.

Then, her eyes started to water.

All of a sudden, my heart felt like it was breaking. I needed to fight these emotions, and there was only one way I ever knew how to do that with Greta: by being an asshole.

I snapped at her. "What are you doing?"

"Chelsea's not the only one who's worried about you."

181

"She's the only one that has a right to be. You don't need to be worrying about me. I'm none of your concern."

My heart was pounding faster in protest of what had just come out of my mouth because deep down, I wanted her to care.

She was hurt. I'd hurt her again, yet I needed to fight these feelings.

"You know what? If I didn't feel so sorry for what you're going through right now, I'd tell you to kiss my ass," she said.

Her words had gone straight to my dick. I had the urge to grab her and kiss her senseless. I had to nip this in the bud.

"And if I wanted to be a dick, I'd say you were asking me to kiss your ass because you remembered how much you fucking loved it when I did."

What the fuck had I just said? I needed to leave before I did something even more stupid, although that one would be hard to top. As I walked past her, I said, "Take care of your mother tonight."

I left her standing in the garden. When I opened the door, I pulled Chelsea into the hardest kiss I'd ever given her in a desperate attempt to obliterate Greta from my mind.

***

The wake had been tougher than I even expected in more ways than one. I refused to look over at the coffin. I didn't know anyone. I didn't belong there.

Voices blended together. I heard nothing. I saw nothing. I was counting the minutes until I could be back on that plane.

Chelsea was keeping me standing.

The only time I ever felt pain was when I'd look over at Greta. The single instance I left to escape everything, I'd ended up running into her downstairs in the basement of the funeral home. She tried to pretend she didn't see me after she exited the bathroom, but I knew it was my one chance to apologize for my earlier behavior.

I hadn't expected her to use that moment to tell me she still had feelings for me.

It had broken all my resolve. Everything about this day had weakened me. Her hair was up, and at one point, I wrapped my hand around her neck. The trauma of this whole experience had totally clouded my better judgment. It felt unreal, almost like I was dreaming. But there was nothing I needed more in that moment.

Chelsea's footsteps interrupted my trance. She'd come down to check on me, but she didn't see anything. I felt ashamed when I looked into my girlfriend's loving eyes. She'd been worried about me and meanwhile, I was in the middle of some kind of wet dream.

I hated myself.

Soon after we went back upstairs, I insisted we leave early and hitch a ride back to Greg and Clara's house. Desperate to wash every shred of Greta off my hands and out of my mind, I practically attacked Chelsea when we got to the bedroom.

I told her I needed sex right then and there. She didn't question it, just started to undress herself. That was the kind of girlfriend she was. She loved me unconditionally even in my manic state.

The problem was...what my body really craved in that moment wasn't in the room.

As I moved in and out of Chelsea, I closed my eyes and saw nothing but Greta: Greta's face, Greta's neck, Greta's ass.

This was the lowest thing I'd ever done. Guilt consumed me, and I stopped abruptly. Without explanation, I ran to the bathroom and turned on the shower. The need for release was enormous. I started to jerk off to a visual of Greta on her knees looking up at me as I dressed her neck with my cum. It took me all of a minute.

I was sick.

After I'd come down from my orgasm, I felt even worse than I had before.

That night, my thoughts seemed to be taking turns obsessing over Greta and Randy. I didn't sleep a wink. Randy won most of the night as flashbacks of him tormented me.

Chelsea would be leaving early to fly out to California in the morning for her sister's wedding. I couldn't fathom how I was going to possibly handle the burial tomorrow without Chelsea there to lean on...or to keep me away from Greta.

***

Scramble the letters of the word funeral; you get "real fun." Of course, it was anything but that.

183

Just don't look up. That was what I told myself. Don't look up at the coffin on the altar. Don't look up at Greta's back. Just keep looking at the watch, and every minute will be one step closer to this being over.

That rule of thumb worked for me until we got to the burial grounds at which point I had the freak out of my life and ended up in Greta's Honda on the road to nowhere.

I needed a smoke, but the craving wasn't bad enough to warrant stopping the car long enough to buy cigarettes.

Everything was a blur: the funeral, my panic attack and now, even the trees that lined the interstate while Greta drove so fast that they blended together into one blurry green line.

Everything was just a fucking blur.

I kept looking out the window for what seemed like hours until she spoke up for the first time.

"Just about another twenty minutes, and then we're gonna stop somewhere, okay?"

I looked over at her. She was softly humming.

Sweet Greta.

Fuck.

My chest constricted. I'd been such an asshole to her up until today, and now, I'd basically hijacked her. She'd saved me from myself this afternoon, and I'd done nothing to deserve her taking the time out to drive me around like this. I didn't have the energy to tell her how much it meant to me, so I just said, "Thank you."

One of her long blonde hairs had strayed, landing on my black pants. I twirled it around in my hands and eventually relaxed enough to fall asleep. It was the first time I'd slept in days.

I woke up delirious. When I realized where she'd taken me, I fell into a fit of laughter.

A casino.

It was brilliant.

When we entered the building, Greta started coughing incessantly and complained about the smoke. It was odd, but my own desire for a cigarette had gone away. The adrenaline of being in that environment had shifted my focus off my problems. I was pumped.

"Try to have fun, sis." I jokingly shook her shoulders and immediately regretted putting my hands on her at all because apparently, my body couldn't be trusted to not react like an animal.

"Please don't call me that."

"What would you prefer I call you here? No one knows us. We can make up names. We're both dressed in all black. We look like mafia high rollers."

"Anything but sis."

"What do you like to play?"

"I want to hit one of the tables. What about you?"

"I just do the penny slots."

The penny slots. God, she was cute.

"The penny slots? You're going wild today, huh?"

"Don't laugh."

"You don't go to a casino like this to play the slots, especially the penny ones."

"I don't know how to play any of the tables."

"I can show you, but first we need drinks." I winked at her. *"Always liquor before you poker."*

Her face turned pink. I'd almost forgotten how addicting making her blush was.

She rolled her eyes. *"God, some things never change. At least you're back to making dirty jokes. That means I did something right today."*

"Seriously, this idea..." I looked at the chaos all around us then back at her. *"Coming here...it was perfect."*

What I wished I could tell her was that unexpectedly getting to spend time with her again was the best part.

We bought some chips, and I'd gone to get us some drinks. I had been feeling really good until I made my way back to where Greta was waiting. A fat guy in a cowboy hat smacked her on the ass as she stood next to him at the craps table.

Without further thought, my body went into fight mode.

"Tell me I did not just see that fucking slob smack you on the ass." I gave her the drinks. *"Hold these."*

I put him in a chokehold. Both hands were needed to fit around his fat neck. *"Who the fuck do you think you are putting your hands on her like that?"*

He held up his hands. *"I didn't know she was with someone. She was helping me out."*

185

"It looked like you were helping yourself." I'd accidentally spit on him when the words came out of my mouth then dragged him by the neck over to Greta. "Apologize to her right now."

"Look man—"

"Apologize." I yelled as I squeezed his neck even harder.

"I'm sorry."

My ears were throbbing. I still wanted to kill him.

Greta was pleading. "Come on, Elec. Please let's just go."

Her scared face made me realize that beating this guy down wasn't worth putting her through this. I took my drink from her and started to walk away.

Then, I heard him from behind me, "You're lucky you came when you did. I was just about to ask her to blow on my dice."

I flipped the fuck out, charging toward him and nearly hurt Greta who tried to use her little body to block my aim. She only ended up getting drenched by the drinks that spilled all over her.

"Elec, no! We can't get kicked out of here. Please. I'm begging you."

I realized in that moment if I even touched him, I was going to either kill him or seriously hurt him. I needed to walk away.

"You can thank her that you still have a face." I was still stewing as we walked out of the room. The only other time I'd put my hands on someone like that had also been in Greta's defense. Was I protecting her now as a brother or an ex-lover? That was the question.

Her hair was wildly disheveled, and her dress was soaked. "Shit, Greta. You're a mess."

In reality, she'd never looked more beautiful.

She laughed. "A hot mess."

"Let's go. I'm buying you a new outfit."

"It's fine. I'm just a little wet."

A little wet. Fuck. Get your mind out of the gutter, Elec.

"No, it's not fine. That was my fault."

"It'll dry. Tell you what, if you win something tonight, you can spend it all on a new outfit for me at one of these expensive shops. That's the only way I'm letting you spend any money on me."

I felt like a douche, and I knew I wasn't leaving tonight until I bought her the nicest dress in this joint to make up for what I did.

After I'd gone to get drinks, I told her it was better if we separated while I played poker. There were a ton of guys who looked like they were on the prowl in the poker room, and I didn't want to have to fuck anyone up tonight. Greta didn't realize how attractive she was.

It amazed me that she even listened and agreed to go play the slots for a while.

When I sat down at the table, my phone vibrated.

Why does it matter to you anymore if other guys hit on me? You're not supposed to care.

Shit. It shouldn't have been a surprise that she called me out on my behavior.

She was right.

I was being selfish. I wasn't really afraid of some guy hitting on her. What scared me was the possibility that I'd have to watch while she returned the interest or entertained it. She was single, and I wasn't. What was to stop her? I was just as jealous as ever, and I had no right to be. It was unreasonable and wrong. So, I didn't respond to the text because there was no good answer.

I couldn't concentrate on the game and kept losing. My mind was too focused on the text and more so on my unacceptable behavior. I took out my phone and swiped through pictures of Chelsea in an attempt to remind myself whom I belonged to. I scanned through the photos: our drive to San Diego, she and my mother cooking Ecuadorian food, she and I kissing, our cat Dublin...the ring she hadn't seen yet. I tried to turn my attention back to the game, but Greta's question kept eating away at me. So, I texted her a non-answer that happened to be the truth.

I know I'm not supposed to care. But when it comes to you, what I'm supposed to be feeling has never seemed to matter.

About twenty minutes later, I was down 200 bucks when she met up with me and waved a thousand dollars cash in my face. I couldn't believe she'd won all of that money on the penny slots.

"Shit, Greta! Congratulations!"

When I gave her a congratulatory hug, I could feel how fast her heart was beating. I told myself it was because of her win and not the same reason my heart was exploding.

We decided to look for a place for dinner and opted for the steakhouse. All throughout our meal, I was obsessing over a strange text I'd received a little while earlier from an unknown number. It was the number 22 and had come in at exactly 2:22. February 22 was Randy's birthday. I was convinced the message was from him, that it was his way of fucking with me from beyond. So, I was barely touching my food.

Greta, on the other hand, had no problem finishing off my steak and hers. She'd drowned the meat in A1 steak sauce.

I busted her balls. "How about some steak with your sauce?"

"I love it. It reminds me of my dad. He used to put it on everything."

Watching her eat had made me smile. She couldn't have known how much her being there for me that night meant. I'd only freaked out in a gazillion different ways yet she was still here…with A1 sauce all over her face.

She noticed me grinning at her. "What?" she said with her mouth full.

I took my napkin and reached across to wipe the side of her mouth. "Nothing, sloppy."

It suddenly hit me: tomorrow could be the last time I ever see Greta.

My entire body tensed up. This day had put me through the wringer of every feeling imaginable. Something else also hit me: the answer to the question she texted me earlier, the reason why it bothered me if other guys came on to her. I was eventually able to let Greta go only because I thought she was happy and that she was with someone who loved her. Everything I believed to get me over her was a lie. Realizing that had now put my feelings back at square one even though I wouldn't be able to act on them.

***

I lay my head back on the couch and let out a deep sigh. This glimpse inside of his head was killing me. I needed to take another

188

break from the book because an incredible amount of anxiety was building about where this story was going.

I was running late for my friend's 30th birthday party at Club Underground on top of that. I couldn't exactly skip out because I'd been one of the organizers along with a couple of my co-workers.

I decided I would take a shower, get dressed then take my kindle with me to sneak in reading whenever I could tonight while I was out. My device showed that I only had 15-percent left in the book. I assumed I'd be fine to finish it in public.

You know what they say about assuming things.

CHAPTER 20

The night was unexpectedly chilly as I stood on the corner and tried to hail a cab. The thin red dress I was wearing was definitely fitting for Club Underground, but I probably should have taken a jacket.

Sully texted me.

Have fun tonight!

I'd tried to convince her to come out with me, but she said she had a date with an electric razor for her monthly "lady parts" grooming night. TMI for sure, especially when in reality, they weren't lady parts at all.

We'd rented a small private room with a bar for the party. This would have seemed like an epic night were I not so preoccupied with finishing the book.

I finally caught a cab.

"West 16th Street."

I slammed the door and immediately wasted no time getting my kindle out.

***

After we left the steakhouse, my funk was back in full force. Greta had gone to get us some drinks while I went to buy more chips.

I sat down at a table to wait for her when out of nowhere tears just started streaming down my face. It made no sense because there hadn't even been a preceding thought. It seemed to just be the release of everything that had been bottled up. This was the last place I wanted to break down. Once the tears started, they wouldn't stop.

In a self-punishing way, I added fuel to the fire and started to focus on things that made it worse. I sometimes blamed myself for coming into the world and making Randy's life miserable. I wondered if he and Mami's marriage would have lasted were it not for me. Deep down, there was always an underlying hope that things would turn around, that he and I could look each other in the eyes someday and see something other than hate—that he would tell me he really loved me even though he didn't know how to show it.

That would never happen now.

I looked up to find Greta standing there watching me as she held a drink in each hand.

I licked a hot teardrop off my lips. "Don't look at me, Greta."

She put the drinks down and immediately pulled me into her.

In Greta's arms, the tears were multiplying. My hands dug into her back in a silent plea for her not to let go yet. I eventually calmed down.

"I hate this. I shouldn't be crying for him. Why am I crying for him?"

"Because you loved him."

"He hated me."

"He hated whatever he saw in you that reminded him of himself. He didn't hate you. He couldn't have. He just didn't know how to be a father."

It surprised me how close to being right she was despite her not knowing my secret. Randy hated what he saw in me that reminded him of Patrick.

"There's a lot I haven't told you. The screwed up thing is, after all the shit we went through, I still wanted to make him proud of me someday, wanted him to love me."

I let out a deep breath because I'd never admitted that to anyone.

"I know you did," she said softly.

Looking into her eyes reminded me that I was staring into the soul of the first person who'd ever actually succeeded at making me feel loved. For that, I would be eternally grateful to her.

"Where would I be tonight without you?"

"I'm glad I got to be the one with you tonight."

"I've never cried in front of anyone before. Not once."

"There's a first time for everything."

"There's a bad joke in there somewhere. You know that, right?"

We laughed. I loved her laugh.

191

"You make me feel things, Greta. You always have. When I'm around you, whether it's good or bad...I feel everything. Sometimes, I don't handle it too well, and I fight it by acting like an asshole. I don't know what it is about you, but I feel like you see the real me. The second I saw you again for the first time at Greg's when you were standing in that garden...it was like I couldn't hide behind myself anymore." I touched her face. "I know it was hard for you to see me with Chelsea. I know you still care about me. I can feel it even when you're pretending you've stopped."

It was the most honest thing I'd said to her all night. Greta always wore her heart on her sleeve, and even though she was trying not to make it obvious, her discomfort around Chelsea had been evident. (Although, Chelsea seemed to be oblivious to it.) I couldn't have imagined how I would have handled it if the situation were reversed.

My tears had finally dried. As we continued to sit in the wake of that embrace, her lips were begging me to kiss them. I wished there were a magic eraser that would have allowed me to experience it just once and delete the consequences immediately after. Of course, that would never be possible. I didn't think there was anyone worthy of those lips anyway, least of all me. So, I just stared at her mouth, wanting to kiss her but knowing I wouldn't.

Maybe she read my mind, and I scared her off, because she got up like a bat out of hell.

The next thing I knew, she'd run off to the roulette table, slapped some of her money down on the number 22, and the rest was history. This girl had a major horseshoe up her ass.

***

Nineteen-thousand dollars. I didn't know what shocked me more: that she won for a second time tonight or that she'd managed to turn my evening around with that awesome play on 22. The mysterious text wasn't preoccupying me anymore. Instead, I was once again stoked to be here and vowed that for the rest of the night in these final hours together, we'd have the time of our lives.

She made me take a thousand dollars cash. I had no intention of spending it. I'd been using my money the entire time. I didn't care if I spent every red cent I owned on her, I couldn't have ever repaid her for being there for me that night. I'd done nothing to deserve it.

We ended up at one of the casino clothing stores, and that was where the mood for the evening shifted to a place we couldn't quite come out from under for the remainder of the trip.

I'd picked out a dress that I thought would look perfect on her, and she'd gone into the dressing room to try it on. I played with my phone to distract from the thought of her undressing just feet away from me.

She was taking a really long time, so I asked, "You alright in there?"

She said her zipper was stuck, so without thinking, I moved the curtain to the side and stepped into the dressing room. "Come here."

The second I got one look at her gorgeous back in that dress, I immediately realized that putting myself in this position was a big mistake. My fingers tingled as they gripped her hair gently, moving it over her silky skin to the front of her shoulders.

As I pulled at the material, her breathing became more rapid. Knowing that my touching her was the reason for it made me breathe faster, too. I was losing control. Salacious thoughts invaded my brain. One in particular had me breaking the dress apart in one violent rip and taking her from behind while I watched her face in the mirror.

They're just thoughts, I told myself. Focus on the task at hand.

"You weren't kidding," I said as I tried my best to fix it so I could get the hell out of there. Finally, it budged. "Got it."

"Thank you."

I didn't have to lower it a few inches but couldn't resist a glimpse of the milky skin of her back. "All set."

It reminded me of every other part of her body that she'd once given to me fully and completely for one night. It may have only been once, but in my gut, I knew a part of her still belonged to me. Her body language proved it and made me wonder if I was the first and last person who'd ever truly pleasured her.

My hands wouldn't leave her shoulders. She was looking down, and I knew she was battling her feelings, too. This was the first time since our reconnection that I truly realized how much

Greta still wanted me sexually. Our desire for each other was so powerful in the confines of this tiny space that you could taste it in the air.

I kept looking at her in the mirror until she looked up and met my gaze. When she turned around suddenly, I wasn't prepared. Our faces were just inches apart, and I'd never wanted to kiss her more than that moment. My eyes dropped to her mouth, and I counted in my head to keep myself in control. The counting wasn't working so I closed my eyes.

When I opened them, I no longer had the urge to just kiss her. It was far worse. Thank God she couldn't read my mind because the image of fucking that beautiful mouth was so clear in my head that I felt myself getting hard and prayed she didn't look down.

I needed to leave but couldn't move.

Chelsea.

Chelsea.

Chelsea.

You love Chelsea.

Having these feelings is okay as long as you don't act on them, I told myself. This is natural. You can't prevent what your body wants, only whether you follow through with it. And I deserved a big shiny trophy for resistance. Instead of the "mirror ball," we'd call it the "blue ball."

The store attendant came by. "Is everything okay in there?"

"Yes!" Greta shouted.

But I knew in her voice it wasn't. This was messing with her mind, and I'd be fucking damned if the night ended in her getting hurt.

Even though we hadn't acknowledged what was happening between us verbally, I instinctively said, "I'm sorry." Then, I slid the curtain and left.

***

We decided to spend the night at the hotel since we'd been drinking. After we'd both separated to shower before heading to the casino nightclub, I met Greta back at her room. When she opened the door, the sight of her in that fitted burgundy dress knocked the

194

wind out of me again. Her hair was still sopping wet, but she looked amazing.

"Wow," I breathed out, not intending to have said it out loud. The word had left my lips before my brain could warn me not to seem so obvious. I needed to make a joke to offset my slip. "You definitely can't pass for an old lady in mourning anymore."

"What do I look like now?"

"You look flushed, actually. Are you feeling alright?"

In all honesty, she looked like she'd just been properly fucked, and it made my dick ache.

"I'm fine," she said.

"You sure?"

"Yep."

"It felt so good to take a shower," I said.

And by that I meant the two orgasms I gave myself thinking about an alternate ending to our dressing room encounter.

"I know what you mean," she said.

"Do you need to dry your hair?"

"Yeah. Just give me a minute."

I turned on ESPN and lay down on the bed.

About ten minutes later, she came out of the bathroom.

"I'm ready."

Her hair was up, her neck was exposed in all of its glory, and I knew I was in trouble for the rest of the night.

I jumped up and turned the television off.

We walked down the hall, and the smell of the soap on her skin was invading my senses. I glanced over at her and wanted her to know how beautiful she looked when I said, "You clean up nice." When we entered the elevator, I added, "I like your hair up like that."

"You do?"

"Yeah. It's how you were wearing it the night when I first met you."

"I'm surprised you remembered that."

I hadn't forgotten one thing.

Not. One. Thing.

We'd started reminiscing about how I used to torture her and at one point, she said, "Well, you weren't exactly as mean as you wanted me to believe you were."

195

I returned that with, "And it turned out you weren't that innocent."

The tone in my voice made no secret of what I was referring to. We looked at each other with a silent understanding that the conversation needed to end there.

If I thought the night was going to get any easier once we entered the distraction of a nightclub, I had another thing coming.

***

We'd been dancing a lot. It was the most fun I'd had all night. The bass was blaring, and I could feel it pumping through me. Dancing bodies tangled together around us, but Greta and I kept a space between each other.

It was necessary.

At one point, I went to the bathroom and as I made my way back through the multi-colored flashing lights, I spotted a guy dancing very closely around her and talking in her ear.

When I returned to the spot where she was dancing alongside him, my conscience gave way to a primal and impulsive reaction. I wrapped my arm around her tiny waist and pulled her firmly back into me. She didn't resist. My arm was still dominantly locked around her when she turned to look at me. I gave her a warning look. In that moment, we were the Elec and Greta of seven years ago. I was jealous, and I was once again making it obvious. Given the not so minor detail of my being in a serious relationship, it was unfair to expect her to accept things that I couldn't, but she cared about me enough to let me get away with this somehow.

We didn't speak about it, and eventually, my caveman moment passed. I let go of her, and we were back to getting lost in the music.

Everything changed, though, when a slow song had come on. People started scrambling to find partners while others left the dance floor. Somehow, it felt like we were the only ones left.

Greta panicked and started to walk away.

I couldn't blame her, but what if tonight was it for us? I wanted this dance.

I grabbed her hand. "Dance with me."

She looked scared but let me reel her into me anyway. A deep breath escaped me when her entire body melted into my arms. She closed her eyes as she planted her head on my chest. My heart was hammering against it as if to tell me that I was an idiot for not realizing that this was precisely what it wanted.

For the first time since we arrived at the casino, thoughts of Chelsea were completely buried by the intensity of my feelings for Greta. Needing to know if she felt it, I looked down and at that same exact moment, she looked up at me. I was losing my ability to breathe. I touched my forehead to hers and just knew. That was the moment I stopped lying to myself. I was still in love with her. I didn't know what to do about it because I loved Chelsea, too.

Before I could think it through, Greta pulled away and started running off through the darkness of the crowd.

"Greta, wait!"

Within seconds, I'd lost her. I made my way to the exit and ran toward the elevators. The doors were closing, and I stuck my arm through the opening to stop them.

She was crying. God, what had I done to her?

"What the fuck, Greta? Why did you run from me like that?"

"I just need to go back to my room."

"Not like this."

Without thinking, I pressed the stop button.

"What are you doing?"

"This isn't how I wanted our night to end. I crossed a line. I know that. I got lost in the moment with you, and I'm so fucking sorry. But it wasn't going to go any further because I won't cheat on Chelsea. I couldn't do that to her."

"I'm not as strong as you are, then. You can't dance with me like that, look at me like that, touch me like that if we can't do anything about it. And for the record, I wouldn't want you to cheat on her!"

"What do you want?"

"I don't want you to say one thing and act in a way that contradicts it. We don't have much time left together. I want you to talk to me. That night at the wake...you wrapped your hand around my neck. It felt like for a moment you were back in that place where we left off. That's sort of how I feel around you all of the time. Then,

197

later that night, Chelsea told me what happened after you got home."

What was she talking about?

"Exactly what did she tell you?"

"Were you thinking about me? Is that why you couldn't perform that night?"

The fuck?

I had no words. The fact that Chelsea told Greta about that private moment actually pissed me off. I was speechless.

"I want you to tell me the truth," she said.

She couldn't handle the truth, and I couldn't handle these feelings for her. But I was pissed that they'd been talking like that behind my back. On top of that, my whole life felt like it had been turned inside out in one night.

So, I lost it.

"You want the truth? I was fucking my girlfriend and could see nothing but you. That's the truth." I moved toward her predatorily, and she backed away. "I got into the shower that night, and the only way I could finish the job was to imagine coming all over your beautiful neck. That's the truth."

It should have stopped there.

Instead, I locked my arms around her as she leaned her back against the wall. I kept going. "You want more? I was going to ask her to marry me tonight at her sister's wedding. I was supposed to be engaged right at this very moment, but instead, I'm in an elevator fighting the urge to back you up against this wall and fuck you so hard that I'll have to carry you back to your room."

My chest hurt. I dropped my arms. "Everything I thought I knew has been turned upside down in the past 48 hours. I'm questioning everything, and I don't fucking know what to do. That's. The. Truth."

I released the stop button because any more time in here would have been detrimental, although being brutally honest for once felt like a huge weight had lifted off of my chest.

When we got to our floor, we both went back to our separate rooms.

Alone in bed, guilt started to really set in and prevented me from sleeping.

I was torturing myself by going through my pictures of Chelsea again.

She didn't deserve this.

I'd tossed and turned, alternating between thoughts of Randy, guilt over Chelsea and my personal favorite: carnal thoughts of Greta. If I didn't care about hurting Chelsea, I would have gone to Greta's room that night. I knew with all of our pent-up frustration, it would have been the best sex of my life. But I wasn't a cheater, and I wouldn't go there. So, I let my imagination experience it.

At one point, the sexual fantasies had gotten so vivid, I tried to undo my sins with a text to Chelsea at 2 A.M.

I love you.

Immediately after, I sent a text to Greta.

If I knock on your door tonight, don't let me in.

***

The cab was approaching my destination, so I thought that was as good a point as any to stop the story since I was going to have to greet my friends soon. It was painful to put it down.

I paid the driver and stuck my kindle in my purse. As I made my way inside Club Underground, the contrast of the darkness and bright lights caused a feeling of unreality. My head had been stuck in Elec's story all day, and it almost felt strange venturing into the real world. It started to make me feel a little panicky with a bit of vertigo, which I got from time to time.

My nervous state improved as soon as I saw two of my coworkers, Bobbie and Jennifer, who greeted me as I entered the private room. A small bar was lit up in purple lighting, and I immediately booked it over there for a vodka soda.

I took a sip. "Is the guest of honor here yet?"

"No sign of Hetty yet," Jennifer said.

Since Hetty wasn't even here yet, I excused myself to go to the bathroom where I promptly picked my kindle up again. Don't judge.

***

I still consider it a miracle that I made it through that night without fucking up. Greta ended up texting me that she was having insomnia. I immediately called her, and we talked until she fell asleep sometime after 4 A.M. I stayed on the phone listening to the sound of her breathing.

The ride home the next morning was downright painful. A chainsaw wouldn't have been enough to cut the tension in the air.

Greta was going to be driving me to the airport. We ended up stopping at her mother's house first. Being back in the place where everything started was harder than I thought it would be.

Greta had served me some of her homemade ice cream. It was nostalgic sharing it with her out of the same bowl. For some reason, out of everything we'd experienced during our little adventure, that moment had meant the most to me and felt like goodbye all at once.

***

I had to put my kindle down when Hetty walked into the bathroom. She must have thought I was pathetic.

"There you are. We've all been looking for you!"

"Oh, I lost track of time. You hadn't arrived yet, so I came in here to chill for a bit before the party started." I hugged her. "Happy birthday, sweetie."

"Thanks. You were reading?"

"Yeah." I laughed and waved my hand dismissively. "You know how it is when you start a book you can't put down."

"Is it smut?"

I had to think about it. "Not really."

"Right. Okay, well, come on! Almost everyone's here now."

I followed her back out into the club and immediately ran to the bar for another vodka soda. Vowing to not pick up the book for at least an hour, I worked the room and found myself looking at people's faces but not really hearing what they were saying. Their mouths were moving, but my brain wasn't processing it; my mind was still with Elec.

200

As soon as my self-imposed hour was up, I snuck back into the bathroom. My friends were probably going to think I was doing lines of coke, but I needed to finish the book since I only had a small percentage left. That way, I could get through the remainder of the night with no preoccupation.

I took a deep breath.

***

Greta wouldn't make eye contact on the ride to the airport. All of the special moments we'd shared, and she couldn't even stand to look at my face now. That was what it all came down to, and I couldn't say I blamed her.

I was breaking apart at the seams and didn't know what to say to her. We'd practically been to Heaven and Hell and back together over the past twenty-four hours and now, I was simply leaving her...again.

When we exited the car at the curb, the wind was wild. It was almost like a scene out of a movie. This would have been the sad part where you'd cue the dramatic music.

The thunderous sound of the planes taking off made it even more difficult to articulate what I wanted to say. What do you say to someone you're abandoning for the second time?

She held onto herself and was looking everywhere but at my face.

Finally, I said, "Look at me."

Greta shook her head repeatedly, and a tear fell down her cheek.

It was official now. I was the scum of the Earth.

My own eyes started watering because I couldn't take away the pain she was feeling, because I couldn't do the one thing that would have achieved that: staying.

She was waving me off. "It's okay. Go. Please. Text me if you want. It's just...I can't do a long goodbye...not with you."

She was right. This wasn't going to end well, so why prolong it?

"Okay."

She startled me when she leaned in and gave me a quick kiss on the cheek. She rushed back to the car and slammed the door before I could even process it.

The remnants of her saliva were stinging my cheek as I walked into the airport in a daze.

I wanted to look at her one last time, so I turned around. Big mistake. Through the glass, I saw that her head was on the steering wheel. I immediately ran back outside to the car and knocked on the window. She refused to look up and started the engine, so I knocked harder. She finally turned to me and got out, wiping her tears. "Did you forget something?"

Before I knew it, my mouth was on hers. My heart was doing the thinking at this point. I wouldn't open my lips because I'd convinced myself that this was innocent so long as I couldn't taste her. It was a firm, desperate kiss, and I didn't even know what it meant.

I felt empty and confused.

She ended it. "Get out of here. You're gonna miss your flight."

My hands were still on her cheeks. "I never got over hurting you the first time, but hurting you twice…believe me when I say this was the last thing I ever wanted to see happen in my lifetime."

"Why did you come back just now?"

"I turned around and saw you crying. What kind of a heartless asshole would leave you like that?"

"Well, you weren't supposed to see that. You really should have kept walking because now you're making it worse."

"I didn't want that to be my last visual."

"If you really love her, you shouldn't have kissed me," she yelled.

"I do love her." It came out really defensively. I looked up at the sky because I needed to think for a second.

How would I explain the realization I had on the dance floor last night?

"You want to know the truth? I fucking love you, too. I don't think I realized how much until I saw you again."

"You love us both? That's messed up, Elec."

"You've always told me you wanted honesty. I just gave it to you. I'm sorry if the truth is a fucked up mess."

"Well, she has the home court advantage. You'll forget about me again soon enough. That will simplify things."

She was getting back in the car.

"Greta...don't leave like this."

"I'm not the one leaving."

Ouch.

She drove off and left me at the curb, which was fitting because I'd unintentionally kicked her to the same place...twice, actually.

I was really tempted to jump in a cab and follow her. But I got on that plane back to California because for once in my life, I needed to do the right thing.

***

My finger kept pressing the next page button hoping there was more to the story. He couldn't have possibly put me through all of that just to end it right where we left things.

When he sent me the manuscript, he said it wasn't finished. It was probable that he didn't feel I needed to know anything more than what involved me. Since the rest of his life would involve *her*, there was no need to torture me with more. I got it now, and I appreciated that. He wanted me to understand what he was feeling all of that time so he could have some closure and move on.

Well, good for him.

I took out my phone and sent him a text that sounded cordial despite my anger.

I finished. Thank you. That was an amazing ride. I'm honored you asked me to read it. The history of your family blew me away and explained so much. I'm sorry you had to go through all of that. I understand so much more now and also why you ended it where you did.

Fuck.

I was crying and had to go back out to my friends.

Devastated, I was determined that the rest of the night would be about forgetting him once and for all.

"Help me drown my sorrows," I remember him saying to me at the casino. Well, that was what I needed right now.

My friends were on the dance floor and cheered when they spotted me. They pulled me in, and we danced together for at least an hour. The more I thought about Elec, the harder and faster I swayed my hips and shook my head around to the point where my hair must have looked like I'd gotten electrocuted. Getting lost in the music, I didn't want to stop long enough to feel all of the painful emotions that his words had caused. I certainly didn't want to accept that the character of Greta Hansen had now been written out of his life.

A half-hour later, my phone buzzed.

What's your theory on why I ended it where I did?

His response stunned me. To prevent myself from losing it on the dance floor, I kept dancing as if nothing had happened. I didn't want my friends to think something was wrong.

I shook my ass and typed.

Greta: Because you didn't want to hurt me. The rest has nothing to do with me.

Elec: You're sure about that?

Greta: What are you saying?

Elec: Stop shaking your ass for five seconds and maybe I'll tell you.

What?

Before I could turn around, the feeling of strong hands grasping at the sides of my dress from behind caused me to suddenly stop moving. They slowly slid down my waist and landed on my ass with a cool self-assurance. That grip. That smell. The way my body immediately responded.

No. It couldn't be.

CHAPTER 21

I flipped around and was met with smoky eyes, incandescent even in the darkness of the club. My heartbeat was so intense, it seemed like it was dueling with the bass of the fast-paced music. Everything around me seemed to fade away upon the realization that Elec was right in front of me, holding onto me as if he knew his presence would jar me to the point that I might collapse and need him for balance.

My voice was trembling. I was so nervous that my first question was a dumb one. "What happened to your glasses?"

"Contacts tonight."

"Oh."

Finally, the shock was starting to wear off just enough for me to attempt to ask something that made sense. "I have a million questions. How did you get here? How did you find me? How—"

"Shut up, Greta." His hot mouth enveloped my lips and abruptly interrupted all further questioning. He devoured me with reckless abandon. If there were any doubt about where things stood between us, the possessive feel of this kiss, the way he pressed his entire body against me, annihilated it.

Without having to say it with his words, the kiss spoke volumes. His tongue lashing at mine, the guttural sounds that came out from his throat as he did it, it was the first time since I'd met him that I'd truly felt it in my bones: he was mine. All of the reservations of the past, every shred of what had been holding us back was gone.

I didn't know the full story yet of how we suddenly arrived at this place, but I wasn't sure it mattered.

My fingers raked through his hair desperately as I pulled him harder into me.

Don't ever leave me again, Elec.

We were still in our own little world despite people dancing all around, bumping into us. He breathed over my lips with his forehead on mine. "I've been waiting for you to finish the book so I could come to you. That was the plan."

"You've been in New York all this time?"

"I was already in New York waiting when I sent it."

"Oh my God." I buried my face into his chest and savored the smell of him sans cigarettes. I looked up at him and had to ask the question even though it should have been obvious. "You broke up with her?"

He nodded his face over mine.

I continued, "But the ending…you said you were doing the right thing. I thought—"

He cut me off with a kiss again then said, "I figured you might assume that. But the right thing…was admitting that I couldn't possibly fully love her if my heart beat faster for someone else." His hands cupped my cheeks. "My heart hasn't shut up since it spotted you standing in that garden. I finally listened. It just took some time to clear my head enough to really understand what it wanted."

I was sure it was a long story, that ending things with Chelsea wasn't easy for him. I knew he'd genuinely loved her and that he'd tell me everything in due time, but now was not the moment for that.

As if he read my mind, he said, "I promise I'll tell you everything about what happened, but not now, okay? I just want to be with you."

"Okay."

I wrapped my arms around his neck and let out a breath so intense, you would have thought I'd been holding it for seven years. Maybe I had been. We kissed like our lives depended on it, not coming up for breath for at least the duration of three consecutive songs. I was sure my friends saw us, but I couldn't take my eyes off him long enough to check for their reactions. They probably thought he was a random hookup, and there would be a lot of explaining to do at work. I pressed my body into his and could feel his erection through his jeans. We were practically making love on the dance floor.

This was surreal.

He spoke into my ear, causing me to shiver. "Do you want me, Greta?"

"Yes."

"Do you trust me?"

"I do."

"I need you to let me have you now."

"In the club?"

He smiled over my mouth. "I wanted you to finish reading, to know everything before I came to you. I've been wandering around this city hard as a rock for three days just thinking about being with you. Your apartment is too far from here. I can't wait anymore."

"Where can we go?" I asked.

"I don't care, but we need to figure it out before I take you right here on this dance floor." He grabbed me by the hand. "Come on."

He ran my fingers through his and led me through the thick humid air of the club. All of the hairs on my body stiffened. What we were doing felt dangerous. Elec was a full-grown man now. When I was last with him sexually, he was practically a boy. I was sure he'd gotten even better in the years we were apart, and I wasn't sure what I was in for. It had been a really long time since I'd even been with anyone. He was going to be able to tell how long it had been.

There was a door leading to a back room, but when Elec tried to open it, it was locked. He looked back at me with a smile that gave me the chills. "You said you trust me, right?"

"Yeah."

"Wait here."

He opened a back door that looked like a fire exit and peeked outside before returning to the spot where I was standing.

"I want to give you a choice depending on what you're in the mood for."

"Okay."

"We can go find the nearest hotel, and I can make love to you in a bed or..."

"Okay. Or?"

"Or we can go outside right now and fuck hard in that alley."

Never had the muscles between my legs throbbed so intensely in anticipation of something. My body had clearly chosen for me, wanting to completely surrender to him. I needed this just as much as he did. I wanted it hard, and I wanted it now.

"I want option b."

"Good choice."

He opened the back door and led me outside. The alley was desolate. A thin layer of fog coated the air. We wandered a bit until we came to a somewhat hidden alcove.

"No one will see us here," he said as he gently backed me into the brick wall. "I'm dying to take you out of your comfort zone."

My chest was heaving from the excitement of not knowing exactly what he was going to do to me. I just knew I wasn't going to stop him. I was going in happily blind. I was shaking a little.

"You're nervous? Don't be scared."

"I'm just excited. It's been a while."

"Your body will remember me."

Elec pulled the top of my dress down so that my bare breasts were exposed. He gently pushed all of my hair back before not so gently grabbing a hold of my neck. It felt good, though. He lowered his mouth to it, grazing me with his teeth.

"This fucking neck…was almost the death of me…my favorite thing in the entire world," he said as he sucked and groaned into it, vibrating through my skin. "I can practically smell how much you want me, Greta. He kept one hand on my neck and lightly pinched my nipple with the other. "Look how hard these are. I don't think I've ever seen your nipples when they weren't hard as steel around me. And I wish you could see your own face. Even in the dark, I can see how pink your cheeks are right now. It turns me on to no end knowing that I have that kind of effect on you. I want you to know I've never wanted anything more in my entire life than to reclaim every inch of you. I'm going to do that now. Okay?"

I nodded, so turned on I could barely breathe. I dug my fingers into the thick black waves of his hair as he kissed upward to greedily feast on my mouth. I savored the sweet taste of his breath, and the scratch of his scruff on my face. There was nothing delicate about being with Elec, even at his softest. I flicked my tongue over his lip ring, and he growled when I lightly pulled on it. I couldn't get enough of his mouth. I wanted it all over me.

Wetness was pooling between my legs as he knelt down on the concrete to lift my dress and slowly pull my underwear down. He looked up at me and flashed his beautiful teeth. "You won't be needing these," he smiled and added, "for at least a week." He promptly put my panties in his back pocket. My legs were quivering.

He stood up slowly, and the sequence of events that followed was nothing short of a perfectly choreographed erotic tease. Every sound, every movement was hotter than the last: the unfastening of his belt, the swift lowering of his zipper, his teeth ripping the condom wrapper as he looked at me, the sound of the rubber spreading over his beautiful cock that had been dripping with precum around the piercing at his tip. I was pulsating with need.

His eyes seemed to have darkened to a charcoal hue. Leaving his jeans on, he lifted me up and wrapped my legs around his waist, backing me against the brick wall. "Tell me if it gets to be too much," he said gruffly.

"It wo—"

Ah!

He entered me in one stabbing thrust. He moved his hand to rest behind my head as a shield because he realized he'd almost given me a concussion.

His mouth stayed on my neck, gently biting as he fucked me, the heat of his cock searing. Each movement was harder than the last and only a second apart from each other.

He groaned loudly with each thrust. Someone was going to catch us. This was the roughest sex of my life, second only to the time he took me on the floor of my bedroom seven years ago. I hadn't had sex in almost two years, and you wouldn't have known it by how easily my body conformed to him despite how massive he was. I think I'd been wet and ready for him since the moment I first spotted him again in the garden.

He continued to fuck me, angrily and unbridled. "No one should have ever had this but me," he said over the skin of my neck. He pushed into me. "I let you go." He pushed deeper. "I threw you away."

I started to move my hips, impaling myself on him. "So, take me back. Fuck me harder."

My words set him off, and he accepted the challenge. He shifted me around so that his back was now to the wall, and he no longer had to shield my head from it. He repositioned my legs around him and wrapped his hand around my neck using the other to hold me up. He looked into my eyes while he moved in and out of me as he choked me lightly, just enough that it was pleasurable. Knowing how much that turned him on made me crazy.

Luckily, no one had come outside. We were still alone in the foggy night. The only sounds were the slapping of our skin, the clinking of his belt buckle and our breathing, which had fallen into a synchronized rhythm.

I reached my hand to lift his shirt halfway up so that I could see his abs. They were harder than I remembered and looked like they'd been cut from stone. I wished we could have been skin-to-skin, but getting fully naked would have been risky here.

"Don't worry. Later, we'll take it off," he said. "We're gonna do everything tonight."

An orgasm was starting to roll through me suddenly. I didn't even have to say anything. It amazed me how well he knew my body.

"You're coming," he said. "I remember how it felt. Look at me."

He held my neck and looked into my eyes as he rocked his hips, fucking me as hard as he could until he shuddered.

It took several minutes for my breathing to come down. He continued to hold my limp body as he kissed my neck.

"I love you, Greta"

I loved him so much that I couldn't even form the words. So many feelings had risen to the surface, but fear had trumped all.

"Don't leave me again, Elec. Don't go back to her," I said.

He held me tighter. "I won't, baby," he said, lifting my face to meet his eyes. "Look at me. You'll never have to worry about that. I'm not going anywhere. I know I have to prove that to you, but I will."

He put me down and fastened his pants before lifting me up again. His feet crunched on the gravel as he carried me in his arms to the nearest sidewalk where we caught a cab.

It still felt like a dream.

In the backseat, I leaned my head against his chest. His heart was beating fast against my ear as he gently caressed my hair the entire ride to my apartment.

When we entered my building, his hands were on my shoulders as he kissed the back of my neck the entire way up the stairs.

I fumbled with the keys and once inside, I had the sudden urge to do something I'd never done before.

I backed him against the door that had just closed behind us and lifted off his shirt. The look in his eyes was a mix of hunger, shock and amusement at my boldness.

My tongue circled along the ring on his nipple and licked down every taut muscle of his chest right down to the two shamrocks. I got down on my knees, and when he realized what I was about to do, his chest started heaving.

"Fuck," he said huskily. "Is this really happening?"

He wasted no time ripping off his belt and throwing it to the ground. I lowered his boxer briefs and lifted his cock out, taking a moment to marvel at its girth, its length, its heat and the shiny ring at the tip. I'd fantasized about sucking him off more than anything because it was the one thing we never did.

He bunched some of my hair between his fingers. "I can't tell you how many times I have dreamt of fucking that beautiful mouth. Are you sure you want to do this?"

Instead of answering him, I flicked my tongue over the metal ring and savored the salty taste of the precum on his tip as I stroked his length. With each pump, with each lick, he became wetter.

His abs tightened, and his breathing was labored. "Shit. That's such a tease."

I stopped and licked my lips as I looked up at him. He closed his eyes in response. Elec was always so controlled, but now he was at my mercy, and that turned me on.

His eyes were still closed when I took him down my throat for the first time. The sounds of pleasure emanating from him were so damn sexy and only encouraged me to take him even deeper and faster. I loved the smooth feel of him filling my mouth. I couldn't get enough and sucked harder. I was so wet and could have come so easily from this if I touched myself.

He dug his fingernails into my hair and pulled on it. "Stop. You're gonna make me lose it, and I want to come inside of you."

I sucked him harder. "No," I said, wanting him to come in my mouth.

His breathing was erratic. "Are you on the pill by any chance?"

I nodded yes. "I have been for years. It regulates my cycle."

He pulled out of my mouth. "Stand up and turn around."

My heart was racing as he lifted my dress over my head. He grabbed my hips and sunk into me. Without a condom, the hot, wet feel of his skin inside of me, and the sensation of the metal ring were almost too much to bear. Every feeling was enhanced.

His hands gripped my ass as he fucked me. I could hear my wetness as he moved in and out. I was ready to come at any moment, so aroused after sucking him off and his taking me bare.

"I can't ever use a condom again with you," he breathed out. "This feels too good."

I was starting to come. "Come inside of me now."

He pumped into me so hard, I was sure I'd have bruises on my ass tomorrow. "Fuck…Greta…oh…" He kept moving in and out until there was nothing left and even after, he continued fucking me slowly for a while.

Elec finally pulled out of me and flipped me around to kiss him. He chuckled. "We couldn't even make it past the front door. Do you realize that?"

"I think I could even go again."

"Good, because I'm nowhere near done with you tonight," he said, dragging me to the bedroom as his pants hung down his waist.

***

Four lit candles flickered around us as we sat in my bed at four in the morning feeding each other ice cream out of a Ben and Jerry's container.

"So, how did you know where to find me tonight?"

"Well, when you sent me the text that you'd finished, I was sitting at a Starbucks around the corner from your apartment. I came straight here since I assumed that's where you were reading. I wanted to go right to you and surprise you. I waited on your steps. This…person…who said she was your fairy godmother came up to me and said, 'Alec, right? I'd recognize you anywhere from the description my Greta gave me. I knew you'd be back for her, you dumb fuck.'"

"Are you serious?" I burst into laughter. "That's Sully. She *is* like my fairy godmother."

"Well, you do realize your fairy godmother has a bigger package than mine, right?"

"Yes, I'm well aware of that. We just don't discuss it."

"You must have given her an earful about me. Anyway, I just needed to get to you and asked if she knew where you were."

"So, she gave you the name of the club?"

"Not at first. I think she wanted to make me suffer."

"What did she do?"

"She made me take off my shirt."

"Are you kidding me?"

"I'm dead serious."

"That was it?"

"I wish."

"What?"

"She made me hold up a sign made out of cardboard that said 'fuckface' and took a picture of me holding it."

I covered my mouth and spoke through my hand. "What?"

"Yeah. Then, she said it was collateral."

"Sully is nuts."

"Well, he…she obviously cares about you. I can relate in that sense. Anyway, it was only after I let her take the picture, that she gave me the address of the club and said, 'This is your last chance.'"

"Wow," I said.

"Yeah."

Elec turned to me. "I need you to know something."

"Okay…"

"Earlier tonight, after we finished in the alley when you told me not to go back to Chelsea, that was hard to hear. There's a part of you that doesn't trust that this is real, and you're still traumatized by my leaving you in the past. It made me realize just how badly I hurt you, how much work I have cut out for me."

"I was just very emotional at that moment, especially after reading your book all day. Every feeling including my biggest fear came pouring out."

Elec took the ice cream from my hands and put it aside. He placed his hands on my cheeks. "There was never any contest. I loved Chelsea, but it was by default. I love you so much more. Every second I was with you again, I had to constantly reassure myself that I loved Chelsea, which is not something that you should have to do. My feelings for you were so powerful that they scared the shit out of me. The second I got on that plane, I knew I was really going back to California to end things with Chelsea. That was the right thing."

"You hurt her pretty badly, didn't you?"

"Yeah. She didn't deserve it."

"I'm sorry."

"It would have been worse if we were engaged or married because I'm not sure the outcome could have been any different. It wouldn't have been fair to stay with her and love you like I do in secret."

"I feel like I know exactly how she must be feeling right now."

"Yeah, you probably do. A part of me will always feel horrible about hurting her, but there was no way to avoid that. It took me several days after I got back to figure out how best to explain everything to her because I wanted to be honest about you. I didn't do it immediately, but I never slept with her again; you need to know that. I made up excuses. The bottom line is, I didn't want to come back here to you until I no longer had any baggage and until you knew everything about my past. So after I moved out of Chelsea's, I spent a lot of time working on the book until I got it to a point where I was comfortable with you reading it."

"Thank you for sharing it with me."

He kissed me. "I love you so much, Greta."

"I love you, too."

"I'm not going back to California."

"What? Not even to get your stuff?"

"No. I put it all in storage. Mami is doing okay for now. We need to go out there soon to visit, though."

"We?"

I wanted to meet Pilar about as much as Dorothy wanted to meet the Wicked Witch of the West.

"Yes. I already told her about you. She didn't take it well at first, but I explained to her how much I love you and that she needs to accept it. She will, Greta. And if she doesn't, it wouldn't matter anymore."

"I hope so. "

"I needed to find another job because I quit the youth center after I ended things with Chelsea. So, actually, one of the things I did over the past few days was interview at a school here in the city last Friday. They offered me a guidance counselor position."

"Are you kidding?"

"No."

"Elec, that's the best news!"

He picked up the ice cream and started eating it again. "I'll need a place to stay, though. Do you know a girl who needs a roommate?"

"Actually, Sully's been looking."

He fed me a spoonful. "I'm talking about another girl. I was kind of thinking of moving in with this beautiful little nymph I know who likes her pussy licked."

"Oh…she might be interested."

"Good, because I wasn't planning on taking no for an answer." He kissed me with his mouth full of Cherry Garcia ice cream. "Hey…you never explained to me what it is you actually do for a living. You say it's an administrative position, but what does the company do exactly? Or are you really an FBI agent or something?"

Oh boy. I was surprised it took this long before I had to fess up. There was a reason I never went into it.

"It's not quite administrative, and you have the agent part right. There's a reason I've been kind of hesitant to tell you. I felt really guilty when we were apart because I wished I could have helped you, actually."

"I don't get it."

"I'm a literary agent, Elec."

He put the carton down on the end table. "Say what?"

"I represent authors, and I think I could actually help get some of your work published, particularly *Lucky and the Lad*. I work closely with a major publishing house's young adult imprint, and I think we should submit it to them."

"Are you fucking shitting me?"

"I'm dead serious."

"How did you get into that?"

"Actually, I fell into it. I was looking for a job out of college, started as an intern and worked my way up to an agent position. I'm newer, so my clientele is still growing."

"Please tell me I'm gonna have to sleep with you to get ahead in my writing career."

"That's definitely part of the deal."

"Wow, in all seriousness, I'm so proud of you."

"You have no idea how guilty I've felt this past year when I'd see writers not nearly as talented as you getting deals and having success. I didn't know how to contact you or if you'd even want to pursue anything because I knew how private you were about your writing."

"You know I would never expect special treatment. You don't owe me anything."

"Your writing blew me away long before this career. I believe in you. We'll work together. If nothing comes of it, then at least we tried."

"If nothing comes of it, I'm still the luckiest man in the world." He whispered to himself, still thinking of my admission. "That's wild."

I got up to straddle him and brushed my finger over his side. "Speaking of lucky, I noticed this new tattoo right here."

He started to tickle me. "Oh, you did, did you?"

It was a small *Lucky Charms* cereal box with the words *Get Cereal* above it.

How cute but bizarre.

Even though it went along with the Irish theme of all the other tats, it made me chuckle. "What's the significance of this?"

"Honestly? I just got this recently. It reminds me of you and the horseshoe up your ass. Also, you're my lucky charm. More than once in my life, you turned something miserable into something magical for me. He pulled me into a deep kiss then said, "And if you scramble the letters of *Get Cereal*, you get our names."

Get Cereal=ElecGreta

Oh my God. I loved him.

"That's my favorite anagram you've ever come up with."

"It was either that or *Rectal Gee*, which made no sense. Then I would have had to get an ass tattooed on my side. That wouldn't have worked."

***

A few months later, it was Christmas in New York. This was my favorite time of year with all of the lights and decorations adorning the city. This Christmas was like no other because Elec and I were experiencing it together in love for the first time.

We'd be going out to San Francisco to spend the actual holiday with Pilar. Per Elec's suggestion, he had me speak to her on the phone to take some of the edge off. She was surprisingly cordial to me, and it made me feel a lot better about the trip. Things would never be perfect between us, and I was sure she would have preferred him ending up with Chelsea. At least, though, with Randy gone and through the passage of time, she was able to accept me.

A few days before we were set to fly out west, Elec and I were invited to a Christmas party at Sully's.

Sully's apartment was very classic New York, lots of dark wood crown molding and a hefty built-in bookshelf lined from top to bottom with books ranging from erotica to military history. She'd gone all out, hanging plastic mistletoe and white lights all throughout the apartment. There was even a gold banner that read, *Eat, Drink and Be Mary.* She also set out a table of spiked eggnog and assorted appetizers. Elec and I were feeling pretty good after a few mugs of the eggnog.

He looked so sexy in a velvet Santa hat when he led me to a private corner of the room.

I pulled on the fuzzy ball at the end of his hat. "You know you're the sexiest Santa I've ever seen, right?"

His slid his hands down my waist. "Lucky for you, I'll be coming way more than once a year."

I wrapped my arms around his neck and leaned into him. "And I'll be giving you way more than cookies."

"I wouldn't mind spreading some cheer in that bathroom right now," he said.

So, that was what we did.

When we emerged, it was time to open presents. Sully gave Elec his first. They'd actually grown pretty close and were constantly busting each other's balls.

"Oh, Sully. You shouldn't have." The room burst into laughter as Elec lifted a t-shirt that displayed the photo of his bare-chested self, holding the cardboard *fuckface* sign. There was also a mug and mouse pad featuring the now classic image.

Sully laughed. "With all this book stuff, I just didn't want you to forget your roots."

Elec took it in stride then accepted his actual present, which was a gift certificate to Starbucks where he spent a lot of time writing after work. We'd recently inked a publishing deal for *Lucky and the Lad* and a yet to be written sequel he was developing now. He was still working at the middle school during the day.

Elec's present to me was the last to be handed out. I was surprised he even brought something for me since we agreed to exchange gifts in California. Let's just say, once I opened the box, it made total sense. This wasn't my actual gift. It was the last pair of underwear he'd stolen from me all those years ago. They were turquoise lace. I remembered them well and shook my head.

"I can't believe you've held onto this all these years."

"It was the one memento I had of you for a long time."

I whispered in his ear. "You're lucky my ass still fits inside these."

He whispered in mine. "I think I'm even luckier because I fit inside your ass."

I punched him lightly on the arm. "You're so nasty. I love it, though."

"You didn't read the card," he said.

I opened it. It had a picture of an old couple kissing by a Christmas tree. It was one of those blank cards where you could write your own note inside.

Greta,

This Christmas will be the best of my life.
Because of you…I:

Am grateful.
Am happy.
Am fulfilled.
Am at peace.
Am excited for the future.
Am in love.
Because of you this Christmas…I:
Am Merry.

Am Merry.

It didn't register at first until I saw him getting down on one knee and reaching into his pocket.

Am Merry=Marry Me.

"I didn't know what love felt like until you, Greta, not just giving it but receiving it. I love you so much. Please say you'll marry me."

I covered my face in shock. "I will. Yes. Yes!"

Everyone in the room clapped. Sully must have been in on it because a bottle of champagne popped in the air.

When Elec placed the ring on my finger, I gasped. "Elec, this is the most beautiful ring I've ever seen, but there is no way you could afford it."

The diamond was at least two carats and channel set with small stones all around the white gold or platinum band.

He stood up and pressed his nose to mine. "This ring is the one that Patrick gave Pilar all those years ago. Money was no object to him. Mami stopped wearing it after Patrick died but didn't want to part with it. She held onto it all these years. I hadn't ever seen it before, but she showed it to me just before I moved here. I immediately asked if I could have it, knowing I wanted to give it to you someday. She gave it to me, but I insist on paying her back eventually. This ring once represented a lot of pain for my family, but I don't look at it that way now. If it weren't for all of that, there'd be no us, and I couldn't imagine that. This ring is an indestructible piece of light among all the darkness that was my past. It reminds me of your love for me. It is *the* ring for you."

***

A year later, on New Years Eve, Elec and I had a private ceremony officiated by a justice of the peace. I wore my hair up. He was happy about that.

A big wedding wasn't necessary; we just wanted to make it official. We chose New Years Eve as a way of sticking it to fate.

After a nice dinner alone at Charlie's Pub following the wedding, we joined the crowd in Times Square.

When the ball dropped, Elec lifted me into a passionate kiss that more than made up for our lost opportunity here five years ago.

When he put me down, I whispered into his ear and gave him the surprise of his life.

Later that night, he'd put his head on my tummy, and cleverly joked in typical Elec fashion about how we belonged in a reality TV show: he'd now officially become his brother's bastard child who impregnated his stepsister.

EPILOGUE

The Final Chapter: True Romance

"Are you baby O'Rourke's father?"

An unfamiliar twinge developed in my heart upon the nurse's use of that term. "Yes. That's me. I'm the father."

The father.

My whole life had seemingly been defined by being the antithesis of father. I was the son: bastard son, bad son, estranged son. But now, I was the father. It was my turn to be...the father.

"Can I check your identification please?"

I lifted my arm and showed her the plastic bracelet locked around my wrist. I wanted to wear it forever. Gangrene may not have even been a good enough reason to cut that thing off.

"Follow me," she said.

I'd missed the birth. I'd been visiting Mami in California when Greta called me to say her water broke. She was only thirty-four weeks along, so I thought it was safe to take a quick trip out there before my time became more limited than ever.

I immediately packed up and started driving to the airport once I realized she was likely in labor.

The next thing I knew, Sully was calling me to say Greta had been taken in for an emergency c-section. I panicked because I wasn't even on the plane yet. I knew I wouldn't make it in time. The worst kind of helpless feeling came over me. I prayed probably for the first time ever. It's funny how you can spend your entire life wondering if there's a God until suddenly in a time of crisis, you're begging Him for help as if you'd never doubted He existed.

Sully sent me a text shortly before I boarded. It was a picture of my son.

My son.

I remember I'd been walking out of the bathroom and just froze, staring at my phone in awe. I looked around me as if everyone should have known that this was the most monumental moment in the history of the universe. The message said the baby was taken to the NICU but was fine. Greta was fine. They were fine.

Thank you, God. I swear I'll never doubt you again.

Tears stung my eyes as I looked down at the picture while I walked through the gate and onto the plane. I think I must have stared at the photo for the entire six hours.

When I finally arrived at the hospital, Greta was sleeping, and I didn't want to wake her, but I couldn't wait another minute to meet my son.

The nurse led me to where he was asleep in the incubator.

If I thought the photo made me emotional, there was no comparison to seeing him in person, watching his little chest rise and fall.

"He's breathing on his own, and all his vitals are good. He should only have to be in here five to six days."

"Can I hold him?"

"Yes. We just ask that you wash your hands with the antibacterial soap over there and put on one of these masks."

I wasted no time heading to the sink, lathering my hands and placing the paper mask over my mouth.

She took him out and handed him to me. His warm body was swaddled in a blanket and felt light as a feather. Suddenly, I became terrified, not only of keeping him safe for the rest of his life but worried even about the ride home through the city. He was so fragile, and yet this tiny being comprised everything in the world that now mattered to me. Talk about holding the world in the palm of your hand. I wished I could carry him home in a breathable non-destructive display case with a lock. I wanted to shield him from everything this crazy world had to offer.

Looking down at his little face made me truly realize that everything I'd been through in life was supposed to happen exactly as it had. It couldn't have transpired any other way if it meant that this little person never came to be.

He had Randy's nose, which was also Patrick's. It was uncanny. With his lighter hair, he looked even more like them than I did. How ironic that through all of the hate, love was spawned in their likeness.

Chills ran through me when I realized today—his birthday—was the 22nd but didn't let it bother me one way or the other.

"Hey, little buddy. It's Daddy. I'm your daddy."

His eyelids flickered, and he started to squirm in my arms.

"You don't have to wake up. I'll still be here. You won't be able to get rid of me for a very long time."

He opened his little hand, and I watched his tiny fingers close around my pinky. I wondered where any of my inspiration to write even came from before him. I knew that from now on, every last bit of it would be derived from my son.

Letting go of all lingering anger from the past was going to be more necessary now than ever. There would no longer be room for any of it in my heart. I needed all the room for him. It was in that moment holding my son when I knew I had to truly forgive Patrick and Randy. They'd schooled me on what not to do as a father. I'd make up for their mistakes by giving my own son more love than he'd know what to do with.

It may have seemed strange, but I quietly thanked Randy for what he had given me. In life, he led me to my one true love. In death, he made it possible to find her again.

Through death there was life. Through hate there was love. I looked down at my son. "In the end, there was you, and that made it all worth it."

In the same way that you can easily switch the letters of a word around to see another hidden meaning, such is life. A life can be defined by its hardships or its blessings. It's all a matter of how you look at it. So, while this book was once setting up to be a tragic tale, it turned into a love story, an imperfect but unconventionally epic romance.

Scramble the letters of romance, you get Cameron. Greta came up with that one all on her own. It was her very first anagram.

Romance=Cameron.

I love you, Cameron.

THE END

MY SKYLAR
A USA TODAY Bestseller

From the author of the #1 bestselling romance, *Jake Undone*, comes a friends-to-lovers story of longing, passion, betrayal and redemption...with a twist that will rip your heart out.

Skylar was my best friend, but I secretly pined for her. One thing after another kept us apart, and I've spent the last decade in fear of losing her forever.

First, it was the cancer, but she survived only to face the unthinkable at my hands. Because of me, she left town. For years, I thought I'd never see her again.

But now she's back...and living with *him.*

But now she's back...and living with *him.*

I don't deserve her after everything I've put her through, but I can't live without her. This is my last chance, because she's about to make the biggest mistake of her life. I can see it her eyes: she doesn't love him. She still loves me...which is why I have to stop her before it's too late.

My Skylar is a standalone story and a companion to the novel, *Jake Undone*.

Contains graphic sexual content and harsh language. It is only appropriate for adult readers age 18+.

***

JAKE UNDONE
An Amazon #1 Bestseller in Romance

Nina Kennedy was alive…but not *living*…until she met him.

Planes, trains, heights…you name it, Nina was afraid of it and led a sheltered life ruled by irrational fears and phobias. When she moves to Brooklyn for nursing school, that life is turned upside down, as she develops an intense but unwanted attraction to her gorgeous roommate, who's pierced, tattooed and just happens to be the smartest person she's ever met.

Behind Jake Green's rough exterior and devilish smile, lies a heart of gold. He makes it his mission to change Nina's outlook on life. When he agrees to tutor her, they forge a bet and the stakes are high as Jake forces Nina to face her demons. He just wasn't expecting to fall hard for her in the process.

What Nina doesn't realize, is that Jake has been living his own private hell. Once he drops a bombshell, will their love survive it?

Told in two parts from both Nina and Jake's points of view, *Jake Undone* is a standalone story and a companion to the novel, *Gemini*.

***

GEMINI
An Amazon Bestseller

Diner waitress Allison Abraham had no idea her mundane life was about to dramatically change the day she serves a devastatingly handsome customer.

Allison is immediately captivated by the mysterious man who stared through her soul with his electric blue eyes. After he abruptly leaves the restaurant, she can't get him out of her head.

She has no idea that he had actually come on a mission to find her.

Cedric Callahan wasn't expecting to fall in love at first sight with the pretty waitress he'd set out to find. In fact, she was the last woman on Earth he should be having feelings for. But his selfish heart had other plans. Feeling compelled to know her before revealing himself, he makes her believe their meetings are coincidental.

After a passionate romance ignites, Cedric's lies and secrets are finally revealed, changing both of their lives forever.

***

AND COMING IN EARLY 2015:

JAKE UNDERSTOOD

From the author of the Amazon #1 Bestselling Romance, *Jake Undone*, comes a full-length companion novel.

A different side to the story: Jake's side.

"We're getting a new roommate," they said.

I thought nothing of it…until she walked in the door. Her hand trembled in mine as she looked at me with fearful eyes. My entire world spun on its axis.

Nina...

It was a mismatch made in heaven: innocent girl from the boonies moves in with tattooed, pierced, badboy engineer.

I came up with a bet, a plan to tutor her in math and coach her through her phobias. What I wasn't betting on was becoming addicted to her.

But I was living a double life on weekends, and once she found out about it, she'd be gone.

I had to protect myself and that meant one thing: I couldn't fall in love.

**In *Jake Understood*, pivotal scenes from *Jake Undone* are retold from Jake's point of view, combined with all-new material that will give readers a never-before-seen glimpse into Jake's past, present and future. It can standalone, but if both books are read, should follow *Jake Undone*.

Contains graphic sexual content and harsh language. It is only appropriate for adult readers age 18+.

ACKNOWLEDGEMENTS

First and foremost, thank you to my loving parents for continuing to support me every day in every way.

To my husband, who puts up with a lot of crap so I can live out this new dream …thank you for your love and patience.

To Allison, who always believed in me back when all of this was simply about telling stories and to Harpo, my agent in heaven: love you both.

To my editor, Kim York, thank you for your undivided attention chapter by chapter and for your invaluable facebook chats.

To my besties: Angela, Tarah and Sonia…love you all so much!

To all the bloggers who help and support me: you are the reason for my success. I'm afraid to list everyone here because I will undoubtedly forget someone unintentionally. You know who you are and do not hesitate to contact me if I can return the favor.

To Penelope's Peeps, my facebook street team/fan group: I adore you!

To Donna Soluri of Soluri Public Relations who organized my book blitz and who always dishes out sound advice: Thank you!

To Hetty Rasmussen: for your support and for being my awesome Book Bash assistant!

Special thanks to Aussie Lisa, Erika G., Kimie S. and the two Amys for your endless support!

To my readers: nothing makes me happier than knowing I've provided you with an escape from the daily stresses of life. That same escape was why I started writing. There is no greater joy in this business than to hear from you directly and to know that something I wrote touched you in some way.

To the autism moms (and dads): you rock!

Last but not least, to my daughter and son: Mommy loves you. You are my motivation and inspiration!

ABOUT THE AUTHOR

Penelope Ward is a USA Today Bestselling author and an Amazon #1 Bestselling author in Romance. She grew up in Boston with five older brothers and spent most of her twenties as a television news anchor, before switching to a more family-friendly career.

Penelope lives for reading books in the new adult genre, coffee and hanging out with her friends and family on weekends.

She is the proud mother of a beautiful 10-year-old girl with autism (the inspiration for the character Callie in Gemini) and an 8-year-old boy, both of whom are the lights of her life.

Penelope, her husband and kids reside in Rhode Island.

She is also the author of *My Skylar*, *Jake Undone, Gemini* and the upcoming *Jake Understood* due out in early 2015.

Contact Penelope at: penelopewardauthor@gmail.com on Twitter @PenelopeAuthor or on Facebook on the Penelope Ward Author page. Guarantee you never miss book news by subscribing to Penelope's blog posts at the bottom of the page here at: www.penelopewardauthor.com or simply email Penelope at the gmail address above with the subject line "newsletter" to be added.

Made in the USA
Lexington, KY
04 November 2014